THE SILVER PORTAL

Jim Stein

Digital ISBN: 978-1-7335629-8-0
Print ISBN: 978-1-954788-01-5

First printing, 2021

Jagged Sky Books
P.O. Box #254
Bradford, Pa 16701

Cover art & design by Kris Norris
Edited by Caroline Miller

Magic Trade School

Also by Jim Stein:

Legends Walk

The Space-Slime Continuum

Visit https://JimSteinBooks.com/subscribe to get a free ebook, join my reader community, and sign up for my infrequent newsletter.

1. Weekend Warrior

T HE CONTROLLER RUMBLED and buzzed, wanting to fly apart. I clutched the blue grips tight with both hands and mashed a thumb down on the four colored buttons like my life depended on it.

"It's gonna blow!" Billy yelled in my ear, despite the fact that the big lug sat right next to me on the couch. He slammed his own thumb stick so hard it was sure to break off and launch toward the television. "Scorpion bosses are the worst. Watch the tail!"

My fighter ducked and darted away from the monster's slashing stinger, obeying the commands from my controller while my friend's sorcerer launched a string of fireballs. Our attacker flashed red, bits of its exoskeleton blowing off under each hit. My fighter danced and parried with his comically large sword, occasionally getting in a solid hit, but mostly just sucking up damage and keeping the bug distracted.

The controllers rumbled in stereo. With a mighty whoosh and a roar of bass static, the scorpion went up in flames, rolled over, and died. We'd vanquished the beast.

"Too easy!" Billy beamed, big square teeth gleaming from his big square face.

Introverts like me only held onto one or two friends through the years. It wasn't that I was antisocial. Heck, I'd fallen in pretty easily with the new gang at Attwater Academy. Of course, learning magic alongside a skilled trade pretty much made everyone there a misfit, so I wasn't stepping far from my comfort zone. With one semester of basic classes and spells behind us, we were all chomping at the bit to train with our individual magic, the special talent uncovered by first semester testing.

Still, I'd never had any of my Attwater friends over. It was hard to gain a person's trust, even harder to give it. That made lasting bonds rare. Billy was my one holdover friend from high school and didn't have a clue that magic was real. We'd survived being the odd-man-out in more gym classes and school dances than I cared to remember, led the charge for better workstations in the computer lab, and had been pretty much inseparable since ninth grade.

Billy threw himself back into the couch cushions with a gusty, satisfied sigh, rocking the sofa onto its rear feet. My friend was a big guy. Curly black hair cascaded to a neck as thick as my thigh. From there down he only got wider; not fat necessarily, just big. Those Samoan genes gave him a barrel chest, thick arms, and beefy mitts that screamed old-time wrestler. I'd often likened him to a downsized Andre the Giant, a comparison that never failed to raise a thick, rich chuckle.

At six-three he topped me by several inches. The weak winter sunlight refused to even attempt darkening my Northern-European complexion, leaving me a pale, lanky ghost compared to my robust companion. I wasn't exactly a weakling, but it was easy to feel inadequate around Billy. Conversely, he made fun of the effort and gel that went into maintaining the stylish blond mop above my fade cut and—as

Billy put it—my simmering gray eyes, so it seemed our collective insecurities balanced out.

Despite outward appearances, Billy was pretty mellow, and smart too. He'd mastered computers and their hardware years ago and could run circles around the managers in his IT department. That we still got the odd weekend at my place to hang out and play games helped keep me sane, a mundane bastion from the craziness Attwater had brought to my life.

"Beer me!" Billy's grin was contagious as Amos leapt into action at his command and headed for the fridge.

Amos was the latest in the line of service robots I'd been working on for years. This Autonomous Magic Operating System model was the first to fully embrace my magic talent and compartmentalize it from independent systems that handled gyro stabilization and such. The magic I unconsciously flooded my projects with had made earlier models explode. This design let me pump more complex commands into the unit, but there was still a limit where he'd go kablooey.

I'd assembled Amos in the garage workshop below the apartment I rented from Mom and Dad. Another unit was in my tiny workroom back at school. Upgrades from prior series included wide hinged footpads that helped with stability and a torso made of midnight-black industrial PVC, though I'd carved up the sixteen-inch diameter pipe until it was hard to pick out. Both arms ended in dexterous three-fingered hands with an opposing thumb. The squat silver helm that was his head swiveled three hundred and sixty degrees, giving my Amos robot improved situational awareness.

The more efficient design didn't clash as badly with my magic, but also called for a larger percentage of electro-mechanical parts. With all the extra hardware and electronics, I'd just about given up calling my creations automata. My early work tended toward bulky and awkward, but the trim Amos torso allowed for expansion with several onboard tools. I hoped to move him beyond the bottle opener stage soon, but was proud of how my robot glided back with Billy's beer. I'd finally nailed the right proportions for arms and legs that balanced utility with bipedal stability.

"Hey, robo-boy is rattling," Billy said, taking a swig. "Don't look at me like that. His real name sucks. Something's loose."

"Shouldn't be." I ignored the jab at my naming convention and sent a mental command for Amos to circle the room, only remembering at the last second to back it up with words. "Amos, take a lap."

I shot a glance at Billy. He hadn't seemed to notice that Amos started off before the verbal command. Magic wasn't something I shared outside of school, not even with my good friend.

Amos clunked and scraped as he skirted the stairs and passed the kitchen in my studio setup. Had he been damaged during our last trials? Experimenting with new capabilities and programming tended to take up way too much of my free time, so I was used to making adjustments on the fly. But something was off. The sounds didn't keep time with his pace.

"Amos, stop." I listened close. The scraping came again, louder this time. "Did you close the garage door when you came up?"

"Thought I did. Maybe a cat snuck inside."

I headed to the stairs with Billy in tow and Amos bringing up the rear. Follow mode for my bots was a no-brainer and gave me the opportunity to catch and correct issues that might crop up.

Downstairs, the garage smelled of burnt solder and PVC dust. The white plastic tubes tended to be my go-to material for projects. Even Amos was half plumbing supplies. Dim light poured in through the high row of windows along the main door. As usually, gaming had sucked away more hours than ought to be possible. The sky was growing darker by the minute, and a glance at my phone confirmed it was past six.

I hit the light switch at the base of the stairs, throwing the room into brilliant white contrast. My shelves full of supplies, the workshop, and the obstacle course test track taking up the center of the floor left no room for my car.

"Yes, I did close the door." Billy looked unduly proud of himself until he followed my gaze to where the side door to the walkway stood ajar. "Ah…I did however go back to grab the snacks from my truck."

A crash behind and to our left had us both spinning around. I grabbed a pair of flashlights from the wall charger, pushed one at Billy, and motioned him to circle around the far side of the shelves along the back wall. Our lights panned over the dim space behind the boxes lining the bottom shelf, but nothing looked out of the ordinary. Scratching and a metallic jingle were followed by a soft thump, and I ducked my head around a trashcan bristling with segments of white pipe just in time to see the side door swing open a few more inches.

A familiar loop of rainbow ribbon disappeared around the door's bottom edge. My eyes snapped to the key hooks by the door where the lanyard with my car keys should have been hanging. The little wooden plaque shaped like a rainbow trout—a holdover from Dad's fly-fishing days—held only empty brass hooks.

"Damn!" I darted out into the gloom in time to see a small critter scuttling away on all fours. My keys jangled across the concrete, the colorful lanyard trailing behind the animal as it took a left and headed along the gutter.

"Is that a raccoon?" Billy shined his light along the side of his truck, but the thing was fast.

"Come on! The little thief stole my keys." I jogged out into the street, spotted the burglar, and took off in pursuit. "My school badge is on that too."

My mind raced, trying to think of the best way to deal with raccoons. I'd always assumed they just stole food, but apparently they also liked shiny objects. School had done a good job drilling in the danger of getting rabies from wild animals, so I didn't want to risk a bite. If Billy wasn't following along, an elemental spell from common core might pluck the keys back on a well-timed air blast. Maybe I could pull it off without being obvious, make it look like a lucky gust of wind.

Billy crashed into a metal trash can and lost his balance. He cursed, but came up grinning with the lid held like a shield.

"What?" He asked when I shook my head. "Need *something* to tame the beast, unless you plan to sweet talk it. Oh, he took the alley behind the schoolyard up ahead. We've got him cornered."

The alley in question actually ran behind the local daycare. But Billy was right, the broken concrete ended at a block wall with a pair of big green dumpsters nestled into an alcove. At least, I assumed they were green. It was hard to tell in the rapidly failing light, and the undersized bulb in the sole streetlamp near the drive entrance seemed to blanch at the thought of illuminating the area. Since trash trucks had to back in with their harsh reverse alarms bleeping the whole neighborhood awake at six in the morning, the approach was plenty wide with ample room to skirt around the dumpsters.

I let Billy take point. After all, he had the trashcan lid. As he passed I saw he'd also grabbed a length of wood and brandished it like a club, or like a flag. Tattered strips of cloth dangled from his weapon as if it were maybe the leg of a broken up chair.

I hung back, blocking the exit and hoping he'd flush the coon out so I could use a tiny whirlwind to snag the keychain. As I reached for the tingling bit of power and tried to clear my mind, I couldn't help feeling as if someone watched. My neck prickled, the hairs raising as imagined eyes bored into the back of my head. I turned slowly, casually, as if in no hurry at all, and found…Amos swaying from side to side as he made tiny adjustments to his position.

I'd totally forgotten the little guy was in follow mode when we dashed from the garage. Amos definitely wasn't rattling because I hadn't even noticed him. Magic might not be needed at all, assuming we could corner the animal before it got smart and took to the trees lining the property.

I dropped the elemental spell and mentally compiled a few simple commands that would send my robot to fetch the keys without overloading the delicate magic-machine balance and turning him into slag. Melodramatic? Not really—it had happened before.

"Here, kitty, kitty." My giant friend crouched behind his makeshift shield and crept between the dumpsters, holding the length of wood before him like a pike.

"It's not a cat," I reminded him as Amos and I fanned out to keep our quarry from bolting.

"Well it's definitely not a raccoon either." Billy's deep voice rose half an octave and took on a distinct quaver. "It's smooth instead of fluffy. And what's with those teeth?"

"What the hell are you talking about?" I angled the beam from my flashlight between the dumpsters adding it the light streaming down the length of his stick.

Two red reflections shone from the darkness at about knee level, feral eyes set in a pointy, furless face. The word possum jumped to mind, but it was too big, and the swaying lights caught a pair of hands held against its chest, curved claws running along the bare belly. It sat on its hindquarters, a snarl rising deep in its throat. Possums had truly nasty looking teeth, but they were little needles, not the tusks that scissored together near the point of the animal's snout as it chewed out its warning growl.

"Whatever you are, mutant beasty, you're giving back those keys." Billy raised the club and stepped forward.

Something about this didn't feel right. My eyes streamed as if with allergies, and the animal waivered in my vision. Heck, the whole scene blurred. I wiped at my face. Billy hoisted the stick high, but the trailing material got caught on the edge of the dumpster to his right. The open lid slammed shut with a hollow boom. My vision wavered again, and I blinked in confusion. The big square container...moved.

Billy tried to pull the club free, but long claws sprouted from the metal and hooked through the material. A thick stubby arm swung in from the far side of the shifting mass, slamming across his back and driving my friend headfirst into the other dumpster. Billy's head hit with a hollow boom, and he crumpled to the ground.

2. Dumpster Fire

T HE THEIVING CRITTER stalked forward, eyes gleaming and long digging claws poised in front of it like a velociraptor.

The dumpster Billy had collided with sensibly remained just a trash receptacle, but the other sprouted dull green fur and took a lumbering step toward his fallen form. Stubby legs matched the wide, flat arms, and eye slits the size of bread loaves gleamed above a gaping mouth.

These are lurkers!

The demon's shape made it well suited for its disguise as a trash can. Big and blocky, it had to weigh in at a ton and would crush Billy in the blink of an eye if I didn't do something. Lurkers were a mid-level class of demon, and we hadn't learned much about dealing with them during my first semester. They tended to be ambush predators ranging widely in form and magical ability. This wasn't something I was prepared to tackle, but if I could get Billy on his feet, we could make a run for it.

"Amos, go!" I sent him in fast, arms flailing and brandishing the bottle opener like a switchblade. I really should have equipped him with better tools.

Amos closed in with big strides, harassing the monstrosity with silent swipes as I dredged up a spell. The little whirlwind was still in the forefront of my mind, so I let it fly. But in the beam of my light it only managed to ruffle the monster's long fur. On the plus side, our massive attacker did turn away from my fallen friend to focus on me. The depthless pits that were its eyes had my heart leaping into my throat as I struggled to think of a better spell. Unfortunately, my signature talent of fixing broken items wasn't going to be of much use.

Fire! Fire would be best.

It took a critical few heartbeats to mentally shift gears and draw upon the reserve of energy roiling under my sternum and another long moment to gather heat from the surrounding blacktop that had soaked up the afternoon sun. The huge demon stomped toward me, shaking the ground with each step.

Amos streaked in again, putting himself in harm's way. The bond between us flared. Without proper guidance he'd gone fully autonomous and was making too many judgement calls. The tinker magic infusing my creation throbbed, threatening an overload that could result in anything from Amos simply switching off to a low-yield explosion. Tinker energy was meant to fix things and didn't play well as a motive force in my projects. I couldn't afford to lose another robot. Aside from the time that went into construction, losing a creation hurt—a lot—like being kicked in the stomach and gutted. Amos was more than a possession; he was a part of me.

The small demon thief shot forward, sweeping Amos's legs and sending him crashing to the ground. My spell casting wasn't nearly as fast as others at school, but I managed to get a shot off when the giant was ten steps away. The flaming orange ball whooshed forth, splashed against the shaggy green wall bearing down on me, and went out with a muffled *phhtt.*

The smell of burnt hair washed over me as I fell back, knowing I was too slow.

The high-pitched whine of an electric motor split the air, and a black shape the size of a go-cart zoomed between me and the demon, nearly running over my feet. *What the hell?*

Long spikes along the front of the little car raked across shaggy knees, and the dumpster demon roared. The cart was fortified with black armor and sat maybe three feet tall. Someone had painted flames down each side, a wicked smile above a spiky grill, and eyes around the headlights. How could the driver see without a windshield?

A wide green paw slapped down on my rescuer, putting an end to further speculation. The flattened little car sat motionless when the hand pulled back, but the armor hadn't even been scratched. A panel slid open, but instead of revealing a cockpit and driver, two metal arms extended from the recess. Each arm ended in a circular saw with jagged teeth. The motor hummed loud as the cart suspension raised the chassis back above the tires and the blades whirled.

Robot battles had been a short-lived television phenomena, one of the few geeky pleasures that crossed over into the macho crowd at school. This was a killer robot if I ever saw one.

I searched for the operator and spotted a woman standing near the mouth of the alley. The lone streetlight illuminated long blond hair draped to either side of a narrow face with brow furrowed in determination. Oddly, she didn't hold a remote. Her robot slashed at the demon, spinning blades carving through fur and flesh above its short legs. The howl that rose had me grabbing my head, and unfamiliar magic flared.

There was no time to second guess her motives. I rushed to Billy. The smaller demon came in from the other side, but shot past and jumped on the robot, tearing at its dome. Sparks flashed from the raptor claws with each strike.

"Amos, help it!"

Bottle opener slashing, my creation went to the killer bot's aid. He got a few good jabs in, forcing the little demon to give up its attack to counter. Satisfied the two robots had the creatures' full attention, I turned back to my friend and shook his shoulders. Billy moaned and waved me away, eyes still closed.

"Ten more minutes, Mom." He rolled over on his side. A dark, wet spot matted his wild hair above the right ear. "Beer me. Dancing raccoons. Pancakes."

"Come on, dude, snap out of it." There was no way I could drag the big lug off to the side, let alone carry him home.

A quick glance showed that the killer bot was down to one sawblade. The other arm ended at a jagged break and withdrew into its compartment. A three foot pole extended from the top of the dome, surprising a yelp from the digger demon still perched there. The little demon clung to the pole and glared at Amos, who'd shifted tactics and was now lobbing rocks.

At first I thought the robot had deployed a lance, but instead of a point, the pole ended in a horseshoe that arced blue sparks as it rammed forward into the belly of the dumpster demon. Fur sizzled and smoked, and the creature howled in pain.

"Time to go." I heaved on a beefy arm, managing to get Billy to sit up.

"Wild night." He swayed, but opened his eyes with a little coaxing and basically crawled to his feet using the dumpster for support.

His eyes still didn't seem to focus. I shot a worried glance over my shoulder as metal screeched followed by pounding footsteps. The demons had disengaged. The small thief scurried from the alley while casting venomous looks back. Amos continued to pelt it with golf-ball-sized stones. Cut and bleeding thick ichor, the hulking pile of shag thundered after the small lurker, nearly knocking the woman over as it fled the scene.

If it was possible for robots to look smug, the pair preening in the alley did. Amos tossed aside his last stone, and stowed the bottle opener with deliberate care, while the killer robot cart pulled in the cattle prod and tucked away the working saw arm. Something told me the pair would have high-fived each other if they could.

"What the hell is that?" Billy blinked and shook his head, then winced in pain. "When did you build another robot?"

"Not mine. It's hers," I said as the newcomer approached.

She wasn't as tall as I'd first thought, probably about five-five. Even under the weak light, her sandy blond hair was thick and lustrous, framing a narrow face with wideset eyes and a sharp, petite nose. She wore jeans, a black top with thick long sleeves, and a padded denim vest.

"Thanks for jumping in. I'm Jason and this is Billy." I extended my hand, but she was laser focused on her robot.

A pool of liquid formed under her bot. Sharp bits and pieces littered the pavement. She opened a small compartment revealing the glow of what was probably the onboard monitoring system. I shifted uncomfortably as she continued to ignore us, and felt an unreasoning guilt that I wasn't doting on Amos. Stupid, because he'd sustained little more than cosmetic scratches. Magic let me check on his status without getting close, but of course the woman didn't know that and probably thought I didn't care about Amos.

"Roxanne Debove," she finally said as she closed the panel and stood. "Call me Roxy."

"Well, thanks again," I said.

This time she shook the hand I offered. A spark zapped between our fingers as they touched, not the nebulous sexual attraction romance novels spoke of, but a literal spark of power—of magic. My eyes went wide as I looked from her to the robot. Was that why she didn't have a remote? Could this woman be a tinker like me?

The puzzling thoughts had me grasping her hand too long. The second time she tried to pull away, I let go and shoved both hands in my pockets. This was no place to ask about magic, especially with Billy blinking at the awkward exchange. How much of the battle he had seen and understood remained unclear. From all appearances he'd been out cold until the very end when our ambushers broke and ran. Billy still swayed and held the lip of the remaining dumpster for support.

"I better get this guy home before he falls over." I jerked a thumb at Billy, who responded with a dazed grin, then shined my light on the growing puddle under her robot. "Looks like your bot cracked a cooling line or something. My shop's just down the street if you want to patch him up before taking off."

Roxy smiled when I used the word him, but shook her head. "That would be patch *her* up. Probably a good idea, but first I've got to recover something that little thief stole."

Crap, in all the excitement I'd forgotten about my keys. There'd been no sign of my lanyard, even before the living dumpster took out Billy. Roxy turned, strode past us, and knelt at the block wall at the back of the alley.

"Stay here," I told Billy before following, then as an afterthought, added over my shoulder, "Amos, keep him on his feet."

Two cinderblocks were missing at the base of the wall. The alcove they left was covered with branches that must have been newly stripped because the woody breaks looked bone white under my flashlight. Roxy pulled the branches out, followed by a small pile of old candy and fast food wrappers.

"Ah, here we go." She yanked out a toy car, then a handful of marbles, then an empty wallet followed by a small purse. Her arm was elbow deep as she continued to rummage around. "I've been tracking that little burglar for days, but kept losing him in this neighborhood. Here it is!"

She pulled out a small wooden jewelry box with a carved top and delicate scrollwork on the brass latch. A final sweep of her arm brought out a handful of odds and ends, including my rainbow lanyard holding my little credit card pouch and the keys for my beater Ford.

* * *

"How is he?" Roxy asked as I clomped down the stairs to the garage.

With the demons gone and our respective items recovered, she'd taken me up on the offer to at least get the coolant leak on Mindy fixed. Yep, she named her robots, same as me.

"I think it's only a flesh wound." I waited for her eye roll to subside, a sign that she had good taste in old movies. "He'll be fine. No double vision or anything, but he's napping. I'll get him home in the morning. She all patched up?"

"Good enough to get home. You've got a pretty sweet setup here." Her wave encompassed the work area and Amos on his charging station. "That dude has sick balance. I've always wanted to take the plunge into walkers, but wheels and weapons are shiny objects. You know how it goes."

I did. It was always easier to load big payloads on a rolling frame because weight limits and center of gravity didn't drive design nearly as much. Aside from my little exploding robot problem, equipping Amos with better tools would make him more versatile. And tonight's encounter had me thinking more toward offensive capabilities if this was a taste of what being an Attwater grad was going to be like.

"So where do you live anyway?" Battery technology had come a long way, but she'd been tracking the little lurker on foot and couldn't have come very far.

"A couple miles in toward the city. Not gonna say exactly where." She gave me a mischievous grin that for some stupid reason had me smiling in return. "We just met."

"Fair enough." That explained why I hadn't seen her around, but I had a more pressing and delicate question. "Mindy there reminds me of an old-time battle bot, but I noticed you don't use a remote…" I let the unasked question hang for a moment, but she didn't bite. "Amos can take voice commands, but we've got a special…bond that's way easier."

I'd sensed magic during the confusion in the alley and assumed the demons were its source. But that spark when shaking Roxy's hand told me that at least some of it had come from the woman who now eyed me cautiously. That she hadn't gone off the deep end after encountering that pair of demons said a lot about her character and backbone. But her guarded expression might mean the adrenaline was wearing off and reality was about to come crashing down.

"I should be going." She stepped left, putting herself between me and her machine, as if worried I'd somehow hurt her killer robot.

"I'm not judging." I held up my hands in apology, dancing around the question I wanted to ask. Might as well go for broke. "You have a special bond too. It's how you control Mindy, right? I…just wanted you to know you aren't alone."

As cool as it had been to find I possessed real magic, not being able to talk about the awesomeness, my fears, and the countless burning questions outside school was an emotional anchor that could drag anyone down. The gang at school would agree; our abilities came complete with on-again, off-again depression as we each struggled with our newfound lives.

"It's just"—she looked to the floor, voice catching and dropping to a near whisper. "Jason, what *were* those things? I figured we were chasing a destitute street urchin, but that monster—they were both monsters. I feel like I can't trust my own eyes, can't trust anything."

Her shattered look had me rushing over, but I stopped short, hands at my sides and cursing my overprotective reaction. I'd just met this woman and couldn't exactly wrap her in a hug. I wrestled with my stupid male ego for a good ten seconds, trying to untangle my motives. Sure she was lovely, a petite dynamo that could bend machines to her will. Not only had Roxy bested a powerful lurker, she'd tracked a thieving demon that had clearly been fleecing my unsuspecting neighbors.

The dark alley and bold actions had me assuming Roxy was in her thirties. But standing so close, vulnerable under my workroom lights as she wrestled with the night's impossible encounter, revealed a woman in her early twenties, perhaps only a couple of years my senior.

"Crazy, I know." As nice as it would have been to hold her, I settled for a reassuring pat on her back.

Still looking down, she sighed and rested her head on my shoulder. Her thick mane of hair draped across my chest, smelling of honeysuckle and pepper. The subtle waft of burnt rubber would have been from whatever repairs she'd had to make. My heart ached for her.

More than anyone, I knew it was possible to possess magic, even use it, without knowing. A feral need to keep Roxy safe while she discovered her abilities rose with each passing moment we stood close. Without thinking I slipped my arm around her shoulders. "I know a place that can help you, a school that can explain all of this."

3. Back to School

I MAGINATION, THE POWER to be whomever you'd like, to explore actions and ideas without ramifications. Imagination, that unique human faculty that also lets us forget, to bury deep the things that might otherwise consume our fragile equilibrium.

Returning to school for second semester, pretending nothing unusual had happened, acting as if it was perfectly normal to step into a tiny dilapidated brick building each morning to train as a welder—that took hard-core imagination.

Six months ago, I would have been hard pressed to imagine the doorway to the old Beer Barn as a portal to the Attwater Trade School, an ancient academy that prepared its students for more than simple careers. Sure, Attwater trained us, but it also cultivated our supernatural talents and expected us to wield our magic for the greater good after graduation.

I fell through my first day back, numbly following a skeleton schedule plucked from the whirling gears of a brass and steel machine that spit out the enchanted page. Classrooms and times printed in neat blocks on the heavy stock would change of their own accord to accommodate additional classes and student needs, so it was important to never assume you'd memorized everything. I'd yet to catch the ink flowing, but the entire schedule could rearrange itself in the blink of an eye.

I wandered under the dangling glow bulbs and tangled piping, plodding from class to class, hoping to run into one of my friends. Open pipes and ventilation gurgled and sighed overhead, testifying to years of upgrades to the old building and sitting at odds with the stone walls and slate floors making up the concentric rings of classrooms. Generally speaking, outer rings were accessible by all, but badges were required to gain access to the deeper reaches of Attwater.

I waved the yellow side of my badge over the proximity sensor to the right of a banded steel door and was rewarded with a metallic snick and green light on the slanted panel. My picture stared from the backside of the laminated badge, another new security measure that proudly displayed my name, Jason Walker, in bold text underneath the image.

Announcing "picture day" ahead of time would have given me a chance to pick something nicer than the white tee-shirt and jeans that I'd sweated into under my welding smock before they snapped photos. I hated the way the V-neck collar accentuated my pointy chin. I was no sun worshipper, and an early winter had eradicated any signs of a tan. The white shirt managed to wash the last vestiges of color from my narrow face and messy straw-blond hair. I considered myself passingly handsome, but the overexposed image turned me from a lanky, broad-shouldered twenty-one-year-old into a washed-out cadaver. I'd apparently been pissed off too, because stormy gray eyes glared out at the camera. All in all, the photo would have done the Department of Motor Vehicles proud.

As first year students who had signed our contracts, my friends and I wore the laminated yellow badges that let us go a level deeper into the bowels of the school. In six months, we'd get green badges, but even then, there were corridors and offshoots requiring special permissions keyed to a handful of closely guarded proximity badges.

Despite its deceptively simple design, Attwater remained a maze to the uninitiated. Higher corridor ring numbers sat deeper in the nested pattern. I currently only had access to the first two rings. Our school was a big old castle of a building, but I couldn't imagine the architecture accommodating more than three or four full rings of classrooms. The security doors helped keep newer students from getting themselves into too much trouble.

For now, I was done with the second ring and more than ready to find a corner and put my feet up. I shrugged at my angry image and pushed the thick door open to the hustle and bustle of other students rushing along the hallway separating our common core classrooms from the commons area that acted as cafeteria, student lounge, and general decompression zone.

At least Dean Gladstone hadn't stationed guards at the entrances to those inner sanctums—yet. After our crazy first semester, students were now screened in person each morning after stepping through their respective portals. Not everyone entered Attwater through old beer distributors outside Philadelphia. My friends came from all over the United States using facades that ranged from strip malls to barns to get to school each day. Attwater had satellite buildings everywhere and magic at its disposal to whisk students across the nation the moment they crossed the threshold. *Talk about distance learning!*

"Hey, Jay Walkie, can't believe you didn't flunk out first semester." Larry Ashburn pushed through the doorway from behind, a perpetual sneer making his flat brown eyes nearly disappear behind the curve of his pudgy cheeks. "Nobody sucked at common core classes like you."

Larry had been a childhood bully, but we'd reached a kind of detente back in high school. At a stocky six feet, he had a couple of inches and several pounds on me. He'd rebranded himself with thick gold chains, a buzz cut, and mannerisms that had to come from some old boyz-in-the-hood type movie. I was pretty sure he'd be laughed at down in the city, but as a geeky science nerd who liked to build robots I tried not to be too judgmental—tried.

I hadn't seen Larry much after graduating high school. Imagine my joy three years later to discover the only other student to be invited to Attwater from my area had gotten even weirder. It was hard to picture Larry—or Lars, as he now called himself—as special, let alone having magic talent, but Attwater didn't make mistakes. Even so, Lars had done only slightly better than my mediocre performance in our common core class.

We'd all run through the gamut of generic elemental magic that gauged a student's affinity with Fire, Water, Earth, Air, and Spirit. Pretty cool stuff that taught a few core spells we each mastered with varying degrees of success. More importantly, the combination of how weak or strong an individual proved in working with each element and its associated spells built an arcane fingerprint the administration used to pin down a student's specific magical talent. That talent, in turn, pointed each of us at a matching vocation.

My talent had been a letdown. I was a tinker, someone who fixed things magically. *Lame, right?* It gets worse. My odd jobs since high school branded me the neighborhood handyman extraordinaire, but in my spare time I built little robots with fewer electronics than should have been possible and a flare for catastrophic failure. Experiments at Attwater revealed that those tinker abilities didn't match well to building my automata. So the dean decided I should train as a certified welder instead of something more central to robotics. Still, I'd learned a few tricks to keep my creations from undue explosions. The adjustments limited their range of abilities, but I was hopeful for further improvement.

"Happy first day back to you too." I decided to take the high road and ignore the stupid schoolyard nickname Lars kept trying to resurrect. It barely even sounded like Jason Walker. "Spring will tell."

Semesters ran July through mid-January, and mid-January to June. The starter schedule stepped us through extra-long blocks of vocational instruction and supporting classes, which for me meant level two welding and a couple of mechanical classes. As a budding motorcycle mechanic, I'd hoped my friend Owen would be in one of those, but no such luck. I was more than ready to add in second term common core magic and the other supporting classes, so I'd have a familiar face or two in class.

Lars opened his mouth as if to make a nasty reply, but looked as weary as I felt from the day's introductory classes. He blew out a disgusted breath, shrugged, and jangled his way toward the common area with an awkward sliding strut. I shook my head, wondering what ancient god or keeper of fate had decided it was a good idea to give the idiot a magic talent. And what exactly was his talent? Cultural misappropriation?

The uneasy knot that always sat in the pit of my stomach after a Lars sighting unraveled when I stepped into the busy commons and spotted two young women and two men sitting at the table by the central stone column. Despite the hundred or so students crowding the room, chattering and drinking coffee, my friends had managed to snag our favorite table. Schedules and course material sprouted from the tabletop in front of each like they were about to embark on a magical quest in some massive board game. The thought of Owen—prematurely jaded and cynical at the ripe old age of twenty-five—playing D&D had me grinning as I threaded my way over.

"Choosing an elective sucks," I said after exchanging greetings ranging from Bethany's squeal and hug to Owen's barely perceptible head nod. "Sucks big."

The fact that we each needed an elective wasn't a problem, but it wasn't fair that we could only pick one. How was I supposed to choose between things like Magical Creatures, Occult Journalism, and Extinct Fantasy Races? I wanted to take them all. Who wouldn't?

Unfortunately, most of our class time at Attwater Academy would be consumed by common core class, trade training, and our first foray into the special magical talent we each possessed. That left only a two-hour block of time for extras.

"Load of crap, if you ask me." Owen blew out a gusty breath and slammed his course catalog on the pale wood tabletop.

If not for the press of bodies, the sound would have echoed around the open area, which was easily twice the size of my high school lunchroom and had twenty-foot-high ceilings to boot. We'd coordinated by text the night before to gather after class and discuss schedules. Phones didn't work in Attwater, thanks to a suppression spell that kept students from getting distracted. But as we'd found out during holiday break, it also kept you from calling for help in the event of trouble—unless you had the security prefix to cut through the spell.

Five of us sat around the polished wood lunch table that we'd made our own during first semester. Owen's light brown hair shot off in different directions, bedhead turned stylish and a shade darker than the thick straw-blond mop sitting above my own fade. He stood maybe an inch taller than me and was a few pounds heavier, most of it lean muscle across his chest and upper arms. At twenty-five, Owen was four years older, but tended toward aloof and maybe less mature—in a too-cool-for-school sort of way. The leather riding jacket, boot-cut jeans, and engineering boots played to his jaded demeanor, but our more than exciting first term had proven he did in fact care—even while actively trying to convince the world otherwise.

Owen Jones was destined to be a motorcycle mechanic. I hadn't heard a specific name for it, but his talent was fixing engines. He could apparently get anything to run, but had to rely on mundane methods to troubleshoot all the supporting systems in modern vehicles. An added bonus that probably swelled the guy's head even more was the fact he'd ranked second only to Bethany in common core spell casting during our initial evaluations.

Chad Stillman sat across from Owen, a strapping six-foot-two cowboy from Montana, complete with wide-brimmed hat and button up plaid shirt. At ease as usual, Chad reclined against a stone column that stretched toward the ceiling to disappear among pipes and ventilation. His hand rested fondly on the smooth stonework. Every once in a while, he'd pat the stones, and a purring sigh would escape from the ventilation system overhead. Our cowboy had formed a unique bond with the living building that housed our classes.

Though surely magical, the bond had more to do with his penchant for adopting strays than his magic talent of predicting the weather. In a pinch, Chad had even managed to throw lightning, which wasn't something any of us had been taught in common core. Of course, he'd been deep in some sort of trance, communing with whatever passed for Attwater's consciousness, and we suspected the school itself had lent him a bit of oomph.

A tap on my left hand pulled my attention down to find the Magical Creatures class in my own booklet had been circled in red. Beady dark eyes looked up from the fearsome figure standing next to my hand. The gargoyle was about a foot tall with a blocky face and jagged tusks jutting up from his lower jaw. Although he stomped about on two thick legs, Mortimer didn't wear clothes, and a whip-like barbed tail trailed behind his squat body. I could just make out the print on the page beneath him because the little guy was a tad transparent. He was Bethany's favorite drawing, made of colored pencil and graphite and twisted into three dimensions by the will of her scriptomancy magical talent.

Mortimer had used the tip of a wickedly long claw to circle the elective, leaving a tiny portion of his own substance behind. Bethany could replace any missing bits when the need arose. I was happy to see the gargoyle's left arm and hand fully intact. It had taken her several attempts to replace the limb after it was severed during last semester's craziness.

Bethany's bright smile stretched wide as she nodded at the page. "We both should learn about enchanted animals."

"That might be great help with magic drawings." I eyed the description with skepticism. "But I'm not sure how it relates to my tinker skills. We repair and build."

She shrugged, and the dark braids piled atop her head swayed precariously. With skin the color of cocoa and high round cheeks, Bethany Daniels had a bit of a baby face. As a recent high-school grad she was the youngest of our clique, but despite her five-foot-four frame and sunny demeanor, the girl and her living drawings could scrap with the best of them when things went south. A thick spiral sketchpad rested by her right hand, home to Mortimer and several of Bethany's other creations.

I promised to think about the course, which for some reason made the last person at our table snort out what might have been a giggle. Mon Kimora, the dark-haired Asian girl to Bethany's left, remained a walking contradiction. A slim, sharp nose sat in the center of Mon's porcelain features. Her delicate neck rose like a swan's from a dark crop-top with a black vest and dangling chains. The girl's crimson-black lipstick only served to highlight the contrast between her alabaster skin and wardrobe.

Aside from the goth outfits, Mon tended to morose brooding, interspersed with giddy little bouts when a through struck her as funny. Usually it was something the rest of us missed, or maybe something that didn't exist at all. Her course of study was cosmetology, but none of us knew what Mon's magical talent might be. Even Bethany pled ignorance when pressed.

"If you both take Magical…" Chad trailed off, his mouth dropping open as he gazed over my head toward the entrance.

I laughed, figuring he was up to some sort of mischief until I realized the room had grown quiet around us. I swiveled at the sound of clattering and chairs scraping across tile, following his gaze.

Six people stumbled and limped into the commons, heading for the kitchenette. All were dressed in black outfits reminiscent of commando uniforms. Shirts and trousers bore tears and ominous dark stains, and the smell of scorched leather followed the battered group into the room.

4. Returning Troops

A FAMILIAR WOMAN led the black-clad students to the table nearest the fridge. She handed out water as her charges sagged onto benches. Judging by the green badges that looked to have been hastily clipped to sleeves and collars, these were all upperclassmen.

"Gina?" I pushed to my feet and hurried over, my friends close on my heels as dark murmurs rose around the room.

Gina Williams was in her last semester, about to earn her welding certification. She'd helped with my technique in my first welding class, and admitted she'd done independent study with Dean Gladstone, same as me, which I suppose made us both teacher's pets. Most evenings I'd found myself hanging around the commons right up until the eight o-clock curfew imposed on new students, just to see her warm smile and dimples, a combination that never failed to make my pulse race. We'd talk for ten or fifteen minutes before she had to get to night class, at which point I'd sprint for the exit.

I'd never quite worked up the courage to ask her out. Now, Gina would be too busy with her own classes to step in as a teaching aide. I still hoped to parlay my newfound curfew-less evenings into spending more time with her.

"Hey, Jason." Gina gulped down half her drink, then wiped the frosty bottle across her face.

Ash and soot ran down to the point of her chin. She'd pulled her frizzy rust-colored curls back into a tight little ponytail. Unlike her fellow students, Gina's outfit included a leather welding tunic with heavy gloves looped through a web belt. We used similar protective gear in class, but these had been dyed midnight black to match the tactical outfits. She gave me a tired smile that barely touched her eyes, and swayed on her feet.

"You're hurt!" I reached out and guided her to a seat before she keeled over.

"Just wiped and a bit scorched." Gina waved at the bedraggled crew she'd come in with. "We're the lucky ones. A little hydration and we'll be right as rain. Two others are in the infirmary with our instructor, but I think they'll be okay."

The room had been of two minds on how to handle the unexpected disruption. Half seemed to have faded away, deciding there were better places to be. My friends and the rest crowded close, trying to look nonchalant as they listened in.

Attwater was big on hands-on learning, which meant we'd all get a chance to apply our growing skills in the field during our second year. If this group had been with a teacher, it meant they were out on a raid. But as far as I knew, raids seldom led to serious injuries.

"What happened?" I asked.

Rather than answer right away, she took a long drink and considered the question. The silence stretched on, and the room held its breath.

"I should really wait for our debriefing." Resolve settled over her features, and she squared her shoulders. "Screw it. You'll all hear soon enough. It was a lurker raid gone bad. We were supposed to have the drop on a nasty little low-level reptilian harassing workers at a power station. But our man on the ground had bad intel, or he simply missed the nest of wyverns. At least that's what the lurkers looked like, fierce mini-dragons."

We'd only gotten the basics so far, but demons came in three classes: shadows, lurkers, and mimics. Shadows were weakest and considered a simple nuisance—although, as we'd found out last term, with the right guidance they could cause serious problems. Lurker was a broad category that covered an array of grotesque creatures. These ugly things used their magic to hide in plain sight and excelled at ambush tactics.

Lurkers could seriously threaten infrastructure points like the power grid, transportation, you name it. Mimics were the worst because they impersonated people. I think they were the brains behind the whole demon wave that had become increasingly active over the past ten years. Throughout history there'd been demon problems, and safeguards like our school had been established to counter them.

The situation had apparently been status quo for the last few centuries until something went wrong a decade back. Now demon hot spots were cropping up faster than the three schools positioned around the globe could handle the problem. Similar issues plagued the three mystic strongholds at the world's edge. One ancient order had vanished completely. The remaining two struggled to keep the bulk of demonkind from ever setting hoof or claw on Terra-firma.

"More power grid problems," I mused, thinking back a few weeks. "Didn't you head out on a similar mission last semester?"

"That was a substation, just a trio of shadows we mopped up easily. They're definitely getting bolder, and this was a bigger operation, like they were testing—" Gina cut off the sentence with a shake of her head. "That's definitely straying into a sensitive topic. Gotta get washed up and go see how the others are doing. The dean's head of security will have to decide if more details can be released."

"No problem." I jumped up as Bethany opened the fridge and helped her pass out another round of water. "I think we got the gist of it. Just glad no one was seriously hurt."

As I handed her the last water bottle, Gina placed her hand over mine. "Thanks for caring."

I blinked at our hands as warmth spread up my arm and our fingers laced together. "Uh…no problem."

With no further gritty details coming, people lost interest and began filing out of the room. The big burnished clock on the wall over the kitchen read seven o'clock, so people were likely heading home for the evening. I sat down while Gina finished her second drink. She didn't let go of my hand, and I had no desire to pull away even when Bethany decided to plant herself on my other side.

When they'd come in, the raiding party had been on death's doorstep, but the water revived them. Several cleaned up in the sink and rummaged through the cabinets for food. Even outside of meals, Attwater always kept plenty of snacks on hand.

"Sounds like this mission was a setup," Bethany whispered under the cover of crinkling cellophane and loud crunching. "Like someone leaked plans for the raid."

"Most of the team never knows the specifics until we portal in." Gina's lips compressed into a thin line, and her fingers tightened around mine. "Oh, sorry." She gave an apologetic smile and let go of my hand. "Only a few folks in security and the team lead know ahead of time."

"I'm guessing you're the team lead?" That conclusion stemmed from the way she'd led the group into the commons and her heavier outfit. I rubbed my fingers to get the blood flowing after her death grip, wishing I could reach out and take her hand again.

"Until I get replaced." She nodded. "I definitely didn't spill the beans. Even so, it's a good thing this one didn't get assigned to another class."

"Why's that?" Bethany leaned forward, sandwiching me between the two women.

"The other two teams are led by a water jockey and a flyer. Lurkers don't strategize much. Usually it's just brute force and vicious hand-to-hand. But this group had a plan. After a brief skirmish, they retreated. We followed, figuring it was an easy win despite the bad information. But they drew us into a trap and blew a pair of those big transformers to fry us."

"Crap, the other leads wouldn't be equipped to handle that," I said.

"My salamanders earned their pay." Gina grimaced, maybe realizing she'd divulged more than she'd meant.

Gina's welding certification matched her magic talent better than mine. As a pyromancer, elements of fire obeyed her command. I wasn't sure of the mechanics, but Gina saw and controlled salamanders, mystical elemental creatures that crawled around the coals and flames of any fire. A strong water mage might have been able to protect the team from simple fire, but countering explosions and a conflagration summoned through magic would have hands down taken a talent like hers.

"Regina, we should go check on our wounded." A stocky guy with short blond hair interrupted our discussion.

"Everyone, grab what you need. It's going to be a long night." Gina gave me a grimace of apology as she stood.

"Don't look so glum. You'll get a taste of dealing with demons firsthand this semester. Nothing quite as dramatic as tonight's mission. But even controlled encounters can get exciting."

With a last glance back to ensure her team was ready, Gina headed for the hallway. If I didn't know better, I'd say she was enjoying herself. I smiled at the thought and her words. Even though I'd been a total newbie six months ago, handling demons wasn't exactly a foreign concept. I couldn't help wondering if Gina would be impressed by what my friends and I had dealt with right here in the school last semester. Of course, the Dean had sworn each of us to secrecy, so we could only talk among ourselves. Even Mon was excluded from those discussions.

"I think she means our Practical Exploration class." Bethany gave me a knowing grin, and I pulled my eyes away from Gina's retreating form. "Rumors are floating around about field trials."

"Guess we'll see." I turned to see where Owen, Chad, and Mon had gone and spotted them ransacking the snack drawers. "Bring that stash over and let's pin down those electives."

* * *

The first week flew by, a blur of new classes, old friends, and frantic second guessing over wasting my one elective on Magical Creatures. I really should have taken something more practical. Our instructor was a short, squat man in his mid-forties. With his wide, lipless smile and bulging brown eyes, Mr. Grawpin reminded me of a toad—a mild mannered, pleasant toad—but a toad nonetheless. From his wide flat fingers to the few wispy hairs clinging to a shiny dome mottled with early age spots, the image was hard to shake.

"Good morning, everyone, I am Harold Grawpin," he croaked in his gravelly voice at the start of class, drawing out the "aaw" sound to the point we wondered if he enjoyed making fun of himself.

Only eight students chose Magical Creatures, a testament to the better choices being offered. Theo, a curly haired redhead in his mid-thirties from our common core class had enrolled, so it was good to see another familiar face in addition to Bethany's.

"Fairies, trolls, silkies, and more will be exposed to you this semester," the teacher continued. "Although many of the races we will discuss haven't been seen in centuries, rest assured that all of them shared our world at one time or another. I like to think learning how they came and went is important in managing our own existence and offers insight to dealing with the array of demons pressuring the world."

The first three classes continued along similar lines, setting us up for what was to come. The fact that most of the course would be history of now extinct races was a letdown. But Mr. Grawpin excelled at storytelling, and our small class couldn't help being drawn into the visions he painted, from unicorns and fancy to darkness and chaos. If nothing else, the class promised to be entertaining. As long as the exams weren't bad, I expected to actually enjoy the Magical Creatures curriculum.

When it came to launching into training of my magic talent, things got more muddled. Attwater had only seen a couple of tinkers in its long history, so it wasn't like a room full of us could learn mending and repairs together. I landed in a class of five misfits, those of us who didn't cleanly fit into the more common talents. The lesson plan for the next several weeks concentrated on learning focus, gaining a feel for our individual talent, and getting used to tapping the associate magic. The instructor would have to be a mental gymnast to keep up with the diverse group, but Cindy Horton's sunny demeanor and can-do attitude kept spirits high even as we struggled to understand what would constitute progress in her class. Meanwhile, the school was actively working to bring in a dedicated teacher more versed in the tinker talent.

In those early days, I managed little more than simple repairs on a few broken contraptions that Ms. Horton brought to class. Of course I'd spent the better part of my life willing a kind of life force into my automata, little robots that eagerly did my bidding—right up to the point my mismatched magical talent got overloaded by too many instructions and caused them to explode.

I'd developed a feel for the prickly sensation that meant my tinker abilities were flowing, but couldn't see how that might help when facing a snarling lurker demon. For that matter, what good would Owen's ability to jumpstart dead engines be in the same circumstance? Bethany's talent remained the one best suited to take on demons. Her drawings could go toe-to-toe with the creatures, so I figured Owen and I would be relegated to supporting roles when push came to shove.

Common core continued as our first class of the day, so we'd get to hone our skills with basic elemental spells with the lovely and distant Ms. Schlaza, a cold-hearted task master I'd dubbed the Ice Queen our first semester. In those early days our secondary instructor, Mary Eisner, had been relegated to quietly sitting in the corner or handing out supplies.

Something in Ms. Schlaza's recent ordeal must have softened her frozen heart a little because Mary was now allowed to be more hands on. Her kinder, gentler approach to teaching paired with Schlaza's militant demands for repetition and perfection actually struck an effective balance that at first blush seemed to help even the slowest of us succeed.

The real surprise was to find that the biggest bang for our magical buck second semester would come from Practical Exploration class. The mysteriously named unit was added to my, Bethany's, and Owen's schedules from the start, and we'd spent the break in a texting debate over what the class might entail. The course turned out to be another focused on our magic talents. Instead of individual training, we'd be learning to apply what came naturally in a variety of simulated situations.

I'd seen our teacher, Everett Manning, at the beginning of the year. He'd always seemed to be helping Gladstone wrangle guests or set up for lectures, so I assumed the man was a member of the admin staff. Mr. Manning had a laid back attitude and an interesting accent with British and Caribbean undertones. Between his scraggly beard, dark-skinned complexion, and silver-rimmed glasses that constantly slid down his nose, the man had me thinking writer or artist. Even so, his easy nature exuded quiet confidence. Considering he planned to dump a bunch of newbie mages into crisis situations with actual demons, that confidence would be sorely needed. The rumors and Gina's hints had been confirmed on the first day of class. We'd get to try our own small missions this semester in Practical Exploration. The thought was both daunting and exciting.

5. Dean's Office

MY BRAIN REBELLED at the riot of color and shapes strewn around Dean Gladstone's office. I was used to seeing half-completed projects scattered across the long workbench on the left-hand wall. The bins of gears, sprockets, and sundry parts taking up the wall shelves were to be expected. A neat line of tools stood at attention along the bench's backboard. I'd been in the office workshop often enough that little surprised me, but today was different.

Three massive gears leaned against the edge of the polished wood desk. Two were fully metal, probably cast iron. The third looked more like an old wagon wheel with heavy wooden spokes and an outer hoop around which a continuous strip of metal teeth had been wrapped. Each of the monsters had to weigh a hundred pounds.

The nook between desk and window, where I'd spent many a morning pouring a cup of rich Colombian, held a rolling easel covered in bright maps. Two more sets of maps had been pinned to either side of the door, so that it felt like I walked in between palace guards. Something about the geometry of the entire arrangement felt planned, as if it mattered greatly that the spurious pieces of this life-sized puzzle sat precisely where they did.

"Ah, Jason, come in, come in." Dean Gladstone stepped back and stroked his pencil-thin moustache as he turned back to studying the map behind his desk.

Impeccable as always, the man's snow-white hair had been combed to perfection, its color matching the thin strip of hair perched above his sly smile. Thin, tall and dapper, the dean was nearly six-foot. His brown leather vest with its double row of buttons and matching pants said louder than words that he'd be engrossed in his work for the morning. The outfit blurred the lines between welder and train conductor while still managing to look classy. If there were meetings on his calendar he'd have been wearing a dark three-piece suit.

"Sorry for barging in, but I've been wanting to talk with you," I said to pull his attention away from the map.

"No trouble at all." He turned his long face and friendly eyes on me. "About our Mr. Gonzales, I presume."

"Have you found him?" I blurted out.

"Not yet, but he's still in the states."

Gladstone waved at the map by the window. North America and Hawaii floated in a sea of blue. A handful of red pushpins looked to have been randomly tacked up, one of them sitting in the waters off Florida. Red, green, and yellow strings formed a cat's cradle as they crisscrossed between pins.

The longer it took to find him, the less likely we'd be able to separate the man from the monster he'd become. I knew that in my heart, and the confusing array of markers did little to instill confidence that the dean was getting close.

"I thought your device could track him." I scanned the room and spotted the gadget in question, a squat silver rocket two feet tall with meters set in the hull near the top and a miniature radar dish protruding from the nosecone. "You had his magic signature."

"It has not proven easy." The dean crossed to the detector and ran a hand over one of the three fins holding it upright. "Our former maintenance man is on the move, quite rapidly. I suspect he has access to more portals."

Portals seemed to be the bane of the magical community. Even with all the expertise within Attwater's halls, magical gateways presented a unique vulnerability. Along with the increased security, the school's magic wards had been shored up to prevent new incursions, but they would do nothing to pin down my former friend's location so we could help him.

As the school's maintenance manager and a prior student years back, Mike Gonzales had access to every part of the school, and the demons had capitalized on his position. I'd trained with the man, learning about the school's systems and foibles. We understood each other, and quickly became friends. I still didn't know at what point he'd become an inside agent for the opposition. Maybe he'd been one from the start, but I had to believe the man I admired was still in there somewhere. We just had to find him.

The dean's clear blue eyes regarded me as I struggled with the memories. I didn't bother kidding myself that he'd expended so much effort to find Mr. G. simply to cure my friend. The dean was a practical man with responsibilities to the network of institutions that protected the world from the demon hordes. Dean Gladstone would do what he could to help Mike Gonzales recover—after learning everything possible about the demons' plans and any other tidbits of information the sleeper agent might possess.

"If he's hopping around that much, why not just grab him at a place and time you're sure he's been?"

The clocks around the room represented more than the dean's hobby. His magic was intimately entwined with the passage of time, and I suspected he could do more than he let on.

"If it were only that simple." He arched an eyebrow in challenge.

"Isn't it? Unless I miss my guess, you can jump back in time. I've felt it."

Just once, but I let the sweeping statement stand. In truth it had only been a déjà vu moment, but a powerful one. Unfortunately, I'd been the only one to notice, which still had me scratching my head.

"Anyone blessed with such an ability would have to wield their power with extreme caution and only after all other options had been exhausted. The science fiction stories you enjoy are riddled with paradox theories and cautionary tales, which any mage would do well to heed." The dean held up a hand to forestall argument. "I am confident we will catch up to Mike sooner or later."

"What about the Shadow Master? How do we get him out of Mr. G.? There was that group of European monks who dealt with him before. Maybe they can help."

An ancient book from the restricted section of the library had shown red-robed monks tossing those touched by shadow into a burning pit. But the text also implied the Shadow Master who controlled the demons possessing the others had been vanquished. As last semester wound down, Bethany and I had ducked back to the library stacks to do more research, only to find someone had taken the book.

"The Chrono-monks of Skellig Michael are a thing of the past, and the two remaining strongholds don't have their depth of knowledge." Gladstone hung his head in what might have been reverence. "We will have to forge our own way forward on that front also. I have already contacted the Bashar and Chingyow schools. Chingyow has their experts researching exorcisms that might work on such a powerful being. Once Bashar gets its situation under control, they'll also jump on the problem."

I looked to his wide leather belt, to where the small bronze hourglass had dangled the last time he'd gone up against the Shadow Master, but there was nothing there. A similar item hung from the rope belts of those red-robed men in the missing book—Chrono-monks, he had just called them. That *had* to be more than coincidence. But if Dean Gladstone was a member of some secret society, why not use the power I was certain he had to find and cure Mr. G? And what was going on at our sister school?

6. Classwork

"**A**GAIN!" MS. SCHLAZA slapped the back of her right hand down on her left palm, making several students cringe. That's how most of us had been our first semester. I grimaced in sympathy for the ones with shaking hands that still struggled to cast the water spell.

"Your girl certainly has the knack," Bethany whispered.

Bethany had insisted on keeping me company to ensure I wasn't late for our Practical Exploration class. We stood at the back of the room, quiet observers hoping the Ice Queen wouldn't take offense. I'd stayed a few minutes extra after our own class to see how Roxy was acclimating given she'd started the semester late. Even with my sponsorship into the school, administrative hurdles and the approval process had taken almost a month.

"She's not *my* girl." I rolled my eyes at Bethany's smirk.

"You found her, so in my book that makes you responsible even if Dean Gladstone gave the green light for a late admission. How'd you swing that?"

"It wasn't like it was hard," I scoffed. "I mean, look at her."

Roxy stood amidst the new students grinning like a madwoman with one arm extended and holding a crystal clear ice ball in her open palm. She'd gotten the water spell to work on her first try, maybe even better than Bethany had. I'd let my mind drift on my first attempt at that particular spell and ended up nearly giving myself frostbite. It was good to see that Roxy was as strong in magic as I had thought—stronger even.

"Very impressive, Ms. Debove." Ms. Schlaza smiled with a reassuring nod at Roxy's accomplishment. "Another excellent spell right off the bat. I'm happy to see Dean Gladstone is finally bringing in high-quality students."

Schlaza glared down the line and huffed out a disgusted breath, her glacier blue eyes keen with angry disappointment. That was the kind of treatment I was used to from our Nordic ice queen. This semester she was notably more cordial toward us in class, but I'd never been on the receiving end of the kind of admiration she directed at her new star student. The squirmy feeling that suddenly crept through my gut was probably just hunger, not jealousy at all. I'd missed the morning snack we often grabbed after Common Core class.

Roxy caught me watching, half turned, and flashed a thumbs-up. Her lips curved up into a sexy little smile conveying gratitude and fierce pride. Despite my much rockier introduction to magic, I couldn't be mad at her for being too good. I nodded and chuckled when she shook out her hair. Lustrous, ridiculously thick locks spilled down over her narrow shoulders and fell across her face. Hair covered the excitement brimming in her dark eyes, to the point it was like looking at the back of her head. She quickly swept her hair back, managing to keep hold of the ice ball, and turned her attention back to the instructor.

"You keep looking at her like that and you'll have some explaining to do to Gina." Bethany said.

"What? No."

"Sure, my mistake." Bethany shook her head, grabbed my arm, and propelled me toward the door. "Just keep your wits and be aware of who might get hurt. Meanwhile, we have to get to class."

The halls were empty, a rude wake-up call that had me worried about walking into class late. Our instructor, Mr. Manning, had only worked through the briefest of introductions during our initial Practical Exploration classes, but promised a mini-exercise today. The heating ducts chuffed overhead as we hurried to the nearest entrance to Attwater's inner ring of classes. Three horizontal bands affixed with rivets the diameter of golf balls reinforced the big metal door.

"Is the dean making any progress finding Mr. Gonzales?" Bethany swiped a yellow badge trimmed in red across the proximity sensor.

The gears in the door turned in response, followed by a metallic snick and green light on the lock. Bethany stepped through, and I swiped my all-yellow badge before following so that the system properly recorded our entry and wouldn't give either of us grief if we left separately.

A few students needed special access for their classes, which was why my friend's badge looked different than mine. Bethany didn't talk much about what went on in the wing where classes building up her scriptomancy talent were held. The only other person I knew with a red border around the first-year keycard was Mon. Both of them attended classes down the same restricted corridor—through another security door that I and the others didn't have access to. The door in question sat off to our right alongside a sister access, but for now we skirted past the pair and headed for the end of the long hall where Practical Exploration was held.

"The dean doesn't know much yet," I said. "His tracking device always seems to be a little too late to be any use. Mr. G. is hopping around fast, probably using more portals."

"Like the gateway to the demon realm?" Bethany covered her mouth.

"Maybe." I forced down the images that tried to claw to the surface. We'd taken care of that particular problem. "I don't know. Could be just portals like we use to get to school every morning. Either way, they can't pin down his location long enough to go get him."

"You think he's up to something?"

"Maybe he's just looking for support. That old book we found didn't say much about the Shadow Master, but I bet he's stuck coordinating now with the other demons." I cut down the hall to our right. The Practical Exploration classroom was just ahead.

"Next time you talk with the dean ask him if there are any known hot spots near where the Shadow Master visits." Bethany's dark eyes smoldered like hard lumps of coal. More than any of us, she had a score to settle with the demon possessing our friendly maintenance manager.

"Mr. Gonzales is still in there—somewhere." I hoped. I also hoped she didn't get her hands on him before they had a chance to separate man from demon.

Class had of course already started by the time we sheepishly slunk through the door. I blinked at the new arrangement. Our antique desks that usually formed neat rows were pushed off into groups of three or four and scattered about the room. A small knot of students stood around each cluster, working with cards, manipulating blocks, or simply writing.

Everett Manning, an unassuming black man with a scruffy beard and wire-rimmed glasses strolled around the room and stopped to converse in soft tones with a group by the lockers. On one hand, the classroom looked like any other, with student storage along the back wall, white boards up front and antiquated desks with ornate metal legs. But the ring of doors set along the curved stone wall opposite the entrance set it apart. Four metal ovals were spaced evenly along the arc of the far wall and set a good eight inches up off the floor.

The raised threshold around each door meant you'd have to step up and over to pass, reminding me of hatchways from old-fashioned warships. The big metal arm running across the center of each bolstered that impression and operated the six aluminum bolts latching each door shut. My metallurgy class came in handy for identifying materials, and if I didn't miss my guess, the doors themselves were made of chromoly-steel. More like blast doors, these certainly didn't lead to simple storage closets—unless the items being stored were military-grade explosives or charging rhinos.

"Over here." Owen waved us over to our cluster of desks. "You two took your sweet time."

He managed to work a leer into the comment that had Bethany blushing. Heat rose along the sides of my neck too, despite the fact Bethany and I weren't into each other—at least not in *that* way. Owen just liked to get under our skin. He knew damned well why we were late. I'd just been watching Roxy to make sure she was acclimating. The heat intensified and crept to my ears.

"What's the deal?" I figured we had catching up to do.

"Gotta work through these." Owen pushed a short deck of gold laminated cards into the center of the tabletop formed by our desks. Print and pictures decorated each. "Some sort of bullshit exercises. Decide what order to tackle them, then work through all ten." He looked at the brass-trimmed clock hanging over the front desk. "Forty minutes left."

Colorful blocks, paper, scissors, and miscellaneous odds and ends were stacked at the edge of our desks. The instructor's credit card was probably still smoking from his craft store shopping binge.

I fanned out the cards and read the titles. "True lies, save the egg, trigger time, build a bridge—that's got potential. Construct a bridge using only paper so that it's strong enough to hold a brick."

"How about we start with something less engineer-y?" Bethany pulled a card toward her. "Here's one. We each make letters with our bodies, and the others have to guess. Sounds fun."

Ordering the cards was actually the first task and had its own card with a big number one stenciled in the upper left corner. We stepped through a quick discussion about each task and argued over the order to try them in. Five minutes passed in the blink of an eye. Time was of the essence, and it became apparent we'd only be able to give each exercise a token effort.

Body letters did look like the easiest, so we went with Bethany's suggestion. Contorting ourselves into tortured shapes approximating letters—you couldn't just use your fingers—had us howling in seconds.

The bridge turned out to be tricky, and we only achieved success by incorporating short paper struts rolled into columns to support the span along with Owen's thinly folded suspension strips. Even then, the brick teetered precariously as we urged Mr. Manning over to give us the thumbs-up so we could move on.

"Okay, next one's true lies." Owen didn't have time for his glib sarcasm as we hit the eighth task. With the finish in sight and time ticking, we glistened with sweat, grinned, and leaned in close. "Two truths and a lie each. Statements can't be obvious. Others need to spot the lie. Jason, go!"

"Uh…okay. I've only got one friend left from high school. Dad doesn't know about my brush with the law and is super proud of my training because there's a critical shortage of skilled tradespeople." Now I needed a lie. Why the hell was that harder? "And I floss twice a day, morning and night."

"Floss!" my friends called in unison.

Owen pointed to Bethany.

"I love butterflies. Mom's finally coming around to how good Attwater is. Let's see." Her brow furrowed in thought despite Owen's rolling hand motion for her to hurry. "I think I kind of like Mon."

Oh, now those were interesting options. The last one brought out Owen's friendly smirk despite the time crunch. He had a knack for being simultaneously insufferable and endearing, something few could pull off. Yet he did it with ease, and Bethany's cheeks darkened with a blush.

But she'd told us before there was nothing between her and our Asian enigma. Sure they were friends and both ended up with special access badges, but I couldn't picture them together. Mon was unpredictable to Bethany's reliability, dour to the other girl's humor. Heck, the girl wouldn't even tell Bethany about her magic talent.

"Nope, can't see you and Mon." I shook my head.

"For a guy, you're blind as a bat," Owen said. "Her Mom's not coming around anytime soon. Don't you remember that woman on family night?"

We both looked to Bethany.

"You win." Bethany gave Owen a nod and avoided making eye contact with me. "I don't see Mom ever having my back."

Huh.

"Okay, times wasting." Owen crossed his arms and fired out his three. "Project bike's almost done. I caught two girls we know kissing near the end of last semester. And everything's just peachy with Dad; hell, he's practically begging me to move back home."

"I get the feeling 'almost' is a relative term given how much restoration that old Indian motorcycle needed," I said cautiously.

Up until a second ago, I would have pegged his second statement as the lie. That last comment about his dad came out dry and bitter, and I wasn't willing to touch it with a ten foot pole. I didn't know much about Owen's past, but he occasionally dropped hints. His mom had died in a terrible car wreck ten years back. Something about the incident led to an estrangement with his father, who resented then fifteen-year-old Owen for surviving the crash. It wasn't the kind of thing you could just come out and ask about. I figured it was enough to listen when Owen got into a funk.

"I seriously doubt you saw what you think you saw." Bethany wasn't going for the bitter, low-hanging fruit either—smart woman.

"Yeah, well." Owen looked like he might launch off on a tangent, then looked at the clock. "Close enough. Let's move on."

The final card had us playing a kind of reverse Jenga game with the blocks, each of us trying our best to prevent the next move from toppling the structure. A couple other groups had kept that one for last too, and the hollow crash of toppling towers were followed by curses as teams restarted the task. We managed to use up all our blocks on the first try without a disaster—at least until the instructor came over, gave a nod, and deliberately bumped the table. We laughed and scrambled to pick up blocks that managed to roll everywhere in spite of their squared-off edges. As we neatly stacked our materials at the edge of the table, I gave our cards a quick count.

"Hey, there's only nine," I said.

"Correct, Mr. Walker." The teacher smiled and lifted his eyebrows high, looking across the top of his glasses at the room. "We'll do the last one together, a challenge I like to call hot potato."

The class groaned, and my mind flashed back to the stupid ticking ball that we'd occasionally thrown around gym class on rainy days. You had to pass the thing on quickly because getting stuck with the "hot potato" when the timer went off meant childish ridicule followed you for the rest of the day.

"Give it a chance." The teacher turned to his desk, but instead of picking up a simulated scorched potato, he turned back holding a handful of black masks, blindfolds. "In this case the goal is to *not* drop the potato. This is a test of trust. Mr. Walker, would you give me a hand?"

I resisted clapping, but it was a near thing. When I stepped forward, I figured Mr. Manning would blindfold me, but he instead put one on himself, crossed his arms, and turned away from me before falling over backward. *Holy crap!*

I scrambled forward and caught the idiot under the arms, but the back of his head bashed into my nose with an audible crunch. I grunted and lowered him to the ground. He kept stiff as a board with heels together, only reaching up to remove the blindfold after I'd laid him out on the cold stone floor.

"Excellent, Jason!" Though he rubbed the back of his head while I blinked watering eyes. "Trust will be critical in this class and your careers. Everyone gets to try this. Believe in your teammates. Two people are waiting to catch you, have your back. Do not ridicule anyone who needs extra time, come back to them after the others have gone.

"From a safety perspective, keep your heels together, arms crossed, and for heaven's sake stay ridged. Going limp will get you hurt. I want the two catching to say 'we have your back' when they are in position and ready. Before you fall, call out 'I trust you.' The words are an affirmation, but also an important protocol to make certain there are no accidents. And not to worry." He grinned and held up a small white box with a red cross on the lid. "I have Band-Aids."

7. Makeover

M ON BRUSHED A bit more blush on her subject, a warm neutral cinnamon to complement the red tones in the woman's auburn curls. She herself gravitated toward a starker palette with dark accents, but matching the tones to the person presented an irresistible challenge.

Reading people came as second nature, a skill that played well into cosmetology. Hacks in the local beauty salons could hawk color-coordinated makeup all day based on a cheat sheet and one-size-fits-all chart of skin tones. Mon's talent went deeper, much deeper, blending external perfection with the inner core that she sensed within everyone who passed beneath her brushes and applicators.

Some features called for accentuation, others to be delicately feathered into obscurity. She was still learning, but any initial doubt about the calling Attwater had selected for her had vanished weeks ago.

"Those high cheekbones are looking lovely today, Ms. Doe." It was always easier to exchange pleasantries while she worked. "I could just eat you up."

Mon found it so much easier to talk to people who didn't talk back—at least not often. Ms. Doe simply lay quietly, resting with eyes wide as Mon worked and prattled. Beauticians seemed to have a driving need to prattle. The concept was alien to Mon. Growing up under a strict father meant children, especially daughters, were to be seen and not heard. In fact, they were often encouraged to avoid even the former.

"I have a secret about that girl I mentioned yesterday, but I won't share just yet." Speaking aloud was also part of her training to fit in. Apparently people didn't trust quiet salons. Surprisingly, she found the practice oddly therapeutic. Ms. Doe already knew more about Mon that any of her friends, even more than sweet Bethany. "Oh now, you won't pry my secrets away that easily," she chided, selecting sheer lip gloss with just a hint of sparkle to match the woman's unblinking hazel eyes. "But I might share tomorrow. There, all done!"

Mon stepped back and admired her work, plastering a strained smile in place as the instructor glided from the shadows to cast judgment. No footfalls echoed off the cold stone as the woman approached, quiet as death. Layers of black lace covered her teacher from head to toe. Mon had never seen the woman's face, only piercing gray eyes, eyes that looked through rather than at you. Her gaze was a steely pin, and Mon a bug skewered in the display case.

"A well done static presentation." The woman's voice came as a dry wind, and Mon swallowed her sudden craving for a cool glass of water. "But we must work on thinner transitions. Product that is troweled on thick will crack rather than flex with the delicate skin at neck, ear, and nose.

She traced the stark white nail of an overlong finger down Ms. Doe's jawline, then tapped the surface of the stainless-steel gurney the woman rested upon. Mon winced in sympathy since the other woman could not.

"Yes, Mistress. I can do that."

Her teacher had never given a name. "Mistress" seemed enough and fit all too well. The woman exacted perfection, and as far as Mon could tell, only had one student. Mistress never roamed Attwater's halls nor attended any school functions alongside other staff members.

Mon had come to accept the peculiar sessions, even look forward to them. She ought to feel special. Mistress seemed to have been brought in solely to train her in the use of cosmetics and the magic talent revealed by Attwater's tests—although they had yet to delve into the latter. Still, Mon shivered in anticipation of rebuke. Mistress never raised her voice; her mild words cut quite deep enough when needed.

"Do a thorough scrub before putting her back in the refrigerator. Removing powder and paint well is nearly as important as applying them properly." Mistress did not choose the lash today, but her next words filled Mon with equal parts dread and excitement. "We will start with a clean slate tomorrow and, perhaps, encourage our Jane Doe to take a short walk."

8. Practical Exploration

"**I** CAN'T BELIEVE you guys dropped me." Owen rubbed the back of his head with his right hand and gripped the bright yellow demon trap in his left as he glared at us.

"Stop being such a baby," Bethany whispered.

Mr. Manning worked his way down the three other groups waiting to enter their respective doorways. He gave each team their own trap along with a few last words of encouragement. The traps were like foot-long batteries, as big around as my wrist with two metal stubs jutting from one end. Except for being painted bright yellow, they were much like the devices Mr. Gonzalez had used to catch gremlins and small demons.

"You could have given me a concussion." Owen's petulant response had me wishing I wasn't standing between him and Bethany.

"The teacher said not to go limp," Bethany hissed. "You went limp."

"One last time." Mr. Manning stepped to the middle of the stone wall so that two oval doors stood to either side as he addressed those of us who were about to go through. "This is a training exercise so you will only be facing low level demons, glumps as they are commonly called. But stay alert. For most of you this will be your very first encounter with other-worldly creatures. When the adrenaline flows, mistakes can happen.

"Always be certain of your target. Do not use magic if a teammate is in the way, or in the background. Remember, air spells will work best to drive your glump toward the trap, and each trap is primed to trigger on its own once the demon is close enough. Even low level shadow demons are immune to fire, so don't bother with something that dangerous, but be prepared to improvise if needed. Now, is everyone in the first wave ready?" Determined nods met his question as we all tensed. "This is a timed exercise. Your exits will reappear in fifteen minutes. Good luck, everyone."

The cross bars on all four doors swung up in unison. I took point, pushed the heavy door open, and stepped over the raised threshold. Bethany followed, and Owen brought up the rear, dogging down the hatch as we'd been instructed. When he stepped back the door faded from sight leaving a wall of cut block.

"Looks just like our classroom," Bethany whispered.

Except in this room the desks were still lined up in three neat rows, and there were no doors. The lighting was different too, whiter. It took me a minute to put my finger on it.

"No glow bulbs." I stared up at the long fixtures above. "Just fluorescents."

Most of Attwater's illumination came from what could have been simple Edison bulbs. But closer inspection would reveal the filaments in each moved, crawling about like brilliant glow worms. I'd yet to find an explanation or to learn how they were made. Magic, of course.

We stood still warily scanning the room, but nothing seemed out of the ordinary. With commando hand gestures stolen from the latest combat video game, I motioned the others to fan out and search the room, adding in the peace-sign to the eyeballs motion and jabbing a finger at the brass clock above the lockers just because that move always looked so cool.

A quick sweep of the desks yielded bubkis, despite opening every top and checking under each seat. Bethany came up empty on the storage cubbies at the back of the room, and Owen returned my raised eyebrow with a shrug after looking through the teacher's desk drawers and behind the charts hanging up front. We regrouped mid-room.

"Doesn't seem to be—" A screech from the snack fridge at the back of the room cut me off.

The big white cube rocked from side to side as if someone was trapped inside. With another screech of the damned, the through-the-door dispenser started launching ice. Cubes spilled onto the floor in an icy avalanche. The torrent stopped as a black bubble plugged the chute. The bubble expanded, popped from the dispenser, and plopped onto the floor.

The dark blob jiggled, then rose on two stubby legs, a shadowy outline that tapered to a domed head with a slit mouth, glowing red eyes, and short, flipper-like arms. With the plug removed, ice spilled over the little shadow demon until the fridge's hopper ran dry.

"Glump." The foot-tall creature turned at my whisper, then squawked out a hiss of indignation and dove to the left as an orange fireball roared past me and slammed into the fridge.

Owen's spell exploded against the white appliance, and the air filled with the stench of scorched paint. He fired off a second shot, which thankfully splashed harmlessly against the stonework, barely missing the wooden storage cubes.

"Hold up, cowboy." I grabbed Owen's outstretched arm and forced it down as he tracked the little shadow waddling between desks. "What didn't you get about the no fire rule?"

"Sorry. Overreacted." He had the decency to look embarrassed.

"Ya think?" I pointed to the storage trap in his other hand. "How about we try the non-destructive approach?"

"You two set the trap up in the corner. I'll drive it over." Bethany's hands glowed with subtle power as she called on the air element.

Owen nodded, slid over to the back corner, and sat the trap out with the contacts facing up like Mr. Manning had demonstrated. I was getting much better with air spells and called up my own just in case.

The whirlwind Bethany released was only visible as a hazy cylinder where the air currents swept up dust and dirt from the floor. The glump was on the move, plodding to our right when it bumped up against the invisible barrier. Red eyes blinked in confusion as it stumbled, then lurched forward to again be rebuffed. Bethany walked it backward with constant pressure from her spell. The little demon must have sensed the trap because it shifted course short of the corner and headed off along the back wall.

I'd been ready for the move and brought my own miniature tornado to bear, blocking its path. Together, we herded it into the corner. When the demon was six inches from the trap, the contacts glowed a dull red that grew brighter and whiter. The glump's body stretched, pulled like taffy toward the trap's electrodes. Its little legs pumped, its feet desperately scratching for purchase. No use.

Once its smoky black outline touched the top of the trap the capture only took seconds. The demon's essence flowed into the corner, its substance sucked into the trap until the face and glowing eyes disappeared with a quiet pop. Thin curls of smoke rose from the contacts atop the trap.

"We got it." I checked the wall clock. "Three minutes to spare. Go team!"

I grinned like an idiot as we exchanged happy nods. The glump hadn't been the first shadow demon we'd dealt with, but the smooth capture was certainly a morale booster. Suddenly, it didn't seem so improbable that the general populace remained clueless about the quiet invasion taking place under their noses. Attwater grads took care of business. And with the right training and tools, we'd continue to keep ahead of the demon menace.

"Icy cold," Owen said, scooping up the trap.

As we high-fived each other and laid friendly bets about when the exit door would reappear, the printer on the teacher's desk whined to life. I walked over as a sheet of paper stuttered its way out of the machine, print head buzzing. But the random letters, lines, and blocks of color made no sense.

"If someone's trying to send us a message, they failed." Owen held the page up, and the printer drew in another blank sheet. "This is gibberish."

The second page came out just as muddled. While the printer tried to spit out yet another page, something gave way inside, and the access panel on top of the white box popped open. The grinding of plastic gears was accompanied by puffs of color as ink shot out of the open panel.

"Shut it off!" Owen cursed as he caught a face full of magenta that had him spitting purple globs while I mashed down the power button.

"That isn't going to work." Bethany let out a high-pitched whistle to get our attention.

She stood at the edge of the desk, the printer power cord dangling from her left hand. *What the hell?* Unplugging the machine hadn't stopped its wild attempts to print nor the jetting ink, but the next sheet stalled halfway out. A dark stain oozed across the white page. Rather than stop at the edge of the paper, the ink flowed onto the desktop.

No, not ink. The black blob grew thick and rose on stubby legs—another glump.

"Did it escape or are there two of them?" Owen raised his hand as if to cast a spell.

"No fire!" Bethan and I yelled together as the demon jumped to the floor and headed for an electrical panel near where the door would appear.

"Ah crap." A stream of cyan ink slashed a line across my stomach and coated the hand I threw up for protection. "Take care of that thing while I shut this printer down."

"How?" Owen inspected the top of the trap, then held it out for me to see. "Indicator says the first one's still in there."

"How should I know?" I looked to the clock, which saved me from getting blinded by an atomized puff of black that would do a squid proud. Unfortunately, I felt the ink cloud dust my right ear and neck. "Be creative. The door's going to appear any second."

I sensed them both calling up whirlwinds. Without a spare trap, the best they could do was drive it back from the doorway so the thing didn't dart into our classroom. I turned my attention to the rogue printer. Aside from turning me into a Picasso, the stringent buzz of the jammed print head was making it hard to think straight.

The top third of the machine was hinged for easy access to service the unit and change out cartridges, but lifting it to get a look at the problem turned out to be a bad idea. More ink than should have been possible sprayed from the row of cartridges as their cradle zipped back and forth in its frantic attempts to print. My eyes slammed shut a moment before multi-colored ink spritzed my face.

All my life I'd dealt with broken machines and equipment. Nothing quite as haywire as a possessed printer, but my tinker instincts still flew into action. Independent study with the dean and class practice with my talent had me grabbing the thread of intuition. I let my tinker ability pull me toward the issue. My magic rose in response and flowed across the small control circuit deep in the printer.

Directing elemental magic was a chore that took concentration and drained the limited wellspring of power we each possessed. By contrast, my tinker magic rose with an effervescent fizzing to energize me like I'd grasped a live wire. I mentally smoothed that power across the circuit board, letting it seep into transistors and the conductive traces to dampen the bogus electrical signals.

The printer calmed, and I cracked open an eye to ensure the seizures had stopped. I ran my tongue over my lips, tasted ink, and immediately regretted the motion. But at least now we could turn our full attention to the—

"Hey, get back here!" Bethany stumbled as the glump reversed course, ran along with her spell, and shot between my friends as their magic collided.

The damned thing waddled straight at me. I still crouched over the printer and fumbled for a spell, but my magical muscle memory grasped at the tinker power instead of an element that might be useful in driving the thing back. With a leap, it dove off the floor straight at my head. I spun away just in time, and the small shadow demon kind of splashed into the open printer.

The cover slammed closed, the printer sprang to life, and the shadow flowed back out of the discharge slot. The glump tore off toward the smoking fridge, darting and weaving as it danced across the room. It all happened in the blink of an eye. Bethany and Owen looked like school kids chasing a chicken. They'd never catch the thing.

Bethany must have thought the same thing because she dropped her spell, rummaged around in a desk, and came up with pen and paper. Her hand flew across the page, scribbling out a picture faster than most of us could jot down a short grocery list.

She set the pen down, and her magic blossomed. Scriptomancy was nearly as rare a gift as the tinker ability, and her power flowed across the page, twisting the outline she'd drawn into three dimensions. The unicorn stood about eight inches tall, a ghostly blue outline with just the slightest blush of color along sides and flank where Bethany had hastily filled in with broad sweeps of the pen. The drawing's eyes shone golden and azure, colored by her magic more than the ink. Its long spiral horn flared as the picture leapt to the floor and charged the little shadow demon. The glump shied back from the slashing horn until it bumped up against Owen's whirlwind.

"The door," Owen called, one eye on the glump as it attempted to scurry around his spell.

A faint outline of the heavy door we'd come through had appeared and grew more solid with each passing second. Maybe we should just leave the glump to its graphic design aspirations and be happy with the one we'd caught. But our grades might take a hit. This had to be part of the test. And what if the demon snuck out with us?

"Keep it away from the door!" We didn't need any more demons running amuck in Attwater.

Arghh. It was too hard to think with the buzzing printer needling my brain. I slapped out with tinker magic and silenced the stupid thing, which was easy after just having been in there.

Our exit turned more solid with only the slightest hint of stone showing through the last vestiges of transparency. Bethany huffed out a startled breath. Rather than trying to get at the door, her quarry again turned toward me. No, those red eyes focused on the printer. The little bastard was obsessed, which gave me an idea.

"Hold him back. Give me ten seconds." I mentally dove back into the printer, looking for a way to make my repairs more...sticky. At first I couldn't find what I needed, but then spotted a set of capacitors and a memory chip that would do the trick. I floated my desire forth and it nestled deep into the circuitry. The demon snarled and spit, trying to claw its way through the buffeting wind to get at the printer. I threw my hands up and backed away. "Okay, let it go!"

My friends dropped their hands, the wind and unicorn stilled, and the glump shot back into the machine. A few seconds later, the printer rumbled and buzzed, but went quiet a moment later. It happened again, like a lawnmower starting but cutting out.

A chime sounded from the exit. Now fully solid, the door cracked open. I warily scooped up the printer between rumbles. When it didn't spew ink and no demon jumped out, I tucked it under one arm and waved the others toward the exit.

We stepped back into our classroom to a smattering of applause that quickly turned to laughter. The line of emerging groups looked like astronauts stepping from their respective space capsules. A student in two of the other groups held their demon trap high in victory, while the fourth team hung their heads.

There was nothing to laugh about—until I looked over at a grinning Owen. He held our own trap high, same as the others, but a deep purple splotch of ink covered half his face like an actor from the movie *Braveheart*. I sagged and ran a hand along my jaw. It came away looking like a rainbow threw up. *Wonderful.*

"Excellent effort, one and all." Mr. Manning took control, and the laughter died off. At least no one could see my face turn red. "I saw a lot of teamwork in there, which was the main point of this particular exercise. Some excellent improvisation too."

He looked our way with his last statement. It shouldn't have been a surprise that the teacher had spied on us. In fact, it came as a relief to know he could have stepped in if things went south or if Owen's fireball had been an issue.

The printer lurched, trying to jump out of my grasp.

"Um, professor?" I couldn't help noticing that none of the other groups had two demons on their hands. Were we the only ones to get a second? "What do I do with this? I'm not sure how long my setup will hold."

Mr. Manning hurried over to examine the printer that now rattled angrily. I felt the edges of the repair loop I'd set in place fraying as the magic failed, and willed him to hurry. After a moment he motioned a nearby student to grab an empty trap from the rack behind his desk. He activated it just as the glump broke free of the printer. The class let out a collective gasp, but the dark shadow never stood a chance. The demon simply slid from the print slot straight into the trap, smooth as silk. I sighed in relief as the box I carried went still.

"How did you manage that?" Mr. Manning asked.

9. Spotting Chaos

"SO YOU PUT the printer into continuous repair mode?" Bethany asked as we settled into seats for our Demonology class—better known as Demon Hierarchy Studies.

Thankfully, there had been time to clean up, but even after painful scrubbing and a roll of paper towels made from industrial-grade sandpaper, spots of color still decorated the folds around my ears and nose.

"Seemed logical once I saw how obsessed that little demon was with sabotaging the printer. He liked injecting spurious commands into the print queue and messing with the ink tanks, so I tied off a bit of my tinker repairs to reset and reseat things. It was just an old monkey trap."

"Monkey trap?"

"Like the humane ones using a gourd or clay pot." I pressed on when she arched an eyebrow instead of agreeing. "No, really. You just need a container with an opening big enough for the monkey to reach its hand in, but too small to pull out its closed fist. Hunters used to put fruit or some other irresistible treat inside the trap. The monkey reaches in, grabs the bait, and then gets stuck because the opening is too narrow to pull its hand out. It's kind of weird. Monkeys are smart. They even use tools. It would be easy to drop the bait to get free, but hunger or some primitive obsession drives them to hang on to their prize despite the danger.

"Same with the glump. It just *had* to mess with that printer. Every time I fixed it, the demon couldn't help itself; it just dove back in to sabotage things again. My magic was about to fail there at the end, but with the repair loop active, the shadow demon pretty much trapped itself."

"Too bad catching the Shadow Master isn't that easy," Bethany said.

"Hell, we've got to find him first." I slapped the table in annoyance. "I know the dean is working on it, but there's been no word for two weeks now."

"Do you really think Mr. Gonzales is still—" Bethany blew out a breath. "You know, in there?"

Doubt churned in my gut, but I pushed it down, trying to focus on the positive. The glimpses Dean Gladstone had caught with the help of his tracking device still showed the maintenance manager I remembered. The Shadow Master had stretched and perverted the man's outward appearance to the point he'd barely looked human when he vanished. If the man was gone, fully consumed by the demon, he'd still look…wrong. At least that was the hope I clung to.

"So what're we talking about?" Gina slid into the seat to my right.

Instead of individual desks, the class used long, slate-topped tables that sat three to four across. The arrangement made it easier for the three of us to talk before class. Gina would graduate this semester, but had put demonology off to the bitter end in order to squeeze in a specialty welding class, which was fine by me.

"Mr. Gonzales," I said to answer her question. "There has to be something we can do to help locate him. Sitting around sucks."

"I hear you." Gina rocked left and bumped shoulders with me, her smile warm and supportive. "I've been pumping the Dean for information every chance I get. But I think that's backfired because he seems to be avoiding me now."

"Thanks for trying." I bumped her back, the closest I'd gotten to actually taking some initiative. "In other news, we caught a couple of glump demons today."

"Practical Exploration, I'll bet." She sighed and shook out her curls with a smile. "You never forget your first."

Bethany squawked and jerked a thumb to the back of the room, cutting into our exchange. "How the heck did *she* get into Demonology?"

"Who?" I swung around to find Roxy taking a seat between two twenty-something guys that were way too happy to scoot their chairs over and offer her the center spot. "No idea. Pretty early in her curriculum to drop into this."

"No kidding. She just started." Bethany didn't waste any love on the woman I'd sponsored into Attwater.

Up until Roxy's performance in Common Core, Bethany had been the quickest study Ms. Schlaza had seen in years. I suspected my old friend's problem with my new friend might have a little to do with jealousy. Bethany was usually pretty level-headed, but I'd yet to manage a civil discussion when it came to Roxy. I'd have to corner the other woman after class to see how she'd managed to get a seat. Hopefully that would give me ammunition to smooth things over with Bethany.

Ms. Kilbourne called the class to order, cutting off further speculation about Roxy. "Today we will focus on lineage."

Madalyn Kilbourne had been around the block a few times—more than a few. But being in her seventies didn't slow the stately woman down. If anything, the weathered, craggy skin and white hair pulled into a fashionable bun lent her an air of authority. She might be tall and thin, but her back remained ramrod straight, and this lady was anything but frail.

With a regal wave, a ripple of elemental forces spread through the room. Instructors seldom used magic in class for trivial tasks, but Ms. Kilbourne proved the exception. Currents of air tinged with other elements unrolled a weathered scroll onto our desk. Similar documents popped into existence at each workstation, so that everyone had their own copy.

"These are not as old as they look. We're using copies that have the advantage of being translated and annotated," our teacher explained. "But that doesn't mean you can drool and drip on them, Mr. Ashburn!"

"Sure thing, Ms. K," Lars said.

Instead of the usual sneer, his too-red lips stretched into an ingratiating smile that did nothing to compliment his square face. With exaggerated care, Lars lifted his open can of soda off the scroll and set it on the floor. Gold chains jangled under the wide collar of his v-neck.

Why did the only other guy from my neck of the woods have to be such a jerk? I amended the thought. He *had* been the only other person from Philly until Roxy's admittance. Staying out of each other's way was easier when we weren't forced into the same classroom. I'd just have to do my best to ignore the guy. *Yippee.*

"The scroll before you shows the standard demon hierarchy. We will refer to this often, and I expect you to commit the bulk of the information to memory. You should all be familiar with the three basic classes of demons. Shadow demons are the most prolific and can be found across the globe. Fortunately, they are also the weakest of the demon castes and easily recognizable. Like their name, these creatures are dark and nebulous with close to zero physical substance. They come in many forms, but usually assume the shape of an animal. Physical traps will only work if they are hermetically sealed, airtight.

"Then there are the Lurkers, a more powerful class, but less numerous than shadows. Lurkers tend to be ugly, fearsome creatures resembling what you might think of as gargoyles or gothic monsters."

I cringed at the words and Bethany's sharp intake of breath. Ms. Kilbourne had struck a nerve. Mortimer remained Bethany's favorite drawing, and the little gargoyle was certainly no demon. In fact, he literally ate shadows for breakfast.

"Lurkers are solid and usually solitary, though recently more and more nests are being discovered. As such, they can be trapped like the vermin they are." The teacher held up a warning finger, and her hawkish gaze raked the class. "But some are powerful beings, and you better have a plan for dealing with them quickly or they will surely escape and turn the tables on you.

"Lastly, we have mimics. Trust me, you do *not* want to tangle with one of these on your own. Even ancient texts cannot identify their true forms. They walk among us looking and acting human. Few exist and fewer still have been vanquished. When a mimic *does* crop up, it invariably has insinuated itself into a key position with significant control over an industrial segment of interest to demonkind. Take a moment to study your scroll and review the sub-classes."

Ms. Kilbourne turned to her desk at the front of the room and riffled through a stack of papers.

"Mort is *not* a demon!" Bethany hissed.

"Easy, girl." Gina knew how touchy our friend was when it came to her creations. "Kilbourne is the best there is. She was just trying to paint a picture. You'll love the Magical Creatures unit on renaissance beings. There's a decent body of knowledge on the origin and behavior of gargoyles, even some theories that the statues left behind could be living creatures frozen in time. They had a fascinating society. Scholars think the whole species might have actually been working toward a greater good."

That bit of information did more than mollify Bethany; it had her grinning like a maniac. I took the opportunity to change the topic and traced a finger along the lines connecting the three tiers of demons. The chart was shaped like a pyramid with mimics near the top, maybe to illustrate the relative frequency of each class rather than implying ancestry like you'd find on a family tree.

"Hey, here's the glumps." I jabbed a finger at the extreme bottom of the diagram where a cave drawing had been copied onto the page, which made me wonder what the tech-obsessed creatures went after back in the day. I read off the neatly penned labels beneath some of the other shadowy shapes. "Canids, Sidewinders, Scuttlers... Geez, there's a dozen of them followed by three dots. What, implying even more?"

"Many more." Our instructor materialized at the end of our table making all three of us jump. "It is possible that shadows are constantly evolving. Or perhaps they are not constrained at all by physical shape. The latter may be why they often adopt the form of creatures from our world. Shadows usually tend to be temporary nuisances. The other two types pose a greater threat and possess dangerous magic rivaling our own."

She spoke so that the rest of the class could hear, so I figured our quiet study time was over and asked about the empty triangle at the top of the pyramid. "Why aren't mimics at the top? They're way up there, but it seems like the space above them was left intentionally blank."

"That leaves room for the things we know we don't know," Ms. Kilbourne said. "Demons come from a void beyond our world, a place of which we know very little. What we do know is a force out there" —she swept her hand skyward— "seeks dominance in our world. A malevolent intelligence plots behind the scenes. Here on Earth, mimics represent the upper echelon, but even their presence is more tactical than strategic. They dance to the tune of unseen puppet masters that cannot cross to our world. Those greater powers would leave the void if they could, and I fear we would not hold out against them for long.

"The battle has raged for centuries. Our three schools provide eyes, ears, and defenses on the ground. Attwater, Bashar, and Chingyow place men and women where they can best counter demon attacks on our industries and infrastructure. For years the demons focused on water and power in attempts to weaken humanity, but an alarming recent development is their branching out into information warfare. The threat is becoming more complex and difficult to counter, especially given recent spikes in activity."

"I thought strongholds had been set up to stop them early," Bethany said.

"Indeed." Ms. Kilbourne gave her an appreciative nod. "Three dedicated orders have devoted their existence to protecting the boundary of our lands. A natural barrier, a veil between worlds if you will, exists between our world and the void. Thousands of years ago, darkness swept across the lands, and men of power came to realize the veil had weakened. Led by the monks of Skellig Michael, defenses were erected at points around the globe to bolster the failing barrier. If not for those three mystical orders there would be no Attwater, because all would have fallen into chaos."

Chilling thoughts, but I had to wonder if she'd ever get around to answering my original question. "So were the demons we fight trapped on this side of the barrier? And what's at the apex of this pyramid?"

"Yes, Jason, some were trapped. But others continue to slither and wriggle through. Think of the monks' defenses as a sturdy chain link fence. It stops the nastiest and strongest inhabitants of the void from crossing over. Those are the things that would occupy the top of the demon hierarchy. Be thankful we do not know them well. But smaller, less significant beings can sometimes fit through the wire mesh. These are the demons our three schools are sworn to deal with. It has been an acceptable state of affairs for a thousand years. But a decade ago, something made those gaps wider, the fence more...malleable."

I thought back to the assembly when Dean Gladstone had outlined the school's mission. During the lecture, he'd mentioned that demon sightings were on the rise.

"But if the mimics are so clueless, why worry?" Roxy threw the question out like a challenge from the back of the room. She leaned forward with eyebrows raised, pointedly ignoring the fawning men flanking her. "For that matter, where are these monks now? Everyone knows Skellig Michael is an abandoned island. We've seen those empty stone huts in enough science fiction movies."

Every one of us had had our world rocked by Attwater. We'd all adjusted pretty quickly to the idea of magic and demons, but Roxy had gone from zero to sixty faster than most. Maybe philosophy was her thing or maybe learning about her powers had simply kindled a driving need to understand "it all." Either way, the speed with which she'd come to accept the magical world, to poke the hornet's nest, impressed the hell out of me. Of course, the *Star Wars* reference was pretty cool too.

"Mimics concern us because they are poised to do significant harm, and powers from beyond the veil may be controlling them." Ms. Kilbourne looked to our table. "Much like shadow and lesser demons are occasionally controlled by a master of chaos. This happens infrequently, but the results are devastating."

The student body at large hadn't been told about our run in with the Shadow Master or the dean's continued efforts to locate him. But Ms. Kilbourne clearly knew what was going on. I got the feeling that very little escaped the old woman's notice.

Roxy huffed out a breath, annoyed by the answer or miffed at how the teacher now focused on Bethany and me. She crossed her arms and dropped back into her seat only to have the two stud muffins fall on her like ravenous dogs, each tripping over the other to placate her sour mood. Judging by the satisfied smile that curled her lips, their efforts worked. I might have to let Roxy in on a little of last semester's excitement so that she didn't take the teacher's shift in focus personally.

"We will touch more on the order of monks only as it pertains to preparing you all for your chosen careers and the dangers you may encounter. For now, be assured that the outer protections continue to be maintained, despite what you may see on the big screen." She shot a shrewd glance back at Roxy. "As for the rest of this semester, absorb everything possible about the threat as we understand it. You will be standing upon the shoulders of giants, as the saying goes. I urge you to take full advantage of the opportunity. This knowledge may someday save your life."

10. Wrench Your Ride

O WEN'S PARTNER WAVED for another rag from his spot beneath the car lift. They had the little four-door hatchback up high, which made working on the car vastly simpler than crawling underneath. Danny's beefy hand grabbed the towel Owen passed over, the white terrycloth quickly turning pink as the bearded giant wiped transmission fluid from his face and the underside of the vehicle.

"What were the symptoms again?" Danny asked.

"High RPMs but won't go past third gear," Owen read from the trouble ticket on his clipboard.

Danny probably already knew the problem. He'd run his own repair business for ten years, and was only getting certified so he could go legit—well, that and learn magic. The man was friendly and open, except when it came to his talent. When Owen talked about his own ability to make combustion engines run, Danny just nodded and tugged on his long scraggly beard, politely not reciprocating. It probably didn't matter.

Owen wished cars didn't have so many systems to learn or that his talent extended past the combustion chain. Motorcycles tended to be less complex and were what he really wanted to work on. But Attwater insisted he learn automotive systems too. Danny waved him under the car to check the tension settings for himself.

"Fluid was fine and so are the bands," Owen said after checking the latter. "What's next?"

"You tell me." Danny crossed thick arms in front of the overalls covering his barrel chest and waited.

"Well, the shift signals from the computer were all good." Owen resisted checking the troubleshooting guide he'd been trying to memorize. "Torque converter next?"

"Be my guest." Danny stepped back and ushered him toward the component in question.

Owen sighed, not really wanting to dig into another messy job. It was nearly four. As much as he hated to admit it, meeting the gang in the commons after class had sort of become the highlight off his day. *Talk about lame.* Well, the faster they worked the sooner—

"Hey, Owen, need your help over here." The call from across the room was music to his ears.

"Sorry, bro," he told Danny. "Duty calls."

Being the only person in the shop that could instantly get a car or bike running kept him in high demand. Auto repair tended to be a mentoring activity where students got paired up with each other. When working through difficult problems, they'd sometimes go a week without talking to George Davies, the official instructor. It was a pretty good arrangement that let students learn together and from each other, plus a couple of fully certified teaching aides were usually on hand to help.

But the shop got a lot of junkers through their doors, and most of the time George wanted the engine running so that students could work on those supporting systems.

Occasionally, the teacher wanted the opposite, for Owen to break something specific in the combustion chain.

Introducing problems had been tricky at first because his magical talent liked to fight him, but after a little practice, Owen could dial in just about any issue the boss wanted. This time, George just needed the smoking and coughing delivery van that idled outside the bay doors patched up so it could be brought in as a class project.

"Burning oil like a banshee. The rings are probably crystalized," George said by way of introduction. "The company is loaning it to us for reefer work in the cargo area, and I'd rather not fill the bay with smoke. Mind smoothing her out before we pull it in?"

"You got it, boss."

Owen had the driver shut off the engine because the beast was putting out an ungodly amount of smoke. Hard to believe a business would run their vehicles that far into the ground before having work done. Externally, the panel van was well maintained. Custom graphics wrap boasting colorful flower arrangements and the company logo decorated the pristine white sidewalls. Flower Power Inc. might indeed have been providing quality bulbs, blooms, and blossoms since 1997, but their equipment screamed cut-rate business.

While the driver opened the rear door and pulled out trays of seedlings, Owen popped the hood and got to work. Traditional mechanics often liked to hear and see how an engine ran to aid in diagnosing problems. Checking vibrations, hot spots, and visible issues augmented the quick and easy step of plugging in a diagnostic scanner and reading any codes the onboard computer was throwing.

But Owen's kind of inspection worked equally well with the engine off. Before learning of magic, his little trick of communing with his motorcycle or car had been just that, a last ditch moment of quiet reflection after everything obvious had been checked, a kind of last rights for the vehicle, lawnmower, or tractor in question before biting the bullet and paying a real mechanic. But something odd started happening in his teens. Occasionally, after his moment of silence, one last crank of the engine and the problem would sometimes simply disappear. Trying to "get lucky" and dodge repair bills became a game, until he'd been invited to Attwater and found the miraculous repairs had been his magic talent surfacing.

Knowing about his talent and a few short months of practice let Owen dive into the V8 engine with confidence. The talent avoided pesky things like transmissions and cooling systems, going straight for the heart of the vehicle, the chamber and passages that tamed the exothermic reaction and released raw power, the engine itself. That was where the magic flowed now, correcting the issue almost faster than Owen cataloged what was wrong.

Ten minutes later, he slammed down the hood and fired the van up. A final gout of smoke cleared the tailpipe, and the exhaust flowed free and clear.

"Whoa boy, that's some fine mechanicing," a familiar voice drawled from just inside the bay doors.

At six-two, Chad Stillman had two inches on him. They guy loved to play up that ignorant hayseed stereotype despite being pretty darn bright. His lazy lean against the doorframe, ever present cowboy hat, and plaid shirt—blue and white plaid today—helped seal the deal.

"You really should buy yourself a dictionary." Owen tossed the keys to George. "What brings you down to the lower decks?"

By necessity, the garage entrance sat at ground level. A circular cobbled drive merged with the country road that meandered off over rolling hills. Despite the snowy mountain peaks in the distance, the air only held a slight chill that seemed to be building as the sun dipped below what had to be the school's west wing. Three stories of gothic stonework cast lengthening shadows across the courtyard. Between the topography, dry air, and warm February temps, Owen figured the school must be situated in the southwest, maybe New Mexico.

"We're here for a pickup." The newcomer, a blocky guy barely in his twenties and dressed in baggy black clothes and ridiculous sunglasses, barged out past Chad and headed to the back of the delivery van.

Lars wasn't Owen's favorite person. Hell, the dick wasn't anybody's favorite person. That would be true even without hearing Jason's high-school stories. And Chad certainly didn't seem like the type to hang out with someone that annoying.

"Class assignment." Chad gave an apologetic shrug as Lars proceeded to give the delivery van driver grief. "Picking up those plants. We're paired up in Practical Exploration class."

"Lucky you."

"Sure, rub it in." For all his go-with-the-flow attitude, the brawny guy shifted uncomfortably. "You got Bethany and Jason. I got…him and some gal who talks to animals." He deflated on a huge sigh. "Not that there's anything wrong with that, but can you imagine?"

"Honestly, no." Owen lowered his voice. "Any idea why they paired you with Lars?"

How Mr. Manning had teamed him up with his friends was still a mystery. At first Owen had thought it was simply because they sat together, but that hadn't been true for everyone. And instructors might have different methods.

"Maybe because our talents are related?" Chad shook his head.

"I can see how animals might be impacted by your weather predictions, a little. But what's Lars's talent, rudeness?"

As a rule Owen tried not to care much about how others acted, but it was hard to ignore the crappy attitude the poor delivery driver endured just a few feet away. Bits of the one-sided conversation drifted over full of snotty phrases and accusations that the rack of seedlings had been poorly tended. His gaze fell on the bright pink bouquet of roses plastered above the rear wheel well and a lightbulb went off.

"Flowers!" Owen couldn't help his burst of laughter at the image of a gangsta pretender bebopping along delivering flower-grams. "He's a flower child, a blossom buddy?" Oh the jokes would just write themselves.

"Cowboy, I told you to mind your own business outside of class." Lars stormed over, dark blotches blossoming on his face. "And what are you laughing at, grease monkey?" Lars spun to face Owen, his chains whipping out in an arc. "Not just flowers. I'm into all plants." His face darkened further, forehead wrinkling. "Um...not into, just good with. You know, a green thumb."

"Sorry, my mistake." Owen forced his lips into a tight line, clamping down on any more jokes. He might be an idiot, but Lars hadn't picked his talent. Still, the amusement must have leaked out of his eyes.

"It's botanical magic." Lars scowled and turned his back. "Really rare...and powerful. You'll see. Now how about giving me a hand. These seedlings aren't going to last out in the cold."

"Right behind you." Chad rolled his eyes and watched a grumbling Lars stomp back to the trays. "Oh joy."

11. No Picnic

T HE NEXT FEW weeks blurred past, and before we knew it spring was in the air. I'd taken to dropping in on the Dean once a week before class. My usual routine included grabbing a cup of dark roast coffee and fishing for the latest updates on his search for the Shadow Master. But information was scarce, and I started to think finding the man was a lost cause.

On the bright side, my welding skills had improved immensely from those early days when I couldn't keep the electrode from getting stuck. Better yet, my tinker classes had begun in earnest with a new instructor. Although the magical talent came naturally, training it to do what I wanted after years of unconscious misuse required unlearning half of what I thought I knew. And today was no exception.

"Good…steady," Mr. Girardi coaxed as I worked. "Now let the drum spin free."

The carved music box sitting on the felt-covered work bench was big enough to hold a video game controller. I slid my tinker magic through the mechanism inside, across springs and spiked drum, over metal comb and sounding board.

My instructor split time between three students of varying talents. None of the others were tinkers, but Mr. Girardi had trained as a generalist in Italy, or the "old country" as he liked to call it. His physics-based talent let the man manipulate small objects in metaphysical ways. His magic also allowed him to see the flow and ebb of other people's talent.

"I think that's the last one." The magic felt sticky, clinging to the small brass drum as it began to turn, its tiny metal spines picking out the opening notes to "Edelweiss."

When I attempted to ground the magic as I'd been taught, it slipped from my grasp and plunged back into the music box. The wheel spun faster, the music taking on a stringent edge. Mellow notes turned harsh and the song fell silent with the twang of the main spring snapping.

"Two out of three is an improvement." He picked up the box and moved it to our work-in-progress shelf. "Your magic can be quite stubborn. No?"

To all outward appearances, Marco Girardi looked to be a kindly Italian gentleman in his sixties. The man spoke with an accent from the old country, and mentioned on more than one occasion that he still lived in Europe. His scruffy gray beard would have been considered fashionably short if he were younger. Despite his age and a little trouble understanding the man, I was happy to have his years of experience to draw on.

"Yeah, sorry. I'm just so used to leaving the magic in place. Repair and retreat still doesn't feel natural."

Repair and retreat, or R and R, was the mantra meant to guide me in simple repairs. The stack of broken items we had been working through for the past two weeks ranged from stereo components to plastic toys. Some were magic, others mundane. I could usually fix what was broken, but sometimes the magic still ran wild. It didn't seem to matter if I was working on an enchanted item or not. Just a small slip of concentration or attention, and I'd find myself pumping too much power into what I'd been mending.

"It is your work with robots," Mr. Girardi said. "You are used to leaving a part of yourself behind to animate what you make. Unlearning this will take time and practice. It is like retraining any bad habit, but you are on the right path."

"I'll keep practicing," I promised.

What I didn't have the guts to tell him was that I still worked on my automata every chance I got. The Amos series was coming along nicely, with more tools, agility, and capacities than earlier models. The Amos back in my garage was my prototype. After each success, I made matching upgrades to the model in my little workshop at school. Well, it was really more of a broom closet with good lighting, storage shelves, and even a four-foot workbench.

The dean had been the first to warn me that my robots melted down due to improper use of tinker magic to animate and control them. He'd still encouraged me to keep pursuing my dreams, even if reality fell short. Mr. Girardi trained me to be a proper tinker, but I could well be sabotaging my progress by reinforcing those prior bad habits. On the other hand, a glass-half-full view would be that I was well along my way to learning multi-tasking and mastering both uses of my talent. Time would tell.

"Tomorrow is another day." He shooed me toward the door and winked. "It looks like you have a visitor."

Gina stood by the entrance wearing her black tactical outfit and a big grin. I grabbed my string bag and hurried over.

"Hey, how's it going?" I said, putting my mad social skills to use.

"Hey yourself. Your last class happened to be on my way, so I figured I'd pop in."

I caught my eyes running over her tight fitting tunic and looking to her waist for the black welding gloves. The gloves weren't hooked on her belt, so I figured she wasn't heading out right away. I jerked my eyes up, suddenly worried that she'd think I was checking her out, which I totally wasn't—much. Gina's dark ensemble had seemed out of place at first, but the outfit was growing on me. Who was I kidding? *She* looked better every time I saw her. I kept promising myself that I'd do something about it, but here I was dragging my heels again.

"I'm glad you did." A flock of monarch butterflies battered around in my stomach looking for the flight path to Mexico, and my mouth went dry. "It's your last semester."

Way to state the obvious. Idiot.

"You'll be there before you know it. I need to stretch my legs." She headed down the hall, and I followed. "It's a blast working with the placement office. They can't get too far ahead of graduation, but their goal is to have an entry level job lined up a month before."

"That's great." It also meant in a few short weeks my opportunity to ask her out would be gone. Even if I got up the nerve, was there even time to get things…going between us? The butterflies found my esophagus and began crawling up my throat.

"Don't worry." She misinterpreted my grimace. "They don't hand you a one and done assignment. Attwater's professional network stretches across the country, maybe the globe. So there's a lot of back and forth with counseling. They listen to you about location and stuff. I've even got a couple irons in the fire near the coast."

"Cool. You could look for an underwater welding program."

"You remembered!" She smiled and bumped shoulders as we walked on toward the exit to the outer ring.

We were heading for the commons, which would be crowded with too many prying eyes. To buy time, I slowed to a shuffle and screwed up my courage.

"Hard to forget. You were pretty passionate about it when we were talking big dreams last semester." Back when I should have asked. "So…um, thing is. Do you want to do something tonight? Maybe grab dinner and hang out? I figured we could both take the portal back to my place—uh, to my town, and hit a restaurant."

There, I'd done it, dropped the big question. You'd think the magic that whisked students to Attwater each morning would make getting together easy, but first year students could only go to and from their home locations. Between being an upperclassman and her training missions outside the school, I figured Gina had standing permission to go where she wanted.

The silence was deafening, and we slowed to a stop near a dead-end hallway that led deeper into the school. I edged around the corner and studied the gleaming circle of metal that blocked the end of the hall. The door was a bank vault from those overly-complicated heist movies. In keeping with the school's décor, there were a good half dozen massive gears meshed across the front to drive home the thick titanium bolts. With no hand-wheel or keypad, I wondered how the door operated.

"Beauty, right? Who knows what treasures are squirreled away in there?" She followed my gaze, clearly willing to pretend I hadn't just asked her out. I opened my mouth to agree, but she cut me off. "Tonight's no good."

"Oh, okay." Even worse. So, that was that.

"We'll work something out." She ran her hands down each side of her clothes, showcasing herself and looking perplexed. "I know you noticed the outfit. I'm leading another training mission tonight."

Crap! Women could tell where you were looking.

"A lot of those lately." I tried not to sound sour.

"Just a couple of bad hotspots. We need to encourage the demons to back the hell off. I bet you'll get a team of your own next semester. Classroom work is great, but there's no substitute for rolling up your sleeves." She smiled, her eyes twinkling. "And the best part is the briefings."

"Really?" She was so damned perky that I almost forgot getting shut down on the dating front. "You look like the cat who swallowed the canary. What's so exciting?"

"Jason, something big's going down soon." She grabbed my hands and leaned in close. "Security is planning a raid on the Shadow Master."

"Nah, Dean Gladstone's been at a dead end for weeks." I just couldn't believe the man would be hiding progress from me. "I check in with him on Monday mornings like clockwork."

"And today's Friday," she reminded me. "I'm telling you this just came up. Student team leads have to sit in on the regular security briefings. That helps coordinate activities in the event training missions land near official school operations going after bigger fish. The dean himself is gearing up to lead an extraction mission week after next. Some big hunk of intel came in recently and tipped him off on where to find the Shadow Master."

"Is it near here?" I wondered what had changed. The dean had been chasing shadows since the start of the semester.

"Sorry." She sucked air between her teeth and grimaced. "I've probably already said too much. Locations and times are definitely on the do-not-share list. It's too big of a lead to risk tipping off the quarry." When my shoulders slumped, she checked her phone and rushed on. "I've got a couple of hours before the pre-mission briefings. Let's hunt up the dean, and we can get the story from the horse's mouth, maybe even learn how he got the drop on the Shadow Master."

Wandering into the admin wing wasn't exactly what I'd envisioned for a Friday night date, but I'd never complain about an excuse to spend time with Gina. Unfortunately, the staff had bugged out right at the five o'clock bell, and the offices stood empty. We were just about to give up when a quiet curse drifted in from a small break room just off the waiting area.

"Hear that?" Gina waved me to follow as she prowled toward the door, looking every bit the sexy cat burglar in her dark outfit.

Two long legs clad in brown slacks rose from a stepstool that sat just inside the doorway. The pants merged with torso before disappearing above the lentil.

"Dean?" I'd recognize those brown loafers anywhere.

We ducked around the little ladder into the room to find Gladstone elbow-deep in the big clock above the doorway. To his credit, the dean didn't jump or start at our sudden appearance. In fact he barely reacted at all, except for a slight nod acknowledging our presence while he focused on the innards of the clock.

After a minute, he rolled up the small toolkit he'd been using, slipped it into a pouch on his belt, and moved the clock hands to the top of the hour. A pure chime rang out, an oddly restful sound. The dean closed the clock face and hopped down.

"That should take the edge off people." He turned to us, eyes huge beneath another pair of his magic spectrum goggles, which he quickly stripped off. "Mr. Walker, Ms. Williams, what a pleasant surprise."

"We were hoping for an update on your search." I didn't want to throw Gina under the bus for sharing what she'd heard.

"How timely." His gaze flicked from me to Gina, but he didn't seem upset. "There is in fact breaking information. Shall we adjourn to my office?"

I carried the step ladder as we headed down the hall. The office was a bit more crowded than it had been at the beginning of the week. In addition to the various clocks and projects, the rocket-shaped spectrum analyzer he'd been using to track the Shadow Master had been moved to an ornate wooden pedestal next to his desk. Alongside the pedestal sat an antique globe set in a rolling cart and surrounded by hand-carved gimbals that let the age-cracked sphere rotate on all three axes.

The dean had started using the globe to help track down the Shadow Master. But somewhere in its long life, the magical device had been damaged. Now, the dean relied on the rocket-shaped detector sitting close at hand. The three-foot sphere still offered an accurate map and bristled with little flags marking locations the Shadow Master had briefly visited over the winter. Most of the flags were in North America, but a handful clustered in central Europe.

The globe and detector had been moved to the side to make room for the seven-foot-tall metal framework standing by the fireplace, another new addition to the crowded room. Decorative silver filigree layered with thick patina surrounded a big oval mirror. The entire arrangement felt old and hummed with restrained power.

I peered close and did a double take. What I'd assumed to be a mirror with beveled edges held no reflection. The smooth face of the oval was the flat gray of morning mist. The surface roiled and swirled like the fog it resembled, a hypnotizing depth of motion that made me want to reach out and see if it was solid.

"Not too close." the dean gave me a friendly clap on the back, and pulled me back a step by my shoulder. "The Gate of Heritiese is vital to our success."

I blinked, surprised to find myself being led to one of the comfy leather chairs sitting opposite the desk. Gina took the other chair, while the dean stepped over to the tracker and globe.

"So you *have* found something." I eyed the gate uneasily. Something about looking directly at its surface made me queasy.

"We have a location," the dean said.

"But the Shadow Master never stays put long enough for the school to close in." By the glint in his eye, I suspected the dean had pulled off some fancy magic. "Did you jump ahead? You know, in time?"

"Goodness no. *If* such a thing was possible…well, let's just say it would have to be used with the utmost caution and only in the most dire circumstances." Dean Gladstone emphasized the 'if.' I wasn't buying it, but didn't press. He opened his top drawer and slid two black shell fragments the size of my palm onto his desk. I recognized the quarter-inch thick pieces. They'd come from eggs that had been perverted by the demons. "I've been tracking the magical signature the Shadow Master left in the shattered dragon eggs. His taint is weak but traceable. As you so aptly point out, this has not let us get ahead of the demon lord, and he does not revisit locations in a predictable manner that would allow us to lay a trap."

"But?" I heard a qualifier in the building excitement of his words.

Gina must have sensed it too because she sat forward with eager intensity.

"But there is another magical signature in these fragments. "He waved at the shells then the analyzer. "Subtler, but I managed to isolate the traces and calibrate our mechanism. This is what I found."

The dean turned on the tracking device. The narrow gauges ringing the upper hull lit up and a faint hum filled the room. The rocket shape had me imagining the thing billowing smoke and flying off like a missile.

The three fins supporting it ended with odd little upward sweeps, like hooks curling up from the gleaming wood of the pedestal. The gimbals supporting the globe had strange brackets mounted in a triangle. I snuck a peek and realized the tracker was meant to be mounted on the globe.

But the modern construction would have been a huge anachronism back in the single digit century when the globe had originally been constructed. There was no way these two things were built at the same time, so the tracker must have been made later as an add-on to help drive the globe's magic. The longer I studied the two, the more certain I became. In fact, a small thread of energy connected the two even now.

Now that I was fitting things together, the gate made a third piece to the puzzle. Its filigree and scrollwork matched that carved around the globe, though of course it was metal to the sphere's wood. Still, I could easily see the two pieces being constructed in the same time period.

The dean brought a shell fragment over to the tracker, and needles in the meters jumped to life. The little radar dish arrangement on top swiveled and stuttered, finally settling in on a line pointing toward the door and slightly down. When it went still, the magical connection leading back to the globe grew brighter.

He walked over and spun the globe until a section of the Midwestern United States was positioned directly on top. The area of the map glowed and the air above the entire arrangement shimmered. Soon an image of an unassuming man with dark hair and wearing a pinstriped business suit came into focus. The man sat at a sleek desk and scratched out notes with a pencil. A little white cube lit up at the base of the big rectangular phone to his right. He glanced at the light, but went back to scribbling, so probably had a secretary to handle calls.

"Who's that?" I asked as the scratching sound from his pencil continued. We must be looking into the past because…well, who used a pencil anymore?

"I'm not at liberty to share his name," the dean said. "But we believe he is a mimic, a demon placed high in a global corporation owning large interests in oil production and the U.S. power distribution system."

Okay, so not the past. Hadn't demons heard of computers?

"How does watching this guy write out his shopping list help us catch the Shadow Master?" Gina stood to study the man's face, which was a bit unnerving because it seemed as though he could look up at any moment and catch her spying.

Dean Gladstone chuckled and deactivated the tracker. The image faded, the phone's light winking out just before the scene disappeared completely. An odd little surge traveled through the connection to the tracker and echoed along a similar magical line to the gate. All three components were indeed connected.

"The demon may not be currently engaged in anything of interest, but we needed to be certain. Mimics are notoriously difficult to identify until they tap into dark magic." He powered down the tracker and returned the shell fragments to their drawer. "He definitely had a hand in befouling those three dragon eggs. So I have watched and waited, and my patience has paid off. He plans a meeting of several principals, and our own Mr. Gonzalez is on the list of attendees. With a crack security team and bit of luck, I believe we can grab the Shadow Master out from under the mimic's nose after the meeting. This isn't just a chance to bring back your friend. We'll have the opportunity to gain insight to the demons' plans."

"Useful," Gina mused aloud, then caught herself and spoke up. "Nests seem to be cropping up around key points on the power grid. Knowing what they're up to can only help."

"So when exactly is this covert operation?" The closed look on his face told me I'd asked for privileged information.

"A few more preparations must be made, but if all goes well you will see Mike Gonzales soon." He held up a warning finger. "Keep in mind that we still don't have a fool-proof method for separating demon master from human."

"But you *do* have a plan for that too." I could read that much between the lines.

"Yes, I do."

12. Friday Night

"WHAT DO YOU make of that?" Gina asked as we skirted the atrium and headed for the commons.

I figured I'd stick with her for the last few minutes before she had to go get ready for tonight's field trip. They served decent lunches in the commons, and there were always plenty of snacks to fuel up before the night classes. I slowed my pace, not wanting to enter the open area until I'd sorted out her question.

What *did* I think? That the dean had figured out an oblique way to get Mr. G. back was awesome, but something about the whole thing made me uneasy. Maybe it was because they were waiting until after this mysterious meeting to nab him, or the fact that the dean didn't seem inclined to take on the mimic at the same time.

"It's probably more complicated than I think." Framing the thought aloud was difficult. "Shouldn't they bring down the whole operation? I mean why let the meeting happen at all?"

"The information must be more valuable to the cause than taking down that mimic. Or they're worried the mimic is too powerful." She stopped just outside the open doorway and shot a wary glance at the students scattered throughout the room. "I honestly don't know the last time Attwater people took on a mimic. There's an elite cadre trained to deal with them, so our classes are mostly just about spotting and reporting. We're encouraged to take on shadows and lurkers, but never the mimics."

"The dean must know what he's doing." I went for confidence I didn't feel, still unable to pinpoint the source of my niggling anxiety. "Let's get you fueled up. Can't have the team leader's stomach rumbling and giving away your position."

Gina chowed down on cheese crackers and beef jerky before heading to her pre-mission briefing. Her team and another from the Bashar School were meeting up to take out another nest of Lurkers. This one had been terrorizing workers at a coastal power plant with international interest—thus the other school's involvement.

The two lurkers in my neighborhood were the only ones I'd ever encountered, and I'd never even seen a mimic. Shadow demons were another story. I'd dealt with enough of those to last a lifetime, but there'd be plenty more of all three varieties when I got out into the job market. If nothing else, Attwater would ensure we got placed near the action.

I did the usual macho guy stuff with Gina as she stood to leave, wishing her good luck and that I could come along to help. Why that little part of me felt the need to offer protection to someone better trained and more capable was a mystery for another day. I did clamp my mouth shut before going too far overboard, and settled for her promise to be careful and to tell me how things went on Monday. I would have rather gotten her number to talk over the weekend, but a sullen little voice convinced me that being turned down once was enough for the week.

After she left, I tossed out my half-eaten snacks and headed for the portal home, stomach still growling and shoulders slumped. The outer waiting room at my exit held one bored guard, who nodded politely and reminded me that the portals would be shut down all weekend.

Cold air slapped my cheeks as I pushed through the glass door into a dusting of snow. So much for an early spring. But the tiny flakes drifting through the single streetlamp of the old parking lot melted on contact with the blacktop.

A pint-sized SUV sat a few spaces over from my big beater. The only other car I'd ever run across out here belonged to Lars, and lately he'd been getting dropped off by a buddy. He lived a few miles closer to the city, but I still pitied the poor sucker that had to spend even that short ride listening to the guy's bull.

A woman was hunched low on the driver's side of the SUV, peering into the window through cupped hands. She wore a pink denim jacket and matching knit cap that just covered the crown of her head, leaving familiar long blond hair free to fall in a cascade down her back.

"Roxy?" I strode across the damp lot to see what was up.

She must not have heard me and nearly jumped out of her skin as I came around the car.

"Take it easy." I held my hands out to show I meant no harm.

"Oh, Jason." Her hand went to her chest, and she blew out a big breath. "You scared me. Guess I was too focused."

"I noticed. What's up?"

"My stupid keys are on the wrong side of this door." Roxy pointed inside to where a fuzzy pink keyring sat in the cup holder.

"Can't you just jimmy the door?" My question earned me a blank stare in return. "Maybe with an earth or air spell. Either would work, and I've seen you crushing it in common core."

"Oh, well…" She looked at her feet and that avalanche of hair covered her face, but not before I caught a blush of crimson. "I don't exactly have fine control yet. I'm afraid of breaking something expensive."

"Want me to give it a shot?" I asked.

"Could you?" Her smile was shy and inviting, and that protective streak I'd tamped down at the commons leapt to attention.

Popping the door lock took no time at all, hardly worthy of Roxy's gushing praise. But the fact I'd saved her from having to hitch a ride or brave waiting around for triple-A made me feel useful. I made a show of opening the door and presenting her with the keys.

At first I thought the two-inch furry nugget that anchored the chain was a lucky rabbit's foot, but something jagged pricked my skin as I handed it over. I smoothed back the dyed fur with my thumb. Keepsakes like this were generally manmade nowadays. Hers wasn't, and the rabbit had badly needed a manicure. The white tips of four sharp little claws poked through the fur from the desiccated palm of the hapless animal. I'd never examined a bunny up close, but was still doubtful the paw came from your average cottontail.

"I'll take that." Roxy snatched the keys from my hand, then smiled an apology. "Thanks, I owe you big time. Let me buy you dinner." Something must have crossed my face as I blinked at my empty hand and tried to process her statement because she hurried on. "As a thank you. There must be decent take-out around here. That is…unless you've got other plans?"

Since my other plans—well, hopes—had fallen through, I accepted her offer. We drove tandem to the Panda Pagoda, a lonely place standing on the edge of the town center. The store was mobbed, and for good reason. The Panda served up world-class kung-pao beef and signature dishes. Rather than eating in the car, I had her follow me back to my place.

"Great pad," Roxy said as we exhumed dinner from a paper shopping bag that must have weighed five pounds. "And your mother seems nice too."

Yeah, Mom had managed to make an appearance just as we were ducking into the garage side entrance. It wasn't like I had a complex or anything. I was on good terms with my parents, and just because I rented the apartment above the garage didn't make me a geeky introvert—there were other reasons for that. In my teens, I'd had plenty of experience with momdar, that supernatural ability to sense things like bad grades, Billy sneaking in beer, and illicit parties. Over the years, there hadn't been much call for Mom's superpower to activate due to girls, and she positively glowed with pleasure upon conveniently popping outside to empty the trash just as we dashed for the stairs.

"Yeah, the place has everything I need right now, and the price is right." I decided to dodge the whole mother angle, then realized what my words might imply and rushed to add, "I pay rent of course, but apartments around here are nuts. I could *buy* my parents' place for what landlords demand."

"I get it." Roxy chuckled, and we sat on opposite ends of the couch. "Family is great, but there are limits. Am I right?"

She was too damn easy to talk to, and halfway through my eggroll I found myself describing Christmas break, baking with Mom, and the great spritz cookie catastrophe in agonizing detail. I finished the story acknowledging the stupidity of confusing salt for sugar, and immediately apologized. *I'm such a dweeb.*

"No, it's cute." She waved away my embarrassment and scooted closer. "So what made you want to join Attwater and run off to a glamorous welding career? Clearly not this treacherous home life."

"Well, I'm no angel." I looked into her piercing eyes, that adorable half smile just begging for more details. Details I'd only shared with Billy and a couple of my inner circle friends in Attwater. But I wanted to explain myself, to show Roxy I wasn't a bad person, that I'd just made a couple of stupid mistakes. "Got into a little trouble with the law." I shook my head to clear the fuzz and looked away from her expressive eyes that said louder than words she understood bad decisions.

The temptation to bare my soul was overwhelming, and we hadn't even been drinking. The visceral need to share had to stem from simply having a person outside of school to talk with about magic, someone to share the secrets our normal friends could never comprehend. But wallowing in past deeds wasn't the way to spend a Friday night. Still, Roxy would probably appreciate the technical side of the story.

"You saw my workshop downstairs. My projects have a tendency to be unstable. They kind of…you know, blow up sometimes. I'll leave it at that."

"Magic gone awry, huh?" She patted my hand and a warm fuzzy contentment settled over me. "How's that happen?"

We talked of spells and magic into the wee hours. She seemed genuinely interested, which made perfect sense because Attwater was still trying to pin down her exact talent. Even though she'd aced common core spells like few in the school's long history, something about her magical fingerprint baffled the instructors. Dean Gladstone himself had taken up the cause to help identify her calling. In her shoes, I'd have my nails bitten down to nubs worrying that they'd accepted me under false pretenses.

Sharing misery always helps, so I went into great detail about my tinker abilities and how I misapplied them in my wasted youth. I skirted away from my legal issues, focusing on the technical. And boy did my inner geek shine. Roxy sucked it up—or at least pretended to.

"Okay, watch close this time." I'd gone so far as to walk her down to the shop and run a few demonstrations.

The thumb-sized little bot I sent into the center of my obstacle course vacillated with confusion as it tried to work out the overly-complex problem. These little fellows didn't even get a series name and were the simplest, wheeled automata I built to test the limits of integrating tinker magic. And I'd loaded this disposable unit *way* over the line.

"Use the red lens. It shows the magical pressure wave better." Feedback hummed along my bond, so I knew the bot was about to blow.

Bethany and I had honed and improved a simple shield to protect us from blowback when one of our creations…well, for lack of a better term…died. I'd felt the first explosion as a hollow thud, as if someone thumped my chest, not painful but definitely noticeable. Of course, these were just tiny magical detonations compared to what could happen to full-sized robots.

Roxy peered through the dean's spectrum goggles, her excitement raising gooseflesh along pale arms. She really did dig this stuff. Who'd have thought I'd be proud to show off how thoroughly I could mess up.

"Whoa, impressive!" She clapped her hands and did a little dance when my automated cart blew. "I mean, I know it isn't supposed to do that, but the energy release is phenomenal for such a cute little thing. And that's not harmonized magic. I bet it could slice through just about any spell."

"Well, maybe." I didn't mean to brag, but it was hard not to bask in the way she gazed at me, eyes gleaming with near adoration. "I *have* taken out demon shielding. Really strong ones that elemental magic can't touch." TMI, and I knew it so hurried on. "But that's not what the tinker talent wants to do. The talent is all about fixing things, not destroying or even building. What about you? What kind of talent are you hoping for?"

With one last look at the blackened little circle on my concrete floor, she stripped off the goggles. "I'm not sure I care. Something to make my robots stronger would certainly be nice, but there's not really a need. They already do what I want. Right now, I just like hearing about the demons."

That was the thing we had in common and also a huge difference. If my bots could perform without issue, I'd probably be a lot more receptive to learning the tinker trade. At a minimum, I'd be able to focus better and not risk undoing what I learned in class by misusing the talent at home. But Roxy seemed to get everything right on the first try. She'd rip right in and master whatever talent they settled on.

"So how'd you manage to get a seat in demonology class anyway? None of our first term schedules had free periods and you even started late."

That wasn't precisely true. I'd managed to finagle spare time for independent study with Dean Gladstone and Mr. Gonzales, but that was infrequent and outside regular hours.

"Oh, a girl has her ways." She batted her eyes, and it wasn't hard to imagine the woman getting what she wanted. The thought had nothing to do with sex. Roxy exuded a complex cocktail of competence and vulnerability that just made people want to please her. "Ms. Schlaza helped me place out of a couple of entry-level courses on a trial basis. You know, just to see if I could handle second term classes. That woman's such a dear."

My mouth opened and closed once, twice, three times. I must have looked like a beached fish, but had no idea how to respond. *Ms. Schlaza being helpful?* My does-not-compute light flashed out a warning that swirled away in the wake of Roxy's bright laugh.

"Got any movies?"

"Now that's a question you'll regret." I led the way back up to my private collection that Billy called the eighth wonder of the scifi and fantasy world.

Somehow I knew she'd be into the same shows. After much debate, we settled on a few episodes of *Doctor Who*. Roxy was a good sport when I insisted we watch an old black and white installment from the sixties. For me, the rudimentary costumes and sets fueled the imagination. I wasn't certain if Roxy agreed, but she didn't argue—much.

By the time we said goodnight and she headed home, it was snowing in earnest. Late summer and snows were to be expected in what I'd come to think of as the ice-belt. I smiled at how easily she steered out into the street, turning with the car's little skids instead of fighting them.

My good mood made me snort out a derisive laugh as I thought back to how glum I'd been earlier. A flash of guilt quickly followed. Hopefully, Gina's team hadn't run into any issues. But in retrospect, I'd needed someone to hang out with more than a date. Roxy and I just clicked. So why not be happy? I'd had a really fun evening, just with the wrong girl.

13. Day Job

O N MONDAY THE commons was abuzz with rumors of the spring fling event, which was being held the following Friday. Flyers appeared throughout the school promising good food, music, and more.

"Attwater puts one on every year," Gina said when she joined Bethany and me at our table at lunchtime and saw I had one of the announcements in hand. "It's just a chance for everyone to let off a little steam with dancing, a few stupid games, and social drinking for those interested."

"Dress code?" Bethany asked from my right.

"Basic casual." Gina dropped into the seat opposite us. "Staff will likely be in jeans for the three legged race and volleyball."

I didn't miss her eye roll, eyes shot with red and ringed with bruised skin.

"Rough night?" I asked.

"Try rough weekend," she corrected. "Friday's mission went a little sideways. The lurkers we thought would be a slam dunk had dug in deep and a horde of shadows patrolled the substation. Needless to say we didn't catch the nest off guard.

We ended up trading on and off with the backup team over the weekend. Just verified success last night."

"That sucks." I couldn't even imagine, especially after seeing how tough the couple of lurkers that had crashed my neighborhood had been. "We're still just getting ready for our second simulated encounter in Practical Exploration class."

"Take advantage of those." Gina reached over and stole a handful of chips from my plate. "The practice really is valuable. Helps you get used to magic portals too, so that popping into new locations isn't as disorienting."

"Speaking of which." A big shadow fell across the table with the words.

"Chad!" I cocked my head at the grinning face that loomed over me and Bethany. "Long time no see."

He loomed harder and raised an eyebrow. It took me a minute to catch his meaning. Bethany and I were wedged up against the stone column, that special spot were Chad liked to commune with the building. We were in his seat.

"Sorry." I scooted left and Bethany went right.

"Geez, you look as tired as I feel." Gina eyed Chad, and I had to admit that he looked pretty frayed around the edges.

"They've got me on a hell of a schedule, popping around to stations all over creation and back. The dean calls it on the job training, but I'm getting burned out trying to read the weather in so many spots. If I didn't know any better, I'd say they were taking advantage of my good nature."

He wedged himself between us before we had a chance to make enough room. The big galoot's elbow jabbed me in the ribs as he dug something out of the satchel he had slung over one shoulder. He dropped a rectangle wrapped in cloth onto the table in front of Bethany. It landed with a heavy thud.

"You found it?" Bethany clapped her hands and unwrapped the package to reveal a thick book covered in cracked brown leather.

"Had to do some fancy negotiating with the geosciences department and promise to return it at the end of the semester." Chad wagged a cautionary finger at Bethany. "But you were right, Bashar's library had what you wanted."

"And that is?" I asked.

"Another copy of the *Oculus Demontros*, the book we found that talks about the Shadow Master. Since Dean Gladstone has our copy I figured we might be able to get another from one of the sister schools."

"Conveniently, dropping by Bashar was one of my assignments last week." Chad grinned, then sighed as he leaned back against his beloved column and patted the stonework. "Missed you, girl."

He murmured that last to Attwater itself. We'd all grown used to the cowboy's rapport with the school. No one even blinked when a happy gurgle drifted down from the pipes overhead.

"We might not all be out fighting demon hordes yet." I shot a glance at Gina. "But everyone's schedule is ramping up. Mr. Martin has me penciled in for off-campus repair assists this week. First one is flux welding with a recent graduate this afternoon. Simple repairs, but I'll get plenty of portal jumping in."

"I'm hitting a circuit of graphics studios." Bethany patted the book, and I got the feeling it would be replacing her ever-present sketch pad. "And you can bet I'll be digging into this bad boy."

"We barely scratched the surface last time, but digging out secrets won't be easy." I winced at the thought of wading back into those ridiculous middle-English descriptions.

The fourteenth century text might as well have been in a different language. A few words were recognizable, but Bethany had been much better at gleaning their meaning. She must have been an English geek in high school. Luckily, explanations in more modern English were also included along with illustrations that had proven invaluable last term.

"I want to know how those monks dealt with the Shadow Master back in the day," Bethany said. "Tina almost got a grip on him, but says he's more slippery that a normal shadow demon."

The Shadow Master was an aberration, a higher level demon in his own class. A cold shiver ran through me at the memory of the demon master looking out through Mr. Gonzales's eyes. He'd somehow used normal shadow demons to possess other people too. Tenacious Tina, Bethany's living drawing of a big octopus, had developed a taste for shadow demon flesh, but been no match for the master himself.

The monks in the book dealt with possessions harshly, namely by burning those infected. If they had documented a way to banish the Shadow Master, I hoped it was more humane.

"Mr. Gladstone called them Chrono-monks. Let me know what you find, but hopefully the dean's upcoming raid will put an end to all this." I just didn't know how he planned to deal with Mr. Gonzales once the possessed man was in custody.

Several illustrations in her book showed the arcane order. Each red-robed monk had a bronze hourglass hanging from their belt. I'd seen the dean with a similar device once, which had to mean he was somehow connected to the ancient order.

But whenever I asked about the monks, Dean Gladstone went all cagey and evasive, a sure sign he knew more than he wanted to say.

"Speaking of the dean, Jason" —Gina pushed to her feet— "I've got to drop off a little souvenir from our weekend shenanigans. Care to join me before you go off to weld?"

Chad jerked his chin in dismissal, and Bethany waved me away with a glint in her eye. She knew how much I liked Gina. I grew nervous as the two of us left the table and headed down the hall. It wasn't like I'd cheated or anything, but I *had* spent a great evening with Roxy, an evening I'd hoped to share with Gina. The silence grew awkward.

"Um…so what's the dean got you doing?" I swiped through the banded security door to the inner ring, which was taking us farther away from the admin wing and the dean's office.

"We found an artifact in that nest of lurkers that needs to go into the vault." Gina patted her satchel. "Can't show you here, but I figured you'd be interested."

"The vault?" I hadn't heard the term used here, unless… "Are you talking about that big round door?"

She grinned and walked faster, forcing me to hurry to keep up. We strode on in silence, made a few more turns, and came face to face with the bank vault doorway that sat deep in the bowels of the school.

Up close and gleaming under the Edison bulbs, the thing was even more massive than I had thought. But there wasn't a handle.

"So how do we get in?"

"Like this." Gina laid a hand on the smooth metal surface.

A glow rose under her palm, spread to about a foot in diameter, and faded into the metal. A rumble deep inside was followed by several sharp clicks, and the massive gears set across the face of the door started to cycle. Large gears turned smaller ones with teeth that walked the twin titanium bolts back, unlocking the door.

"Impressive." My jaw must have dropped because she laughed and pushed my chin up with two fingers.

"Not really. The dean gave me access. Think of me as a biometric key."

The door swung outward, forcing us to step back, and lights sprang on inside. I felt my jaw drop open again, but slapped Gina's reaching hand away before she closed it for me. We stepped inside, passing through what felt like a magical barrier, though I couldn't tell its purpose.

"Why do we even have something like this here?" I asked.

The cavernous space within was lined with racks of weapons ranging from medieval to more contemporary. There were fewer of the latter, maybe a half dozen rifles and a pair of handguns that would look more at home on a Star Trek set. Several sets of armor, both plate and chain mail, stood at the base of the ten-foot walls, draped across headless manikins.

"It's an armory." I still couldn't wrap my mind around the fact. "Ms. Schlaza said we only use the tools of our trade."

"Well, these were the tools of someone's trade back in the day," Gina said. "And it's not just an armory. Anything unusual or dangerous can be stored down here. That barrier we stepped through dampens and contains magic. It's an ancient spell powered by Attwater itself, so there's little chance of demons or anyone else sneaking in and causing havoc."

We headed past the racks, and I saw she was right. After a few paces, the weapons area gave way to more traditional storage. Shelving, crates, and displays took up the back three quarters of the space. With its mishmash of items, the back of the room had been arranged with the artistic style of an abandoned storage locker. It wasn't exactly haphazard, but it was far from well-organized. A few blank spots along the wall showed that some things had been recently removed or relocated.

Gina found a tall metal cabinet with long, shallow drawers and pulled open the top one. She gingerly withdrew a golden sphere the size of a tennis ball from her oversized purse and laid it on the red felt interior alongside an array of similar items of varying colors.

"So what is it?" I asked.

"Storage nodules." She tapped the top of her sphere, and it opened like the petals of a flower to reveal a rusty handle with a cracked wooden knob. It was the kind of junk you'd find in a garage sale, some lost handle off an old meat- or coffee-grinder.

"Impressive?" I hadn't meant to make it a question, but...what the hell?

Gina snorted, not taking offense. "I know, right? Demons horde this kind of stuff, enchanted little bits and pieces that I guess they hope to reassemble into something useful. The dean took a look and figured these all go together."

She touched a few other nodules that opened to reveal chunks from what might have been the same piece of machinery, a pitted silver shoot, a worn out worm gear, and a rusty clamp.

"A regular jigsaw puzzle."

"Outside of the nodule and this room, you'd be able to sense the magic in each piece. This one's energy feels oily and black, so gets stowed down here for safe keeping. Others aren't so bad."

I whistled while she put things back as they'd been and closed the drawer. In addition to small storage, there were shelves and boxes big enough for car engines. I made a circuit, just taking in the collection. There had to be thousands of parts and plenty of items that looked fully formed, everything from neatly folded cloaks to an old cider press.

"Is all this stuff magic?"

"Pretty much." Gina walked with me and pointed out a few items she was familiar with. "Storage over there is reserved for what's recovered from demons." She pointed back to where she'd stowed her latest find. "Most of the rest is obsolete though. The schools have kind of evolved. Like you said, we mostly just work with our innate abilities and a few tools."

I stopped in front of a tall box carved from rosewood and inset with large gems. At two feet tall, it resembled a small cabinet standing on three arched legs that ended in tightly carved swirls like the neck of a violin. There were no drawer pulls and the gems were oddly placed, circling the main body in alternating rows of color. The sides had been curved into elegant lines so that there was neither front nor back to the piece. A tray affixed between the three legs formed a little shelf, but I couldn't figure out the thing's purpose.

"What's this?"

"A fancy hat box?" Gina guessed.

I laughed, looking for a seam that might indicate the entire top could be lifted away, but found none. Something bugged me about the thing, something familiar. Next to the cabinet, a round patch of floor three feet across was outlined in dust where another item must have sat next to the cabinet for a long time. An empty section of wall behind the space would have housed something tall and narrow. Small wheels had been rolled out recently from the nook, leaving faint tracks through the dust.

"It's the scrollwork." I ran a hand along the carved wood, remembering where I'd seen similar delicate stencils and inlays. "This matches the globe and mirror gate in the dean's office!"

"The one he's using to track the Shadow Master?" Gina shrugged. "So?"

"It's the original component to that system." I double checked the spiral foot of each leg to verify there were brackets. "This would have fit on top of the globe. The magic detector he's using to track the magic in those eggshells is newer. It either does something different than this piece or—"

I knelt and ran my hands down the sides of the three-legged cabinet. Magically, it was absolutely dead, dampened by the spell protecting the vault. Even so, deep down inside was a jumble of discord. A queasy need settled in my stomach, the same uneasy feeling I got when inspecting one of Mr. Girardi's gadgets that had been deemed beyond repair. He said that was my tinker ability working overtime to override an intellectual assessment that the item in question should be disposed of. Apparently the magic often knew better, knew that it alone could return what had been destroyed to its prior glory. If it could be repaired or not wasn't the point. I'd confirmed what I'd suspected.

"Yep, it's broken good. Somebody built the rocket-shaped spectrometer to replace this piece."

"Impressive deduction. You should be a tinker or something." Gina smirked, then held up a finger. "Speaking of eggshells, they're over here."

She led me to a rolling cart in a nearby alcove. The top had been covered in green felt with dark dragon egg fragments laid out in groups, some fitted together like a jigsaw puzzle. On the floor next to the cart stood the broken remains of two dragon eggs, bizarre beanbag chairs with jagged edges climbing upward. Someone had been fitting pieces back onto the upper edge, rebuilding the shells.

I scratched my chin. "Now why do *that?*"

14. Spring Fling

I REALLY DIDN'T find using portals all that disorienting, at least not any more so than driving to a new location and working with a different mentor every few days. I did find classroom welding differed greatly from onsite repairs. In the field, broken parts tended to be in the hardest to access and tightest spots possible. I actually began to wonder if the certified techs I'd been assigned to had sabotaged the parts in question as some kind of new-guy initiation.

The various disciplines maintained their own portals for training purposes. So rather than use the ones in Practical Exploration, my new assignments had me stepping through a door I'd always assumed led to another welding storage room. The first job on the underside of a bridge dangling over an icy stream had been bad, but the next put me on the scaffolding of a Ferris wheel. On the plus side, if the job didn't kill me, I might actually get over my fear of heights.

Then there was the rust, grime, and oil. In the shop we had the luxury of working with pristinely prepared metal. Not so on site, and scraping off bird poop and less easily identifiable substances came with the territory in order to achieve quality results. All in all, I learned quite a bit and adjusted my expectations, which were of course the instructor's goals.

The whole gang was so busy that we barely got a chance to wave at each other in the halls. At best two of us might take a break in the commons together, but never for long. The honeymoon with Attwater appeared to be good and truly over.

Before we knew it, party day arrived. When I'd first read the posters, the event had seemed a frivolous waste, but with our new grueling schedules, everyone was more than ready to blow off some steam.

"Friday!" Owen launched a can of beer at me as I stepped from his beloved auto shop onto the cobblestone drive.

I ducked away from the projectile, realized what it was, and managed to save the drink with an awkward catch.

White tents stood in a cluster around the field between the wings of the building, crowded with happy students and faculty. There must have been other exits, but the only way I knew to get outside the school was through the garage area. Every other exit connected through the portal system and landed students back at their home Attwater branch office.

"Thanks." I waved the can at him and opened it off to the side to avoid the inevitable spray of disrespected carbonation. That's when the general aroma hit, and my mouth watered. "Smells delicious. What're they serving?"

"Sausage sandwiches, meat on a stick, deep fried you-name-it. Think fair food. Bethany and Chad are around here somewhere. We've got a picnic table staked out. Mon's holding it down for us."

A mix of classic rock and pop played at a respectable volume in the background. They'd stuck to clean lyrics and steered clear of over-modulated grunge to keep both hard rockers and the more sensitive souls happy. I had no idea where the speakers were hidden. The music and occasional announcement seemed to come from all directions.

Booths manned by teachers and students offered midway games and skill challenges. Some were traditional, like ring the bottle or knock over the bowling pins. Other games relied on magic skills. A line of students at a tent to our right battled to grow enough ice to crash the model airplane flying circles in front of each. Farther on, a woman in her thirties attempted to guide a fat feather through rings using delicate bursts of an elemental air spell.

I couldn't help the silly smile that stretched my face, a face I planned to stuff with a messy gyro and side of fries. Dozens of picnic tables sat in the middle of the tents, and Mon was easy to spot in her dark leather pants and matching top. We all must have been on the same wavelength because Chad and Bethany closed in on the table from the far side, arms laden with delicious booty.

"Got your burger and onion rings." Bethany sat next to Mon and divided up her haul. "And a few of these for everyone." She passed out little plastic cups of solidified color.

"Jell-O shots?" I picked up a bright green cup and eyed it dubiously. The contents weren't liquid, but didn't jiggle much either.

"No." Bethany's tongue poked from the corner of her evil grin. "Pudding blasts."

Her eyes sparkled as I raised the little cup to my lips.

"No!" Gina rushed over like I was about to down poison. "Do *not* try your first one standing."

"Party pooper." Bethany crossed her arms and pouted, which earned her a conciliatory hug from Mon.

"Just a precaution," Gina said. "Some of those have a pretty big kick."

"Alcohol?" I eyed Bethany as she picked one up, wondering if the underage thing mattered here in magic land. She stuck her tongue out at me, so wasn't too bent out of shape.

"Nope, emoji blasts," Gina said. "An instructor who shall forever remain unidentified has the unusual talent of triggering specific emotions in people. I don't think anyone besides the dean himself knows who it is. He or she puts a small enchantment on these pudding shots. Each one will give you a short jolt of emotion, potent but fleeting. Once you know what's coming, it isn't a big deal, but I recommend taking a seat, especially for the green ones."

"What's green do?" I shrugged and sat since she'd suddenly stopped volunteering information. "Here goes nothing."

The shot was like swallowing a cool mint snail, refreshing but a bit cloying going down. When nothing happened, I shrugged, crossed my arms, and raised an eyebrow at Gina, who'd obviously played me for a fool. It was the welding job thing all over again, tricking the new guy. Owen and Chad exchanged a glance and looked to Gina. In fact they stared at her, and with a flash of intuition I knew they both were into her.

"Hey, why don't you guys go find Roxy?" I figured diverting their attention was best.

"Nah, she was here earlier, but ran off on some secret errand." Owen waved away my suggestion, his eyes lingering on Gina's waist.

I scooted a little closer to where Gina stood, feeling I should warn her. My friends were decent enough, but Owen was a lone wolf who probably broke hearts on a regular basis. For that matter, Chad had admitted to flirting with women from the city who came to his parents' dude ranch. I could tell he was just dying to get Gina alone. I mean who wouldn't, she was cute and intelligent, a down to earth woman. I didn't like the way she returned their looks with a little shake of the head as if telling each to expect a secret rendezvous later.

Well, that wasn't going to happen. I slapped the table and stood to put an end to this nonsense. I snarled at Chad as I turned on him, opened my mouth, and…blinked, at a loss for words. The cowboy gave me a confused smile, the open honest expression he always wore, not the hungry wolf-in-sheep's-clothing grin I'd been certain he'd turned on Gina.

Owen just looked amused. The man found humor in odd places, but the lusty look he'd leveled at Gina was gone. He did grin down at my side though, and I followed his gaze to find I held tight to Gina's hand.

The next flood of emotion had nothing to do with spiked drinks. Heat rose up my neck and engulfed my ears. I tried to pull my hand away, but Gina held tight.

"Green is for jealously," she whispered, her warm breath making my pink ear even hotter, but still she clung to my hand. "Sometimes it's envy or even greed. Best you could get would have been tranquility. The deeper the color, the stronger the emotion will be."

You'd think evoking strong emotions would be dangerous, but the pudding blast effects lasted just long enough to be embarrassing. As with my initial reaction, the spell tended to bring out a person's deepest feelings, so trying them became a kind of truth or dare game. We spent a good half an hour eating and laughing at the bizarre effects.

Mon braved a bright yellow shot, which had her bubbling over with happiness, doling out hugs, and offering to braid Bethany's hair. It was a terrible thing to do to a goth girl who seemed to pride herself on morose brooding. Her vampire-pale skin lit up like Christmas with her post-pudding blush, but even she was able to laugh the experience off.

The only instance that had me cringing was when Owen downed blue pudding and ended up weeping into his beer. Pining over an old flame or missed opportunity wouldn't have been so bad. But Owen's regret swung toward his estranged father, then honed in on his dead mother. He blubbered and begged for forgiveness, his words largely incomprehensible as he washed them down with great gulps of beer.

Owen's mother died in a car crash ten years back, a tragedy that had scarred him for life and sent relations with his father off a cliff. Owen had been in the car and survived. His dad's blame cut deep, a poisonous sentiment that heaped guilt upon sorrow and drove Owen from home.

Thankfully, as with the other enchanted drinks, the effect passed quickly. Owen wiped his snotty nose with a long draw of his sleeve and crushed his empty can. The muzzy effect of plain old alcohol helped him wave away the experience with a rueful grunt.

Chad jumped on the grenade of uneasy silence by downing a pale blue shot followed immediately by a bright yellow. The cowboy's outpouring of weepy love and teary hugs had everyone doubling over, especially when he howled like a coyote, raised his drink to the building looming over us, and promised he'd never let another structure capture his heart.

I couldn't breathe for laughing as tears streamed down my face. The howl attracted more than a few stares, but with everyone else cutting loose, even that wild display didn't bear much scrutiny.

"Oh, we need to hit the booths," Bethany said when the novelty finally wore off. "I saw something on the schedule that shouldn't be missed."

We left the table to three bearded gents who looked like they belonged in an old rock group and headed between the rows of games. The unmistakable scent of kettle corn filled the air and had my mouth watering again. I was still trying to spot the stand when the game set up between a break in tents stopped me dead in my track.

"I'll be damned." And I meant it.

"It's a fundraiser to upgrade the teachers' lounge." Bethany grinned at the evil smile that twisted my lips. "The entire faculty is taking turns, but I knew you'd like this one."

A half a dozen students lined up, waiting patiently at a folding table manned by Dean Gladstone himself. He took money from the next person in line and handed over three baseballs. The woman took the balls, stepped up to a line chalked on the grass, and settled into a pitcher's pose. Thirty feet in front of her sat a giant water tank. Plexiglas sides rose from the top of the tank, enclosing a little diving board. The Ice Queen herself, Annette Schlaza, sat primly on the board, her glacier blue eyes daring the woman to strike her down.

"That's a bloody small target." Chad pointed to the red plate on the end of the swing arm that would dunk the victim.

"Don't care." I felt in my pocket and nodded at the wad of cash my fingers encountered. "She's going down."

Amazingly none of the people in front of us managed to dunk Ms. Schlaza, which I thought was odd until it was my turn. My first ball dropped low, not a big deal as I was just testing out the range. The second pulled left, a near miss I figured was normal. I grinned after releasing my third pitch, certain it would find the target. But when the baseball curved upward at the last second so that it thudded into the backdrop above the target, I smelled a rat.

"She's using magic!" I should have spotted the elemental air currents earlier. No wonder no one could throw straight.

"This *is* a school of magic, Mr. Walker." The dean grinned from his seat and pointed at the game's banner strung above the table.

"Dunk Tank Magic" was a dead giveaway, but I'd been too focused on the teacher who'd given me so much grief last semester to put two and two together. Aside from the name, a rather blatant illustration showed pitchers using their own spells—represented by little lightning bolts—to counter similar ones shooting from the cartoon character in the tank. At a glance, I'd thought the graphics were simply there for emphasis.

Not to be deterred, I rolled up my mental sleeves, got out another five, and circled around for another try. Fifteen dollars later and back in line, my friends were questioning my sanity. Well, at least Bethany was. Owen and Chad had given up and went off to try their skill at something else. Mon's eyes rolled behind their dark eyeliner at my persistence. She gave Bethany a hug and headed back inside to catch up on a special project. Even Gina took off in search of classmates she needed to talk to before the weekend. Acknowledging that the annoyingly dry Ms. Schlaza's spell work was superior might be the better part of valor, but I needed one more try.

"Last call for our lovely common core instructor," Dean Gladstone said as a girl not much older than Bethany stepped up with her money. "After a short break, Mr. Grawpin will be taking a seat above the icy waters for your entertainment."

Rats! I had no interest in dunking our Magical Creatures instructor and spun away with shoulders drooping. A tug on my elbow had me turning back.

"Look," Bethany whispered.

The young woman paused with her pitching arm pulled back. Energy flowed from her hand, layering shielding over the baseball as if she wrapped it in an onion. Even from a distance, each layer felt slightly different, a harmonized flow on one, scattering energy on the next, and so on.

Ms. Schlaza's eyes narrowed, and her confident smile stretched tight. In the split second after the ball left the woman's hand, Schlaza's smile slipped. Wind battered against the incoming projectile, the energy of Schlaza's spell deflected to left and right as subsequent shields spent themselves against the teacher's defenses.

The baseball smacked square into the target. Nothing in my time in Attwater was as sweet as that pregnant moment between the clang of baseball striking metal and the clunk of the mechanism holding Ms. Schlaza releasing. Her blue eyes went wide, as did her mouth, and the Ice Queen plunged into the chilly water.

She came up sputtering, but actually laughed and gave the girl a thumbs up. *Go figure.*

The dunk tank wasn't our only surprise. Farther down the row a big corner booth sponsored by the school's horticultural department passed out souvenirs. A crown of delicate blue flowers circled the attendant's short hair. He hunched over a planter, coaxing vines to grow into a long rope of pink flowers. He exchanged a few words with his customer, a chunky middle-aged woman with blue hair. A wave of his thick fingers had the vine twisting into a figure eight, then another shoot shot out from each side, blossoming white pedals. Think of a circus clown twisting balloons into animal shapes and you'd get the idea, only without squelching sounds. With one last flourish, the guy held out a colorful, life-sized poodle with a vine leash. The woman squealed in delight and took the animal.

"Remember, these are live plants." That voice was familiar, and gold chains swung out for the attendant's open collar as he handed over the dog. "Misting twice a day will keep him fresh well into the summer."

"Lars?" Oh, this was too good to pass up. I stepped under the awning to take in my childhood bully's situation. "Gangsta turned flower boy. That's quite the twist."

"Yeah, yeah." He got busy straightening supplies on his table, arranging seedlings, bits of ribbon, and assorted jars of glitter.

"No really. Make me a nice little bonnet like yours."

"Jason." Bethany's voice held a note of warning, but I'd waited years for a chance to put this guy in his place, to show him how it felt.

"You ain't funny." He waved a hand, and the first row of seedlings shot up to form a curtain of vines between us.

"You used to dish it out all the time," I said. "Can't take a little in return?"

Leaves curled out along the vines, cutting off most my view, but I caught the hurt look as Lars pulled off his flowery crown and hung his head. I suddenly felt like crap. Who was the bully now?

"Hey, um…" I pushed between the vines thinking to apologize. I could blame it on those pudding shots. "Yow!" I jumped back just in time to avoid getting punctured by the three-inch thorns that burst from the thickening vines

As it was, I came away with scratches along my cheek and right arm. I bit down on an angry comment when Bethany laid a hand on my shoulder and pulled me back.

"This could be just what we need," she said with low urgency.

"What? Being skewered by a *douchebag*?" I threw the last word back at the jerk.

"No, listen!" she hissed. "I'm still working through that old book, but centuries ago the monks enlisted druids to help capture the Shadow Master."

"Lars isn't a druid."

"Maybe not, but the Shadow Master was unnatural even among demonkind. So much so that nature itself proved to be an enemy to his powers. The druids used living bindings to trap and hold him. Forest flora neutralized his powers so he couldn't call more shadows to aid him." She cast a pointed glare at the thorny wall separating us from Lars.

"Did these plants draw the Shadow Master from his victim? Free the host?"

"Well, no," she admitted. "I'm still struggling through the language and footnotes to figure out how they finally banished the master of shadows. But having a way to imprison him would be a good start. The dean might need a cage if they bring Mr. Gonzales back...safely." She'd been about to say 'alive.'

I eyed the thorns and thought back to the dog sculpture trick. Flowers aside, Lars had a pretty kick-ass talent. Anytime I wanted to leap into action, I either needed one of my robots all made up and ready to go or would have to hit the workshop and start building. But plants and seeds were virtually everywhere. Unless it was the dead of winter, Lars could call the things around him to life—assuming he wasn't stuck in a sterile room.

"Lars, I'm sorry." I found that I truly meant it. "Give me five minutes? We need to talk."

15. Better Mouse Trap

"CAN YOU WEAVE the vines like a basket?" I asked. "We need a floor too or it isn't much of a trap."

"You think this is easy?" Lars panted his outrage, scowled, and damned if the plants didn't crawl over one another to close the gaps.

Bethany and I had managed to talk Lars into trying to build a cage to hold the Shadow Master. Of course, we couldn't tell him exactly who it was for or why. I did tell him about the old text and how we'd read druids had saved the day when an unusual breed of demon showed up. The druid label resonated with Lars, so I kept using it, which melted some of his grudge against my earlier teasing. But Bethany had sealed the deal with her feminine ways, appealing to his macho streak and emphasizing how grateful the dean would be if we managed to pull off a contraption that worked.

"How about thick leaves and thorns like you used on Jason," Bethany suggested after the basic cage took shape. "Those will help block magic."

We huddled behind a row of hedges away from the festivities to experiment on the pint-sized prototype. At two feet tall, his creation looked more like a bird cage.

"So how are you going to test this?" Lars asked as he filled out the cage walls and added a little hinged door.

Good question. We didn't really have the rest of the plan worked out.

"Maybe the dean will have an idea." I turned to Bethany. "We can show him what the book says about the druids helping."

"I want to be there." Lars pinched his lips tight, his old petulance emerging. "It's *my* cage, and I'm not letting you hog all the credit."

"I'm not going to hog anything, Larry. But the dean needs to keep security tight. He can't have a ton of people knowing about his covert operations."

Using his real name only fanned his anger.

"If you think—"

"I bet Mort can help test the cage before we go to the dean." Bethany cut into the argument with a withering glare that made me feel pretty stupid. "That is, if you two will stop bickering like little brats."

She was right. I'd provoked Lars on purpose, trying to prove he was a dick despite his grudging agreement to help. Or maybe I just couldn't let go of the past, wasn't willing to see that maybe he'd grown up a little. The stupid loose-fitting clothes and chains didn't help. Who was the guy trying to impress? But then again, his parents were both a piece of work. Maybe he was just wrestling his own demons.

I didn't know what was running through Lar's head as he glared my way. Did he still see the scrawny geek from high school? Or did I come across as a holier than thou know-it-all? We broke eye contact at the same time and both muttered an apology—to Bethany.

"Why Mortimer?" Did her gargoyle drawing have special powers?

"He's gone toe-to-toe with shadow demons and knows their capabilities. He's spent time with Tina too, and she almost got a tentacle on the Shadow Mas—" she bit off the name with a wary look at Lars. "She has an even better feel for their magic. I bet Mort could tell me if the cage has a chance of working before we take it to the dean."

"Wait, who are Mort and Tina?" Lars asked as he struggled to keep up.

"Bethany's drawings." I couldn't help the flood of satisfaction as his jaw dropped open. "It's her magic talent, and Mortimer is pint-sized so he'll fit in there just fine."

"I don't recommend calling him that to his face," Bethany warned.

*　*　*

"Here we are." Bethany stopped outside a recessed door on the second floor and slipped a key from her pocket.

Lars stood behind me holding his thorny cage, skepticism clear on his pale features. He eyed the storage closet entrance. Attwater was huge, but students didn't usually get their own spaces to work in. I'd been lucky because the dean had offered me a similar small room that I used as my workshop. It seemed that Bethany had simply found an empty spot and moved in during first semester. The little room lined with empty shelves gave her a bastion from the pressures of school.

Although the room was empty of supplies, the woman's artwork hung from the shelves. Drawings of creatures mundane and magical, from insects to dragons, had been taped up in a kind of studio display. Bethany had upgraded from the pile of blankets she'd used for a writing nest, adding a makeshift desk and folding chair. The work-in-progress propped on its metal lip was a rigid canvas with a half-formed gazelle drawn in colorful pastels.

"Stay near the door for a second while I let out Mortimer." Bethany pulled her big sketch book from the bottom shelf, the book she'd clung to like a life preserver all first semester. "He's been a little claustrophobic lately."

She flipped the book open with practiced ease, jumping straight to the page holding the gargoyle. A wave of her hand slid the charcoal drawing across the page. The graphite flowed off the edge, swirling into the air and twisting into three dimensions.

Mortimer turned vaguely transparent as he reformed. Standing a foot tall and nearly as wide, he was a squat gray brute with thick legs, dangling arms, and a whip tail that ended in a wickedly barbed tip. Tusks jutted up from his lower jaw, scissoring together with fangs from above when he closed his mouth and scented the air with his pug nose. Then he became a blur.

"Geez!" My gaze shot right and left, trying to track the little gargoyle as he shot around the room like a pinball, bouncing off shelves, jumping on the desk to inspect the new drawing, and finally settling on Bethany's left shoulder.

"Like I said." Bethany patted a dangling leg as the little guy's pointed heel bounced against the spaghetti strap of her camisole. "Mort's getting a bit stir crazy. He can't do long stints on the page anymore."

The statement made me wonder what would happen if the hundreds of images squirreled away in the room got restless. Was the school destined to be overrun by animated drawings?

"Well, here it is." Lars sat the cage down with the open door facing Bethany.

Fast a lightning, Mortimer jumped down and started sniffing around the woven branches at its base. He circled the cage twice, poked his head through the opening, then hopped inside and slammed the door. We waited a good two minutes as rustling from inside the cage grew frantic and subsided.

"So…does he—"

The cage shook and rattled, cutting me off. A clawed hand punched through the leafy wall near the hinges then pulled back out of sight. Mortimer poked through at several more spots. Sometimes it was a hand, other times a foot, and once the tip of his tail.

"He might be finding breaks in the barrier." Bethany seemed uncertain as she tugged on her ear and looked up. "What do you think, Tina?"

"For the love of God!" Lars followed her gaze, yelped, and dove under the desk—and for good reason.

The ceiling undulated and writhed, thick pebbly strips of blue twisting overtop one another. I ducked involuntarily as the living canopy spread to encompass the upper shelves, tentacles looping around the metal supports. I recognized Bethany's other prized creature, but it took conscious effort to tamp down my panic.

"Um…Tina's grown." My voice hardly cracked at all. I cleared my throat with a manly cough and stood up pretending to stretch my back. "Almost didn't recognize her there for a second."

"Yeah, she doesn't really fit on a page at all anymore." Bethany cast her eyes down with a shy grin. "Shadow demons must be nutritious."

Tina had gobbled down a lot of them in her short life, and I took a mental note not to feed her more. Otherwise, Attwater would have to build a new wing to house the massive octopus.

Something must have passed between artist and creation, because Tina flowed down and tapped her wicked beak against the side of the cage. The door opened, and Mortimer stuck his head out. The two drawings faced each other in silence, seeming to commune for a moment.

When the octopus withdrew and again took her station against the ceiling, Lars slipped out from beneath the desk. To his credit, he nodded in appreciation at Tina.

"What's the verdict?" he asked.

"Honestly, they are both impressed." Bethany knelt by the cage, and scratched Mortimer behind his bat ears. "Mort says he could get out easily, but shadows won't like the green taste. There are a couple of places they could slip through, so he wants more leaves. Tina agrees the flavor of this will deter the…one we're after." Her avoidance of using the name had Lars narrowing his eyes.

"He's called the Shadow Master." I bit the bullet and decided to trust the guy. "A wacked out demon that can control other shadow demons and makes them more dangerous. But keep that to yourself. We don't want to panic anyone or tip the dean's hand. He's got it handled. We just want to give him a way to keep the Shadow Master contained."

"Cool. I can easily layer on more leaves. No problem." Lars knelt to examine the spots that Mortimer had punched through then looked past the gargoyle into the cage. "This little guy is handy to— Yow!"

Lars must have gotten too close because Mortimer bopped him on the nose with a claw and slammed the door shut. Lars rubbed his face and pulled the door open, but a skinny gray arm yanked it shut again sealing the gargoyle inside.

"Where the hell did he get furniture?" Lars asked. "There's a little couch and table in there."

"Mort?" Bethany stuck her head down by the cage and turned it to the side as if listening, then nodded. "Okay. I get it." She straightened and shrugged. "He likes it in there and wants you to leave so he can nap."

"But it's *my* cage. And how's Dean Gladstone going to use it to catch this super shadow if your drawing is using it as a playhouse?"

"I'm guessing Mortimer won't be holding an open house for the Dean's inspection," I said. "You'll just have to grow the full-sized one. We'll take that to the dean."

"Full sized?" Lars cocked his head. "I've never seen a shadow demon bigger than a cat. How big are we talking?"

"Big enough for a person." There were of course bigger shadows, but I'd forgotten the curriculum was breaking us in with lower-class demons.

"A person?" He looked at me like I was crazy, apparently not wanting to invest that kind of effort. "Something that big is going weigh fifty pounds, maybe a hundred."

"Oh, right." I hadn't thought of that. "Can you add wheels?"

16. Something Amiss

BETHANY, LARS, AND I left Mortimer to his new digs, which Bethany tucked into the back corner. Lars added a few extra leaves, but also a hinged window so the gargoyle could look out without having to leave his door open. Because it was a living cage, he also recommended adding some enchanted glow bulbs to simulate sunlight for a few hours each day in order to keep the cage healthy. Bethany promised she'd dig some up before heading home for the weekend.

The three of us piled out of the small room and ran straight into Roxy, who stood with hand on hip. She gave a sly smile and counted us with a flicking index finger. She wore a jaw-dropping hot pink mini-skirt and fuzzy white top, an outfit I certainly wouldn't have missed—even in a crowd.

"Hey, Roxy." I figured I had better steer the conversation away from whatever evil thought lurked in the woman's mind, especially given we'd just spilled out of a closet in the dark reaches of the building. "I expected to see you at the picnic."

"I had a few errands to run." She waved away my question. "You can take me down and show me around before they close, but for now I have a more interesting question."

Her smile showed too many teeth and looked a little predatory. Bethany would get the short end of the social stick if rumors started circulating about her being with two guys, even if most of us suspected that she and Mon were already an item. In fact, hearing that sort of rumor could devastate Mon too.

"This isn't what it looks like," I blurted out desperate to protect Bethany's reputation. "We were just…" What? Planning out a demon raid?

"Oh, I know exactly what you were 'just' doing." Again with the devilish smile. "What I want to know is who or what is this Shadow Master you were discussing in there. Unless I miss my guess, I bet it has something to do with the old book that beefy cowboy brought you a while back."

Wow, this was both good and bad. Good that she didn't think lesser of our friend. Bad that she'd somehow overheard part of our conversation and was connecting dots. Bethany and I exchanged a quick glance, silently trying to gauge how much Roxy had heard.

The dean had sworn us all to secrecy concerning last semester's events, but the cat seemed to be slowly escaping the bag. Roxy was too sharp to keep in the dark much longer, especially as she became a regular in our circle of friends. I figured setting the record straight would do the least damage and trusted her to keep our secret. I didn't even need to share most of the details, which were what the dean seemed to want kept under wraps for security purposes.

"Well, the book *is* part of it," I said. "There's an old threat that had to be dealt with centuries ago, and we think it's come back around. How much have they taught you about shadow demons?"

I kept the details to a bare minimum, glossing over the battle that took place inside the school and the Shadow Master's ultimate objective. But to put things in context, I outlined how Mr. Gonzales had been taken over and that the dean planned to bring him back. The information satisfied her curiosity without breaking our agreement with Dean Gladstone too badly. She asked a bunch of questions, but I stuck to my guns.

"Thanks for sharing," Roxy said after I'd ducked her third attempt to wheedle a bit more info. "Your secret's safe with me. After all, who would I even tell?"

"So how long will it take you to build the full-sized cage?" I asked Lars before we broke up.

"For something that big?" He shook his head and sighed. "Two days at least. And don't think I'll spend my whole weekend at school. Give me until Tuesday."

"Fair enough." I turned to Bethany. "We can all meet up and go to the dean after our big Practical Exploration exercise. We need time to prepare for that anyway."

Mr. Manning planned to send the teams on another training mission, this time with tougher opponents on the other side of our classroom portals. He'd recommended we bring the 'tools of our trade,' but I didn't know if that meant welding gear or something related to my tinker abilities.

"Sounds like a plan," Bethany agreed. "If you'll all excuse me, I need to go find Mon before she gives up on me."

"Want to show me around the festivities?" Without waiting for a response, Roxy swept me down the hallway.

"Uh, okay." Lars called from behind. "Good plan. I'll just get to work then."

Tents were already coming down by the time we stepped through the big garage doors into the courtyard. I looked off to the right, trying to see if the popcorn stand we'd finally located might still be open. Roxy snaked her arm through mine and pressed up close.

"It looks like we missed the fun," she murmured in my ear and pulled me off to the left. "Let's see if there's anything entertaining to do."

With Roxy clinging so close, the sudden course change had me stumbling and a little light-headed. I laughed and caught my balance. Clumsy feet couldn't dampen my good mood. We were finally on a path to help Mr. Gonzales, and everything was going along smoothly.

I took about five steps and ran smack dab into Gina.

"There you are!" Gina's hair had escaped its band and whipped in the breeze like angry snakes. "Last thing I knew you were obsessed with dunking Ms. Schlaza. I've been looking for you everywhere."

"Sorry, Bethany and I had to talk with Lars about"— I looked around to ensure no prying ears were close— "that side project of ours."

She gazed past me, surveying the back of the building, and I was stupid enough to bite. I swiveled my head to see what she was looking at.

"That's funny. I don't see Bethany." Gina's left eyebrow arched high, and her gaze fell to where my arm was firmly entwined with Roxy's.

Crap. I disentangled my arm, which was harder than it should have been. Roxy and I kept circling our arms in the same direction, until I finally just yanked myself free. She smiled the whole time, as if playing an amusing game.

"She went to find Mon," I explained. "We were up at her little studio. You know the one?" At her slow nod, I continued. "Discussing something Lars is making for us. I can fill you in."

"I think that would be wise." Her gaze drifted to Roxy, a challenge flashing in her sparkling brown eyes.

"I think I'll just look around on my own." Roxy's smile turned hard with lots of teeth showing, but softened when she turned my way. "Maybe I'll see you this weekend, slugger. You can fill *me* in too."

At the start of the day, I'd toyed with the idea of again asking Gina to hang out, but the wink Roxy added before walking away put the final nail in that particular coffin. I rewound the last couple of hours in my mind, trying to figure out where I'd gone wrong. The look in Gina's eyes as she glared at Roxy then back at me promised that she was more than willing to explain. I honestly didn't know if it was a good thing or not that she didn't.

We ended up cruising the tents as things got torn down. I told Gina what Bethany had found out about druids aiding the monks and how Lars's talent could help. The talk and a complimentary bag of kettle corn seemed to ease the tension between us. Going our separate ways at the end of the day didn't feel awkward, but broaching the topic of getting together outside of school certainly wasn't on the table either.

So I spent a lonely weekend with my robots, except for a few hours of online gaming with Billy. Then there was the unexpected knock on my door Saturday afternoon when Roxy made a surprise appearance with a pizza and six-pack.

After Gina's cold shoulder, I was leery of getting too chummy with the woman. Given she hadn't even texted first, showing up unannounced felt a little stalky. But it turned out she had an issue with one of her own robots and just wanted to talk technical details with special emphasis on how she might bring some of her magic to bear to improve the machine.

All in all it was an innocent couple of hours chatting and eating. No harm no foul, she just picked my brain—thoroughly. My inner geek might have imagined she was flirting, but aside from occasionally leaning in too close or accidentally brushing fingers over the last slice of pizza, the evening was totally harmless.

Bethany grabbed me before class on Monday, shoved me into a corner, and launched into her weekend report. I knew she didn't feel *that* way about me, but a guy could get a complex with so many beautiful women always trying to get him alone.

"I did a ton more reading in the *Oculus Demontros* and came across a bunch of good stuff on those monks. Back in the—" She broke off and snapped her fingers twice, right in front of my nose. "What's with the goofy smile? Stop daydreaming and listen to what I'm saying. There might be a way to separate the Shadow Master from Mr. Gonzales."

17. Wrong Door

"**T**ODAY WILL BE a bit more challenging than last time." Mr. Manning adjusted his wire-rimmed glasses as he strode up and down in front of the portal doors. He wore a powder blue sweater over a white shirt with slacks and brown loafers, looking like the African-American version of Mr. Rogers. I guess that made us the people in his neighborhood. "Trust your teammates and what you have learned. I've had many ask how I chose their group. I did not. Your own affinity for each other, for each other's talent, drew you together. I simply wrote names down so we could neatly track everything. Even if you haven't yet discovered how, your talents complement one another. Don't be afraid to experiment. Seek synergy. Make a whole that is greater than the contributing parts.

"But never forget you are dealing with real-life demons. These creatures will look for any avenue of escape. Your rooms have been altered, so do not rely on any conveniently placed items this time, like say…a printer." He shot a glance my way, but continued smoothly. "You have your common spells, your talents, and two traps. Remember, fire has little effect on shadows, but great potential to get out of hand. Mr.

Jones, what would be a more suitable alternative to trying to burn a shadow?"

Owen blushed at being singled out, but of course he'd been the only one to almost set the practice room on fire last time. I considered his embarrassment a sign of personal growth.

"Wind," Owen said. "Shadows have little substance, so use air spells to drive them into the traps."

"Yes, good." Mr. Manning nodded. "Exploit their nature."

"What about light?" I asked. "Shouldn't bright light weaken a creature of shadow?"

We'd touched on the basics of demon hunting over the weeks since our last excursion, but Attwater seemed to be spooning out information in dribs and drabs. I didn't like the fact that we were simply capturing shadow demons. Why not destroy them?

"You are technically correct. Light can diminish a shadow, but is also a two-edged sword. Shadows are not simply darkness, they are contrast. Light also creates shadows, and if inappropriately applied can strengthen them. Mage light is the exception. By all means, use it to your advantage if circumstances allow, but its effect will be slow and more of a repellant than a weapon. The slightest crack in its surroundings will allow your quarry to escape, which is why even trapped shadows must be exposed to direct sunlight or its equivalent to successfully banish them.

"Let's recap what we know. Shadow demons vary in strength. The lowest classes are largely nuisance creatures that sow chaos, whether simply through their disruptive presence or by damaging machines. Higher up the spectrum from creatures like the glumps you captured are shadows capable of much more, including hurting or killing fledgling magic users."

"And some can possess people," Bethany added.

"That is very rare." Mr. Manning peered through his glasses as if wanting to say more on the topic. Undoubtedly he'd been made aware of the Shadow Master's attack last semester. "A valid academic point, but nothing for the class as a whole to worry about. Your immediate future involves traps and air spells. It is fortunate that these capacitor devices were developed." He stopped at my desk, scooped up one of our traps, and brandished it about. Then he picked up the clear wine bottle we'd been issued. "Bottle traps have been the standard for generations. With the correct type of glass, the reflective properties prevent shadows from escaping. Maneuvering a shadow with air currents can be tricky. This small hole near the bottom allows air to escape so that you may use a simple whirlwind spell to draw the demon in once it is close enough. Any shape of glass container will work, but that simple adaptation allows for natural air flow. Each team will try using a bottle trap at least once to become familiar with the technique. Locking the glass stoppers into place quickly will be key to not losing your catch."

In class we'd practiced drawing our tiny tornadoes through both standard bottles and ones with the vent hole. As usual, Owen and Bethany did much better than me. I'd eventually gotten the hang of it and managed to draw in the smoke we'd used to simulate a shadow demon. Mr. Manning was right though. Without that vent, there was nowhere for the air at the bottom of a funnel cloud to go. It had to be bled out through the neck of the bottle, or you risked the building pressure shattering the glass.

Back before glass blowing became a skillset, lightning glass was highly prized. The natural chunks of melted sand were the best device for capturing shadows, but the method for drawing them into solid pieces of glass was more complicated than a simple wind spell.

"What about handling lurkers and mimics?" A man at the back of the room asked.

"Lurkers take a different technique," Mr. Manning said. "Since they are more corporeal than shadows, cruder approaches work best. Fundamentally they are susceptible to weapons made of steel and iron. Some have formidable magic and are resistant to many spells. We'll learn more about lurkers before you get to meet one in person. For now, think of them as insects with so many evolutionary paths that it becomes difficult to predict what abilities one may possess. I won't really cover mimics in this class. Your advanced defenses class will teach the protocols for dealing with something that powerful.

"Mostly the proper response consists of calling for lots of backup and letting a specially trained security detail take care of the mimic. Now, if there aren't any more questions?" He scanned the class and clapped his hands. "Then let's get to it. Teams one through four, you may approach your doorways. Don't forget your traps and bottle. Leave the rest of your items behind."

I looked back wistfully to where Amos stood guard over a portable tank welder and other supplies. I hadn't been the only one who thought we were supposed to bring tools of our trade, but apparently the instructor had just been thinking of adding the bottle traps.

I nudged a simple mental command at Amos, telling him to wait and that we'd be back soon. Owen and I each held a battery trap, and Bethany had the bottle. When the metal bars on the line of doors lifted, Owen pushed our door open, went through first, and cut off to the right. Bethany followed and went left. I stepped through close enough to hear her quiet gasp and braced myself. Taking point meant I'd also take the brunt of anything that charged the open door, and I had a whirlwind spell at my fingertips, ready to push any shadow back that made a break for it.

But her sharp intake wasn't due to encroaching demons. When Mr. Manning said our rooms had been changed up, I'd assumed he meant rearranged—desks moved, chairs stacked, that sort of thing. The low, dark cavern we stepped into bore no resemblance to any classroom I'd ever seen in Attwater. Torches guttered in their sconces along the roughhewn walls, and the small chamber we stood gaping at funneled into a narrow tunnel just a dozen paces on.

"Hey, what's th—" I turned to call back to Mr. Manning and ask what the deal was, but the door clanged shut and was already fading from sight.

"Well this is going to be different," I said.

"Let's mark this spot in case we get turned around." Bethany hunted across the sandy floor and started building a small pile of stones. "Check the time. We've got a half hour before the door reappears."

I scouted around the area and came back with a handful of smooth stones that looked to have been polished by water.

"I bet we're under the school." Owen ran a hand along the rock walls and rubbed his fingers together. "Wet, like there're underground springs. What's Manning up to?"

"It's definitely different than last time." I stood and dusted off my hands after topping the pyramid with my stones. "This feels more like a treasure hunt. We better get moving and keep a sharp eye out. The flickering torches are going to make it a bitch to spot shadow demons."

"Has to be at least two down here." Bethany grabbed the glass bottle and brought up the rear. The glass stoppers clinked as they dangled from their lanyards around the neck. "Three I bet, given that surprise one last time. That would give the teams a chance to grab two with the new traps and maybe catch one in the bottle."

We crept down the tunnel, jumping at the dancing shadows. I was especially thankful Owen didn't have a fireball spell at his fingertips. As it was, I shot off a gust of wind at one of the many little recesses along the irregular wall, managing to drive a frightened spider deep into the funnel web that billowed in the air currents.

"We've got a decision to make," Owen called back over his shoulder while I was terrorizing the poor spider.

Our little tunnel opened into another chamber after about twenty feet, and two openings stood opposite us. The floor changed from sand to a mix made mainly of damp dirt that had been recently disturbed.

"Someone's been down here," Owen said. "Maybe lots of people."

The signs of passage were clear, but with no distinct prints, just a bunch of scraped and flattened dirt. A line of recesses set high on the wall held old pottery, and low benches were cut into the rock along one side.

"Well, somebody had to come down and light all these torches for us." I stepped into the left tunnel entrance to make sure the glow continued around the next bend. It did, and the dim light also revealed a clear set of footprints. Or more accurately, paw prints as wide as my palm with three toes that each ended in a nasty claw judging by the punctures in the dirt above the prints. "If I didn't know better, I'd say these are lurker tracks. I vote we go the other way."

I backed away slowly and, when nobody agreed, turned to find a blank wall. The way back was sealed off. I was alone.

"Guys?" My voice echoed off the dark stone, but so did muffled voices.

I put my ear to the rock wall that looked like it had been there forever. Mr. Manning must have used magic to spring this particular surprise.

"Jason? Can you hear me?" Bethany's voice cut through the stone.

"Just barely. What the hell?"

"Must be a puzzle," she said. "We'll take the other branch. I bet both tunnels connect up farther along."

"Be careful! There are lurker tracks in here."

"Better in there than out here." Owen's laugh sounded nervous even through a few feet of rock. "Use fire on those suckers, unless you have a weapon?"

I rummaged in my pockets and came up with two prospects of questionable use. "A ball point pen and car keys!"

"I don't think the pen is mightier than the sword in this case," he called back. "Even your lame-ass fireballs would be better."

With limited options, I moved deeper into the tunnel. Our running shouting match might not have been the best idea if there were demons around, but knowing my friends were close settled my nerves. My sneakers let out a sharp squeal as the dirt floor gave way to tile. The rough walls changed to cut block where the natural passage fazed into a manmade structure. The flickering light ahead came from a metal sconce rather than a wooden torch set in the wall.

"Hey, I'm entering a real building on this side. Old architecture, like maybe Venetian. Chad would know. Guys, I see columns up ahead."

"Same here." Bethany's voice grew softer, more distant. "There's thick…"

"Bethany?" Nothing. "Owen?" I gave it a few seconds, before admitting I was on my own.

The pair of columns bracketed a wide entrance to the room ahead, which seemed brighter than should be possible with just wall lamps. Steady light filtered in from the far end, illuminating the domed ceiling a good twenty feet overhead, but I couldn't spot any windows or skylights.

Debris littered the floor: shards of broken porcelain and clay, chunks of rock that had been kicked in from the tunnel, and what at first looked like a pair of big desiccated iguanas. I toed the dried husks and flipped one over. Iguanas didn't have fangs like that, nor did they wear woven belts.

My heart pounded as I studied the pair of dead lurkers; that had to be what they were. A short metal spike stuck from the sunken chest of one, but I couldn't tell what had killed the other. A panicked scan of the room revealed a good half dozen similar shapes laying near the wall behind me as though they had been thrown backward before crumpling into death.

A much larger form sat on a bench where the room narrowed back into a corridor. Much of the light came from that area, and I approached warily, gaze locked on the brown-clad figure. This one was covered in leather, a massive lump of a creature. It didn't move as I drew near, hadn't moved in a very long time.

Up close I saw the lump had legs, stark white bones extending from the ragged edge of the leather—a pair of human legs. One was cracked in several places below the knee, the other intact except for a missing kneecap and three deep gouges across the thigh bone. Any pants had rotted away long ago, but the shin bones disappeared into sturdy brown boots with buckles tarnished black by the years.

What had at first seemed a lump resolved into a person reclining in their final moments. I was no forensic expert, but a claw swipe deep enough to score the bones in his leg would have also severed a few major arteries, the kind that kept you alive. A brown leather duster covered the torso, and a matching narrow-brimmed hat sat low on the chest, the corner of a skeletal white smile peeking out between the two.

The fingers of the man's right hand were hooked on the seam of one of the cut blocks framing the exit, supporting the skeleton on its corner bench. The other hand lay palm up next to a foot long metal shaft with a wide grip and ending in a narrow blade. I wasn't certain if the device was tool or weapon.

To be honest, my mind was on the doorway, not the dead man. Not only did most of the light come from the hall beyond, illumination covered the exit like a curved barrier. I'd grown used to seeing power in spectrums the human eye usually missed. This was magic for sure. The blue-white energy filled the short hallway, bright but translucent so that I could see where the passage opened up again only a dozen paces away. Two people stepped into view on the far side, the larger turning back to the other.

"See? I told you the tunnels would merge." Owen came fully into view, waved, then frowned at the blue energy plugging the hallway.

Bethany stepped up behind him. Both stopped at the boundary of light. Owen pulled something from his pocket and tossed it into the room separating us. At least that's what he tried to do. The small stone bounced off their side of the barrier and landed at his feet.

"It's some sort of force field." I pitched my voice to carry, which proved unnecessary. Although it looked solid, the light didn't appear to block sound.

"Did you do this?" Owen asked.

I ran a hand over the glowing curve facing my side of the room. The warm surface hummed with a barely noticeable vibration, feeling alive and...faintly familiar.

"Yeah, Owen, you caught me." I raised both hands in surrender. "Having an escape route took away the challenge so I sealed myself in."

"This is beyond anything we've learned." Bethany squinted hard at the barrier. "Let me try something."

Power gathered between her hands, and she pushed it forward. When nothing happened, she tried again then shrugged.

"So now what?" Owen looked around the entryway and scratched his scraggly beard. "Someone's been trying to get through here already. Look at all these chisel marks."

I stepped back to stand by the dead man and confirmed that someone had been going at my side too. From the looks of things they'd tried to break through the stonework. The section along the ceiling had received its scars long ago, the marks darkened with age. But fresh chunks were ripped out of the wall. In several spots the damage went into the blocks a full eight inches only to reveal blue energy shimmering inside the stone.

"The force field extends through the walls." I again placed a hand on the barrier. Why did this power feel so damned familiar?

"There's writing above the doorway here," Bethany said. "I don't speak it, but this looks like Italian. And I don't think those are chisel marks."

Great, so we were in Italy? Mr. Manning's portal must have gone haywire in a big way. Could the dead guy be a long lost Attwater student, teleported here by mistake too? I snorted a laugh. That would have had to be a very long time ago. And the guy hadn't exactly been dressed for class. His long leather duster would have protected him from weather, not homework.

I pulled back the bunched up material, which had been thoroughly shredded by the dead things laying at the back of the room or by whatever killed him—assuming there was a difference. A wide belt hung loosely around his middle, weighed down by a series of small pouches and tools looped over the leather: crude pliers, carving implements, a small mallet, and more. An empty loop, larger than the others, would have held the length of metal laying by his hand.

I gingerly lifted the hat away to reveal the man's skull, perfect and intact—except of course for being long dead. It had definitely been the leg wound that killed him, bled him out while he gathered his strength. My eyes followed the bend of his arm to where the hand rested on the wall, right at the edge of the blue shield. No, he hadn't been resting at the end, he'd been casting a spell. The tools, the familiar feel of his magic...

18. The Trap

"T HIS GUY WAS a tinker!" I called across the gap while running a hand over the surface of the magic barrier filling the short hallway. "But why seal off your own exit?"

Power sang beneath my palms, like magic calling to like. The shield triggered a memory because it had the same feel as the energy I pushed into my robots. The spark of life that went into my projects and to a lesser extent my repairs felt like the shield. The more I practiced traditional tinker work, namely mending things, the larger the boost my magic gave those repairs. It was a work in progress, but the level of energy this guy had thrown into blocking off the passage must have literally taken everything he had. Why cast such a big bubble instead of simply erecting a wall?

"Maybe more bad guys were coming for him," Owen ventured.

"Could be." I plucked at the surface with thumb and forefinger. The energy stretched, reluctant but malleable. "But he was already done for. I think this shield took the last of his energy. He died casting it."

The bright blue barrier snapped back into place and vibrated as if struck with a mallet. On the far side of the room

Bethany cursed as a flash of power threw her back to land on her butt. Owen rushed over, helped her to her feet, and steadied the woman when she almost toppled over again. It was good to see him acting all gallant for a change.

"It didn't like whatever you just tried," I said.

"You're telling me." Bethany shook her head and stepped away from Owen. "That thing kicks like a mule."

"I'll try from this end." I massaged the spot I'd been testing and felt the shield relax. "It responds to me."

The sensation was like petting a growling dog to let it know your friends were not intruders. I was even able to reach my hand past the outer shell, though it felt like pushing my fingers through molasses.

"Whatever you're doing, do it faster." Owen peered into the darkness behind him while making hurry-up motions with his right hand. "Something's coming."

Rhythmic footsteps drifted from the hall leading deeper into the ruins. I waved my hand in small circles, stirring the thickened air and willing a kind of peace into the ancient spell. The power relaxed further, perhaps thinking that I was the caster. The outer layer drew back slowly like a withdrawing curtain, and I stepped into the hall, pressing into the lingering power.

The footsteps drew closer, though in the echoing halls it was impossible to tell if they were just around the next corner or minutes away. Dissolving the barrier was slow work, and the seconds stretched by as it took its sweet time.

Without warning, the process halted and began to reverse. I struggled to stay calm, to radiate tranquility so that I didn't end up trapped in the reforming shield like an insect in amber. Scratching and scrambling joined the still distant footfalls, but sounded closer—behind!

I whipped my head around. The fallen lurkers had shifted, two of the crumpled forms at the back of the room pushing up from the debris. I should have checked for live lurkers hiding among the dead.

Sharp claws scratched at the tile like nails on a chalkboard. Three toes on each scaly foot matched the tracks I'd found. They stood on two legs, like little velociraptors that came up to my waist. But unlike the extinct dinosaurs, these had pushed-in faces with elongated fangs and white overlapping plates along their bellies.

I pushed on as the lurkers approached the shield. They snarled at each other and pawed the air, but seemed reluctant to touch the bright barrier even in its weakened state. Ahead at the halfway point sat an open wooden chest. Metal glinted inside. As I drew near, I saw it contained a contraption twice the size of a football. A perfect half sphere sat at either end connected by three evenly spaced rods or pistons. The left hemisphere was chrome or stainless steel polished to a mirror surface. The other end shone like rosy gold. If those pistons contracted, the two halves would form a sphere.

Time hadn't touched chest or metal within the spell's bubble of influence. I gauged the distance to the spell's perimeter.

"He wasn't blocking the hallway," I said as realization dawned. "There's a device here right at the center of his spell. That tinker died keeping the demons from getting their hands on this."

"I'd say they've been trying to get at it ever since." Bethany's spoke over her shoulder as she squared off to face the approaching menace. "That's why they've been chipping away at this entrance from both sides. Whatever it is, it must be important."

We were operating on pure conjecture. It wasn't like the long-dead skeleton in the other room could answer questions. But the very existence of his spell spoke for the dead man. He'd given his life to protect the artifact sitting in front of me, and I'd undone his work. The shield continued its slow withdrawal, and the braver of the lurkers stepped into the hallway.

I didn't have the knowledge to put the shield back in place behind me, and if I stopped placating the spell it would spring back and trap me where I stood. I couldn't help but wonder if doing so would put me in stasis to be revived by the next tinker to happen upon the place in the distant future. Or maybe I'd just die like a minnow frozen in ice. I didn't have the time or desire to stay and test it out.

There was only one way to get the heck out of there and deny the lurkers their prize. The chest would be too heavy, so I snatched up the device and pressed on toward my friends.

The pair of lurkers went wild, clawing faster through the dissipating magic and keening like banshees. Answering cries echoed from down the corridor and the stomping feet picked up their pace. With a final push, the resistance vanished. I stumbled into the cool air of the next room and smacked into Owen's back.

"About bloody time." He spun on his heel and jabbed a finger at the hallway he and Bethany had used. "We need to loop back. Now!"

He pushed me ahead of him. We dashed away from the lurkers fighting through the remaining spell and the unseen ones thundering toward us from the darkness. There was no way to pick out individual footfalls at this point, but I'd eat my hat if any less than six more demons were coming for us. Speaking of which, I still clutched the dead man's hat. No way to return it at this point. I sent up a silent apology, hoping he didn't mind.

"Is the door even going to be there?" I couldn't check the time while running with my hands full.

"We've been gone way over thirty minutes," Bethany said. "Hopefully it hasn't come and gone."

"They're gaining on us." Owen turned and shot off a fireball. "Less wondering and more running."

Shrieks from behind told me the lurkers disliked his spell—and that they were right on our heels. Over the next twenty steps, the tile floor disappeared and the block walls abruptly reverted to irregular earth and stone.

"Not far now." Bethany panted. "Should be up around the next turn.

Torchlight led us into a final straightaway that ended at a small pile of stones, and the door to freedom. Two more fireballs whooshed from my left. Owen's aim was good. The leading creatures went down as fire erupted across their front. The lurkers behind them split into two groups to flow around the pair, but several of them got tangled as the ones that had been hit clambered to their feet.

"I want my money back from Attwater," Owen said. "Either that or Manning has to give us better spells to use on these things."

"You're on a scholarship," I reminded him as we skidded to a halt at the end of the corridor. "But feel free to take it up with him on the other side of—"

The words died in my throat because the heavy metal door faded from sight, leaving us caught between the demons and a blank stone wall.

Bethany slapped at the surface, as if maybe the door had simply turned invisible. "It isn't here."

"Maybe it'll come back?" I didn't know for sure. Mr. Manning hadn't talked about what happened during emergencies.

"Just great!" Owen metered out his shots to keep the group of demons at a respectable distance, but sooner or later they'd figure out we couldn't withstand an all-out rush. "How about a little help."

I shifted the device, looking for a clear spot to set it down. Though bulky, it only weighed maybe five pounds. Bethany rummaged in her pockets, brought out a folded sheet of paper, and used her talent.

A brown rope flew off her page, foot after foot uncoiling and expanding into a diamondback snake with huge fangs. Her drawing dropped to the floor and slithered toward our attackers, striking out with its big triangular head when a demon tried an end run around Owen's fireballs.

Smart of her to bring backup. I'd seen her magic tear through shadow demons and hoped the snake had venom to take out the lurkers. Drawing and demons fell into a silent standoff, and the fireballs stopped.

"Can't get a shot without hitting your snake," Owen said.

Bethany's drawings were susceptible to fire. The lurkers must have finally done the math because they fell on the snake as a group. Fangs flashed, sending one demon to the ground where it lay still, but rending claws tore out hunks of the drawing's substance and in seconds the snake dissolved and was gone. Then their cruel eyes turned on us.

Bethany gasped and clutched her stomach, the loss of her drawing a physical blow. My fire magic wasn't nearly as strong as Owen's, but if the demons were cold blooded like the reptiles they resembled maybe some ice would slow them down. I set my burden down against the base of the wall where it clanged, metal on metal.

What the heck?

A raised iron edge jutted from the stone just above the sandy floor. The metal border swept upward forming an oval, and the door back to Attwater phased into existence. I grabbed the cross bar and let out a relieved breath when my fingers touched cool steel. It was solid.

"The exit!" I jerked the two-foot handle up to release the latches and bent to retrieve the strange device.

A glint on the underside of the doorframe caught my attention. An inch of shiny wire drooped from under the door, but it was thick as my pinky and articulated like shielded conduit. I bent low to find a small lump of metal clinging to the underside of the threshold. Three more arms extended from a black metal body the size of a walnut. It was tucked up tight like a spider or starfish hiding in the rocks. I poked it with the brim of the hat, feeling silly when the inanimate device didn't budge.

"One last volley." Owen put action to words and fired off three rapid shots.

Bethany straightened and lashed out with fire of her own. They both turned my way, scowling. I was a big old roadblock in front of our exit. My gut told me the metal spider wasn't supposed to be there. I used the hat to pry it loose, grabbed the dead tinker's device, and pushed through the door.

I blinked, momentarily dazzled by the brighter lights of our classroom, and slipped to the side making room for Bethany. Owen rushed through last, spun, and slammed the door shut.

"Where the devil have you three been?" Mr. Manning's desk chair went flying as he bolted to his feet to confront us.

Our classroom was empty except for our instructor, who'd been busy at the front desk when we spilled into the room. Sweating and filthy from our ordeal, the three of us must have been quite a sight.

"You tell us." Owen still leaned on the arm of the door latch. He gingerly let up, and when nothing tried to force it open, lifted his hands and stepped back. "You sent us into a nest of bloody lurkers!"

"Impossible." Mr. Manning strode to the door and made a grab for the handle.

"No!" we all yelled, and the startled man found himself blocked by three bodies.

"Owen's not kidding. Ten lurkers were right behind us. They're after this." I held out the device we'd found, then showed him the metallic spider in my hat. "This was under the portal. I bet there's another."

My intuition flared like a supernova. I laid down on the floor, drawing confused expressions of my friends. Sure enough, a matching spider device clung out of sight beneath the lip of our portal door. I pried it off, stood, and held the pair out to the teacher.

"That shouldn't have been under there." Mr. Manning leaned in close to examine the spiders. "My monitor didn't track your portal jump properly. All I could see was an empty room and assumed a glitch froze the image. But when you didn't return with the other groups, I dug deeper into the readouts." He motioned back to his desk and the raised panel covered in knobs, sliders, and meters he had been examining when I stumbled into the room.

"Could these things have hijacked the portal?" I asked.

"Something certainly appears to have done so." Manning scratched his chin. "The only indication of a problem here was a power spike, which told me you had gone much farther than into the practice chamber."

"Italy," Owen said helpfully. "That's where we went."

"Probably," Bethany added. "It was an underground tunnel system that connected up with old ruins. Some of the writing sure looked like Italian."

"I'll get the technology department to dissect these. Mucking about with the practice portals is dangerous. You three could have ended up anywhere." He reached for the spiders, but I clutched the hat, holding them tight.

They were definitely a pair, two parts that worked together. My talent showed me that much, but a thought niggled at back of my mind. I'd seen something resembling the spiders before—recently. But where?

"I think we have a larger problem." I ran through my thoughts out loud trying to stimulate my foggy memory. "I've seen the pattern on the back of these before. There weren't legs, but this bit of spiral scrollwork on the body is so damned familiar."

"Maybe an item in the vault?" Bethany had been very curious about what was stored down there.

The vault held lots of interesting items. For starters, we could have used the swords and maces to deal with those lurkers. Of course that would have meant getting in uncomfortably close, and none of us were trained in the use of medieval weapons. Then there'd been the dragon egg shells the dean or his people were in the process of reassembling and Gina's broken crank handle. The broken guidance system that the dean's magic spectrometer now replaced didn't hold any bits similar to the spiders. But the odd cabinet did have matching scrollwork to the globe back in the dean's office and the—

"The mirror gateway!" I picked up a spider by the legs, holding it like a bouquet so only the body showed. "See the scrollwork around the edge and how it blends into the main body? Without the legs, this looks exactly like one of the nobs at the corners of the dean's gateway. I couldn't place it because those are silver instead of black."

"Does that mean someone's trying to hijack his fancy gateway?" Owen peered over my shoulder at the thing I'd found.

"Don't know for sure, but we have to warn him." I shoved the device back in my newly acquired hat alongside the other spider. "Mr. Manning, I've got to hold onto these for a while. What can we do to make sure no one else gets redirected?"

"Of course." He nodded and turned to rummage through his desk. "Talk to the dean. I can check my portals, but other classrooms could be at risk. I'll notify security so they can do a thorough sweep. Go!"

"Thanks. I'll let you know what the dean says."

19. Five Minutes

W E DASHED INTO the hallway and headed for the administration wing. Being mid-afternoon, chances were high that we'd catch Dean Gladstone in his office. If not, the receptionist would be able to check his schedule. Students rushing between afternoon classes stopped to gawk as the three of us ran flat out, darted through the security door to the outer ring, and tore past the commons.

"Is the dean in?" I asked, barely breaking stride as we hurried through the admin reception area.

"Yes, but you can't go in there." Ms. Glovefire's voice cracked and she shot out from behind her desk to follow in our wake. Her friendly blue eyes looked worried beneath those waves of coppery hair. "Mr. Gladstone is in an important meeting with security. He cannot be disturbed for the next hour. Mr. Walker!"

"Too important." I waved an apology over my shoulder and let the other two drop in behind to run interference.

With the dead tinker's device tucked under one arm, I plowed on like a tight-end heading for the goal. The receptionist squawked in protest but was too far away to physically block me. I gave the door three rapid knocks, waited for a second, and then pushed my way inside.

"Dean, I'm sorry, but there's a problem." I'd braced myself for angry protests from the people inside, but the room stood empty.

New maps of an unfamiliar city and town square had been unrolled across the desk, and a dozen steaming cups of coffee in various states of consumption sprouted from surfaces around the room.

"Dean Gladstone, I tried to stop..." Ms. Glovefire's voice trailed off and a frown creased her forehead as she scanned the empty room. "I don't understand. The last person arrived just ten minutes ago. I'm certain no one left this room."

"Not though the door they didn't," I said.

The shiny metal tracker perched atop the big globe, and one of the magic-infused shell fragments sat in the tray beneath. A pinpoint of light shone along the eastern seaboard near Atlanta. The globe was oriented so that the spot sat directly beneath the tracker, and I suspected the maps would correlate to that location.

A thread of power still connected the arrangement to the ornate silver gateway. I stepped over and laid a hand on the reflective surface, which felt cold and hard—just a mirror.

"Gateway's closed." I sat down the device we'd found and held one of the spiders up to the metalwork. "Yep, the tooling is the same."

"But there're four of them." Owen inspected the other three, looking around the back side of the mirror while Bethany tried to placate the incensed receptionist. "This one's mounted differently."

He walked me around back to where the lower left decorative finial was attached. Sure enough, four tubular legs locked the piece in place instead of the soldered disk used to secure the other three. I pried at the little hooks to see if I could detach the device without damaging it or the mirror.

"Leave that alone!" Bethany came around the mirror and swatted my hand away. "You don't know what removing that device will do. If the dean's team *has* been whisked away to the wrong place, pulling that thing off could trap them."

"Where'd Glovefire go?" Owen asked.

"To call security," Bethany said. "Or maybe to have a nervous breakdown. Apparently she had no idea that there was a portal in here."

"We missed them by like five minutes." I cursed, mad enough to spit nails, which earned me an arched eyebrow from Bethany. "Sorry. Their chance to nab the Shadow Master must have come around."

"From the look of things, they were loaded for bear," Owen said.

"But who knows what they'll encounter instead." I didn't like the helpless feeling that nuzzled down to make itself at home in the pit of my stomach. "This smells like a trap. They could have been redirected anywhere."

"We'll just have to give them time to return," Bethany said, always the pragmatist.

"In the meantime, we better figure out how the spiders work." No way was I just sitting around on my thumbs waiting.

I headed to the dean's workbench and picked through his selection of tools. It took some doing, but I finally managed to detach the spider's back plate and expose its inner clockwork. And it did indeed look much like the inside of a precision timepiece. Two small computer chips were nestled among the gears and springs of the spider that had clung beneath the classroom side of our portal. They were innocuous-looking standard black wafers, but figuring out their function would take more research.

Melissa Murdock, a security advisor, showed up a few minutes later and gave the room a once over. She agreed with Bethany's assessment that the redirecting device on the mirror shouldn't be tampered with until we knew more.

The woman also confirmed that a large security team had met with the dean for an undisclosed operation prior to his disappearance. The rest of the department had been activated in response to Mr. Manning's warning and were busy inspecting every portal in the school. Even if we'd wanted to go home for the night, the student portals had to be cleared first.

We spent the rest of the afternoon and evening by the mirror portal. The deafening sounds of rumbling stomachs forced us to send Owen on a munchie run to the commons, but other than that none of us were willing to break the vigil. Melissa kept us company just in case the portal opened and let something nasty in.

I didn't see any weapons on the middle-aged woman. But she moved with a feline grace that belied her petite five-two frame and salt-and-pepper hair. I'd bet money that Melissa Murdock had extensive combat training under the belt of her casually chic navy-blue pantsuit.

The mirror stayed stubbornly inactive overnight. By morning we knew little more about the spider devices, and the crick in my neck had me viewing the world on an angle.

"Why don't you three go get some food and stretch out before classes?" Melissa had been on the desk phone periodically throughout the night monitoring the situation. "The department hasn't found any more signs of tampering so all the normal portals are back in operation. We've got round the clock watches set up, but I get the feeling you three aren't going to be satisfied letting security handle this."

"It's just that I should have noticed that sooner." I pointed to the fake decoration at the bottom of the gateway.

"Hindsight is always twenty-twenty." She nodded her understanding. "I'll be gone if you stop back—when you stop back. We'll let the acting dean know that you're all welcome to drop in whenever you need to."

"Ms. Robles?" Lately, I hadn't seen much of the woman who occasionally took the reins when Dean Gladstone was away, but I doubted she'd want students and security underfoot constantly. "This office is going to get pretty crowded."

"Actually, the board appointed Mary Eisner. Don't worry about getting underfoot. She'll be working from her own office due to the circumstances here." Ms. Murdock gave a vague wave toward the mirror and globe. "Speaking of which, given the unknown origins of the contraption you found earlier, it would be prudent to store that down in the vault. I can have one of our people come pick it up."

During our hours together, we'd shared the tale of our misadventure in Practical Exploration class. It made perfect sense for security to want my find quarantined, especially given we seemed to have misplaced our top executive. Why take chances? But still...

"No need." I hurried over, laid a hand on each hemisphere, and tucked the device under my arm. "We can take it down. I have a friend with access, Regina Williams."

"Gina?" A smile blossomed on her lips, exposing blindingly white teeth. "That girl's a gem, and going places. She keeps everyone on their toes in the student coordination meetings.

I'll have our folks run her down to save you the trouble. You can meet her at the vaults."

"That works." Guess I wouldn't be ducking out and taking the thing to my lab.

Again, I didn't blame her, but the extra bit of insurance made me feel like she didn't trust me. Gina would have to report when we secured the artifact, so there'd be no way to avoid locking it away. Hopefully Gina could sneak me in to work on it because figuring out its function was high on my list, right behind sorting out how the metal spiders worked. If she couldn't get me access, I'd have to figure out another way. Okay, so maybe the nice lady security officer was suspicious for good reason, but it still stung.

"Ms. Eisner is an unusual pick as back up for the dean," Bethany said as we headed to meet Gina. "I would have thought Schlaza for sure."

"The front office staff will eat her alive," Owen said from behind us. "Remember her holiday cheer charm? The woman is a marshmallow."

"She might be sugar sweet, but she's a damned good teacher." On more than one occasion Mary Eisner had saved my bacon by helping me grasp spells in common core class. "On top of that, she weathered Annette Schlaza in full ice queen mode with demons on top. I bet she's made of sterner stuff than your think."

Roxy intercepted us halfway through the inner ring, stepping out of a doorway so that I plowed right into her. We kind of got tangled, and she grabbed my arm, pulling me out of a stumble before I took a header.

"Geez, sorry," I mumbled through my embarrassment. "And thanks. I would have hated to dent this."

"Interesting design. What is it?" She patted the golden hemisphere, and I forced myself not to pull my newfound gadget away.

"No idea, but it'll be fun to figure out. We found it in some old ruins."

Her inner engineer perked up; I recognized the hungry look. Roxy was even more into robots than me.

Bethany cleared her throat. "We're kind of on the clock here."

"Oh, right." I nodded. "Gotta get this baby to the vault."

"Don't let me hold you up." Roxy gave Bethany an appraising look, waved us on, and then surprised me by falling in alongside. "We can chat while we walk."

The term chat was an overstatement. The first couple of minutes consisted mostly of uncomfortable silence, the same kind of tension that always seemed to develop between Gina and Roxy. By his occasional yawns, I was pretty certain Owen wasn't the source. Heck, he may not even have noticed. But why Bethany would have a beef with Roxy was a mystery too.

Maybe the tension was simply my imagination, but I found myself babbling to fill the conversational void. Roxy seemed content to listen, only asking the occasional polite question. She may have been humoring me.

By the time the vault came into sight, I'd touched on our time in the ruins, finding the spider devices, and how we'd have a temporary dean for a while. I did a pretty good job of leaving out the really sensitive information, so it wasn't like I'd betrayed any confidences.

"Nice job, Jason," Bethany said over my left shoulder, her breath hot in my ear. "But you forgot to outline what Lars is working on. Maybe draw her a schematic?"

"Oh, yeah." I knew I'd left something out. "So Larry—that's Lars's real name. Anyway, he can grow—ow!"

"Sarcasm much?" Bethany whacked the back of my head a second time for good measure, and I swear I heard her eyes roll. "Let's get this football put away."

"Hey, guys!" Gina waved when she spotted us, but her welcoming smile quickly faded. "Roxy."

"Thanks for meeting us on short notice." I edged forward and held up my find to break the glares passing between the women. "This is what we need to stow, but I'm hoping to get access to it occasionally."

"Yeah, looks like Melissa Murdoch will be in charge for a while. She called ahead to make sure I let you guys in, but everyone has to keep their hands to themselves. Got it?" At our solemn nods, Gina opened the big door.

She led us inside past the array of old weapons to shelves near the back that still had a few empty bays. One section had a row of heavy black doors with a thick observation port mounted on the front of each. Gina waved her hand in front of a larger compartment, and the hatch swung up with a hiss from its supporting pistons.

"What exactly is it?" She squinted at the device I held.

"That, pretty lady, is the question of the hour." My grin coaxed a smile back onto her lips, and I sat my find inside the storage unit. "Found it with a long dead tinker. I'll tell you the whole story, but we have yet to discover what this thing actually does." I placed one hand on the golden hemisphere and the other on the silver end, envisioning how it might operate. "I'm guessing these halves come together when activated. The pistons would retract to pull them to the center, making a single sphere. It's strange because I don't sense any tinker magic. It's either dead or just a normal gadget."

"No seams," Gina said, giving the device her own once over. Her frizzy hair tickled the side of my face as she squinted and sighted along the pistons holding the halves apart. "If it's a mundane device, there ought to be a keypad or at least buttons."

"Check this out!" Owen called from beyond the shelves. "They're rebuilding the dragon eggs."

"Make sure he doesn't touch anything." Gina sighed and secured the hatch. "Don't worry, I can sneak you in to study this whenever you'd like."

Her smile held mischief, and I wondered at the underlying subtext. Even if we couldn't date, time spent with her was never wasted. I nodded like a fool, and headed over to find Owen with a black fragment in each hand, trying to fit them onto the partially reconstructed eggs. Roxy pawed through smaller fragments in the lower drawer of a rolling tool chest.

"It's like a puzzle," he said.

"Yes, one that the dean is working on for his own reasons." I took a piece the size of a soup bowl from him, but wasn't fast enough to grab the other before he fitted it into place on the egg to his right. It matched up perfectly, and the hairline crack healed over, fusing the fragment onto the growing shell.

"Another one down." Owen held out his hand for the piece I had.

"No." I pulled the bit of shell back out of reach. "Who knows what putting it together will do."

"True, but haven't you ever wondered what they did with the egg that survived?" He hunted casually around the tray of shards atop the tool chest, caught my frown of disapproval, and abandoned the search with a shrug. "It was just starting to hatch when Gladstone froze it. There might be a lost little war dragon out there."

"The dean was going to get it back to its own kind, see if it could be...I don't know, purified." I could see Chad being worried about a helpless creature, but it was out of character for Owen to get all touchy feely. "What did you do, bond with the little guy or something?" I meant it as a joke, but sobered at the concern furrowing Owen's brow. *Well, I'll be damned.* "I'm sure the dragon is safe and sound back with its own kind. If you're that worried about it, we can ask the dean when he returns."

"Yeah, let's do that." He cleared his throat with a gruff cough. "Just to be sure it didn't escape."

"This is beautiful." Roxy closed the drawer and glided over to the hand-carved guidance unit that originally had topped the globe in the front office.

"Do not touch that!" Gina stomped past, muttering under her breath, "it's like herding kittens."

"Don't get your panties in a bunch." Roxy backed away after giving the ornate frame one last caress. "I don't even know what it is, but the workmanship is marvelous."

"Reason enough not to play with it," Gina said.

"It's already broken." I found myself playing peacekeeper again. "This used to be part of that old globe in the dean's office."

"Oh, the one linked to his portal?" Roxy winked when my jaw dropped. "Don't look so shocked. I got a good look at it while the dean grilled me about hobbies. I think he's sweet on people who build stuff. The old man couldn't get enough when it came to robotic challenges I've entered." She tapped her chin and gave me an appraising look. "With that special talent of yours, I bet you could fix this gadget right up in no time."

Except the dean already had a replacement to guide the globe, and we had more pressing concerns. Saving Mr.

Gonzales and now the dean made for a full plate, even without worrying about the spider devices. On top of it all, the school's security department would be stretched paper-thin. Half the force had accompanied Dean Gladstone and remained missing in action. Melissa Murdock implied the ones left behind were largely inexperienced. Between handling calls from graduates in the field and ensuring the school's portal system wasn't compromised, security was barely treading water.

20. Tangled Web

NOTHING I TRIED made the slightest difference to the spider devices sitting open on my tiny workbench at school. Both remained annoyingly inert, their gears and circuits a mocking reminder of how much I didn't understand about the machine-magic interface.

I'd shown pictures of the electronic components to Billy, but hadn't dared let him see one up close. My friend put his geeky talents to work, dug around online, and confirmed there was nothing special about the two black IC chips embedded in each. One was memory, the other an 8-bit microcontroller—generic knock-offs that could be ordered online for about fifty cents. He'd sprained his brain trying to figure out the power source and couldn't even guess at how what he saw in the pics could function.

In the end I told him there were more pieces sealed in a polymer resin that I hadn't managed to crack open, which mollified him but raised other speculation about heat dissipation. Of course magic would have powered these units, but even my tinker talent couldn't detect any residual signature. It was as if someone had pulled a plug on the spiders the moment I removed them from our portal.

"Would you grab the microscope, please?" I asked Amos.

Talking out loud to my friendly robot wasn't strictly necessary, but for some reason made me feel better. Plus, it gave Roxy fair warning before Amos reached behind her. Even with magic being commonplace at the school, people still tended to freak out when robots leapt into action of their own accord. Someday we'd move beyond the old science fiction prejudice of not trusting machines to make their own decisions.

"You've been at it for a week," Roxy complained. "How much longer are you going to study those things?"

"Until I figure out how to track where they sent Dean Gladstone." I didn't enjoy banging my head against the wall any more than she did, and often wondered why the woman insisted on watching me do so. "And I've got to be sure the one in his office doesn't activate unexpectedly."

Even though we'd worked out how to operate the spectrum tracker and globe combo, the silver portal was no good to us if the spiders could randomly hijack anyone trying to use the mirror. To go after the dean, we needed to activate the spiders just like they had been when his team disappeared. Experts from the technology department hadn't had any success either and wanted to keep the spiders. Mr. Girardi had put his considerable influence behind the argument that a tinker had the best chance of cracking the code on the demon devices and that I should be allowed to keep working on them. I could only hope his confidence wasn't misplaced.

"Meanwhile, your other trail's growing cold. Do you really think your missing staff member will stay put while you figure these things out?" Roxy snorted at the spider I held, but offered one of her cute grins to take the edge off questioning a sensitive topic.

She was right. We kept searching for Mr. Gonzales, but again could only go after him once we were certain the spiders wouldn't interfere. Owen and Bethany had helped test the globe. We didn't dare activate the portal, but by feeding dragon egg fragments to the tracker had indeed found that the Shadow Master was on the move, popping around to different locations up and down the coast. Feeding was an appropriate term because the tracker operated by consuming the magical residue in the objects it analyzed.

As it was, the shells held only the barest trace of the demon lord's power. Each fragment could only be used once before being rendered useless for tracking. We'd burned through the remaining bits at an alarming rate, and I couldn't see breaking up the eggs that were undergoing reassembly. Even if we did, they might no longer hold the dark aura needed. And strictly from a size perspective, wedging the three-foot-diameter reconstructed eggs into the compartment under the globe wasn't happening either. Thinking about it, I bet the shells were being built out of used fragments. That would certainly be one way to keep track of the spent pieces.

"We'll find him again," I muttered, using the microscope Amos handed over as an excuse not to look her in the eye.

"At least give yourself a break and work on something else." Her face brightened. "Why not bring that old globe topper up from the vault? See if you can figure out what's wrong with that and give your subconscious a chance to puzzle out the spiders in the background."

It wasn't a terrible idea, but if I was going to focus on something else it would be catching up on my schoolwork. I'd fallen way behind on the sample welds I owed Mr. Martin and pretty much just been coasting through Magical Creatures class. If I didn't start devoting some free time to studying instead of trying to work out how to reach the dean and Mr. Gonzales, I would be in real danger of failing out.

"We've already got a tracker for the globe." I understood the drive to see elegant old machines working again, but had enough on my plate.

"An ugly one that looks like it came from a B movie sci-fi set." She snorted. "That metal monstrosity clashes with everything in the room. It's an aftermarket so probably doesn't work nearly as well as it should. I bet the original could pin down your AWOL maintenance manager in a flash."

Roxy had been privy to much of our actions and plans, but I'd kept my word to the dean and never divulged the details and full extent of last semester's attack on Attwater. Even so, it became increasingly hard to keep track of what she did and didn't know, especially given how often the woman put two and two together and came up with exactly the thing I'd been dancing around. One such example was her deduction that Mr. G. was bouncing around.

A knock on the door of my utility closet turned workroom saved me the embarrassment of admitting I didn't know what part of the spider device might need inspection by microscope.

"Come in." I slid the instrument out of sight behind a toolbox at the end of the table.

"Owen's driving us crazy asking about—oh." Gina swept through the door, wearing a rather stunning green silk top with metallic embroidery, but stopped short when she spied Roxy perched on the stool at my workbench. "Hey."

"Hey yourself." Roxy's expression was never the easiest to read, but I sensed amusement.

"Anyway." Gina sidled around to stand by me, her lips suddenly drawn into a tight line—no amusement there at all. "Owen says it's time to get off the pot and work up a plan."

"And what does *he* think we should do?" I asked.

"Yank the spider off the mirror, fire up the globe, and charge in, of course." Gina shrugged. "He also says it's Friday night and he wants to get out of here before dark if we're going to keep sitting on our thumbs—I'm paraphrasing to clean up that last part."

"Well, we were just talking about dropping down to the vault." I gave her a hopeful look. "The globe needs a new shell piece anyway."

"They're nearly used up." She sighed at my pleading look and leveled a finger at my chest. "But I guess I can spare a few minutes to walk *you* down. There aren't any night raids this weekend."

Her emphasis wasn't lost on Roxy. "You kids have fun. I've got other places to be anyway."

Gina led the way to the vault entrance and did her thing to open the massive door. Handy having a friend with access, especially when they were the student liaison to Attwater's security department. It wasn't even like we were doing anything underhanded.

"We really are going to be out of options soon." I sifted through the handful of tiny black chips—all we had left of the dragon eggs. "We'll need a handful of these to get a strong enough reading to activate the globe."

The last of the shells were scattered in the long narrow drawers of a rolling cabinet similar what you'd find in an auto shop, except these were felt lined. I'd been putting the spent shells in the lower, larger drawers and was down to sweeping up what was left in the top half dozen. It would have to be enough. Owen was right; it was high time to act.

But before we went off half-cocked, we needed to work through the particulars like who took point, what weapons we needed, and how to use the cage Lars made. I'd been surprised at how thorough our wannabe gangsta had been in constructing the small cell that would hold the Shadow Master. But even with wheels, the thing was just too massive to take through the portal. Plus we'd have to do something extremely clever to trick Mr. Gonzales into the cage.

Of course, we also had the little problem of how to get the Shadow Master to relinquish his hold on Mr. Gonzales. Bethany discovered how the Chrono-monks had managed way back before the invention of indoor plumbing. But their methods hadn't been pretty and were just as likely to kill Attwater's maintenance man as to cure him. She and Mon were busy working out a gentler approach, but we couldn't count on keeping the demon lord sitting in the cage for too long. Having him within the halls of the school was risky enough, and every passing hour would offer an opportunity for him to break through the cage. Not to mention Lars hadn't exactly built a living space up to modern sanitation standards.

I pondered the dilemma while browsing through the vault's other artifacts, my feet bringing me to the compartment housing the find from our unexpected jaunt to Italy. At my request, Gina waved the door open so I could get a better look at the strange device.

"Maybe just pushing the two halves together activates this thing." I knelt for a closer look at the telescoping segments spaced at intervals along the three rods connecting the hemispheres. "Could be different settings based on how far you close it. "

"It's built to look deceptively simple," Gina said. "The faintest ring connects those rods, so maybe the hemispheres also can turn around the center axis."

She was right. The rods penetrated the flat side of each hemisphere through an inset collar the width of my thumb. Assuming it was more than just an etched design, the tight tolerance made the seam nearly invisible on the polished surface.

"No gradations though." I ran fingers over the interior face and circumference of each end, but found no marks or ridges. "Infinitely adjustable?"

"No way of knowing, but you can bet magic is involved. Either that or it's just a decorative piece of artwork."

"That a powerful tinker spent his dying energy to protect?" I cocked an eyebrow.

"Powerful, huh?" She got coy and leaned in close. "Are all tinkers that potent?"

"Well, sure." The room grew warm. When my skill with robots had emerged I'd fancied myself a mighty technomancer like the ones in comic books that built magic armor and weapons. Being dubbed a tinker by the dean had been a pretty big letdown, one that I'd thought I'd made peace with. Apparently the drive to be some kind of badass mage still simmered beneath the surface. "I mean…we can't command mystical creatures like salamanders or anything, but the guy's shield was damned impressive."

I palmed a hemisphere in each hand and experimentally pushed them toward the center. The telescoping rods contracted with a gentle click, reducing the separation of the halves by an inch or so. A mild jolt of energy needled my hands like static electricity. The right golden hemisphere gave off warm sparks, the left silver one a cold tingling.

"Be careful," Gina warned.

I nodded and tried twisting the ends in opposite directions. The inset rings let each half rotate smoothly. Turning them just a few degrees off center had me gritting my teeth. The pent-up energy on both ends of the device spiked to painful levels, forcing me to quickly back off.

"That's potent." My shoulders unknotted as the power sizzling under my palms receded. "Maybe playing around with this isn't the best idea.

I gingerly pulled my hands away, and the rods extended smoothly, bringing the device back to its original width. As soon as the motion was complete, the last traces of magic winked out.

"Ya think?" Gina turned my hands over to inspect both palms, which had a distinctly pink cast to them. "I'd rather not rely on the vault's dampening spell to keep bad things from happening. Let's leave this thing to the artifact experts."

"It just tingles." I pulled my hands away to stop her from worrying at them.

And that was from the very lowest setting. What the hell had I found?

"Gather the shells you need, and let's get out of here." Gina secured the storage compartment with a long-suffering sigh, but I wasn't sure if it was directed at me or the football—our new name for the strange device.

Back at the rolling cabinet, I worked through the drawers, sweeping fragments to the front of each. Gina pulled the last drawer open until the stops engaged. I doubted the few bits of shell embedded in its felt liner would be enough for a full charge. We'd be able to activate the tracker and globe two or three more times at most.

"What's that?" I'd caught the flash of metal at the far back.

I craned and squinted into the back of the narrow opening while Gina lit the interior with her phone's light. Gold glinted from the far corner where a metal band was wedged under the felt. I tugged the ring free and brought it out into the light.

"Gaudy," Gina said when I held it out for her inspection. "Definitely a man's."

A flat disc of opal or mother of pearl sat on top of the wide gold band. Two amber gems cut into the shape of interlocking diamonds were mounted on the disc, surrounded by squiggles of silver metalwork resembling runes or hieroglyphs.

"This belonged to Mr. Gonzales." I looked from ring to storage drawer.

"Are you sure?" Gina asked.

"Positive, but how the heck did it get in there?" Mr. G. wore it last year. I remember because he had to take it off when working on pumps." She gave me a funny look. "You know, for safety so it didn't get caught on the rotating shaft and tear his finger off? Anyway, he stopped wearing it altogether near the end of the semester, and I think I know why. The design should look familiar." I traced the air above the double diamonds.

"The shadow demon sigil." Gina gasped.

"Not a good sign."

"But a handy source of the same magical signature that's in the egg fragments." Gina's eyes shone. "Can't you feel it? There's a ton of magic in this puppy."

21. Lock Down

"**S**TUDENTS AND STAFF will both be subject to these new measures. It's vital that you all keep your eyes open and report any suspicious activity to Ms. Murdoch or Ms. Williams." Mary Eisner waved to the two women flanking her on the stage.

As acting dean, Ms. Eisner had called an assembly to fill everyone in on the dean's disappearance, outline added security measures, and—most importantly—quell rumors that had spread through the school like wildfire.

"Gina's moving up in the world," Bethany whispered from her seat on my left.

Between the missing personnel and continued troubles outside the school, security was stretched thin. Melissa Murdoch was the acting commander and had basically deputized our friend as her second in command. The dean had taken the department's top people with him, but recruiting students showed the situation was desperate.

"Ms. Murdoch needs someone she can count on. I just hope this doesn't delay Gina's graduation."

She'd already become pretty scarce after hours. Demon raids were occurring almost daily with coordination delegated to Gina, while Ms. Murdoch handled investigating the dean and administering the increased security.

"I want to emphasize that the school is safe, and we intend to keep it that way." Ms. Murdoch held up her security badge. "You'll be tracked at all access points and portals. Enter without leaving, we'll check on you. Swipe into an inner ring but never out, we'll check on you. Please, be polite and comply with requests from security. This isn't easy on them either. New photo badges are in the works, but will take time to coordinate. These are sad times, but stay strong. We will bring our people home and get through this—together."

After a few more announcements, Eisner and Murdoch took a handful of questions. The acting dean kept a firm lid on speculation, and shut down a couple of doomsayers who tried to say the sky was falling.

"Ms. Eisner did well." Bethany jostled alongside as we left the auditorium.

The emergency meeting had been called abruptly. The rest of our gang had been scattered around the room and would be rushing back to class. We'd get a chance to compare notes later. Who knew when I'd catch up with Gina?

"She's got what it takes," I agreed. "And so does Ms. Murdoch. Gina's getting run ragged, but it's easy for her to update her boss on progress with the spider devices."

Or lack of progress. Maybe it was time to focus on finding Mr. Gonzales.

"Speaking of which, why is Roxy always in your shop?"

I'd made the mistake of recapping my latest efforts while we'd waited for the assembly to start. I hadn't thought twice about mentioning Roxy, until the frown Bethany had graced me with earlier.

"She's interested and has a knack for machinery." I didn't know what else to say. "Sometimes two heads are better. Right?"

"Get Owen's gearhead instead." She grabbed my arm when I snorted. "I'm serious, Jason. We hardly know anything about her. That woman's *too* interested and too good at...being in the wrong place."

She'd probably been about to say too good at magic but didn't want to look jealous. Still, her concern ran deeper than that. Heck, I'd questioned Roxy's persistence myself, but saw her more as a glutton-for-punishment engineer than anything worrisome.

Bethany was an artist, unfamiliar with the insidious power technical riddles held over engineers. Sleep was a rare commodity when something went wrong with one of my creations. Insomnia was a constant for engineers worldwide— failed tests replayed behind your eyelids add new experiments percolated as you desperately tried to count sheep, picture restful woodlands, or imaging flowing rivers—a technique that always ended with me rushing to the bathroom. The damned engineering drive was that strong.

Bethany bit her lower lip as I tried to frame my thoughts in a way she'd understand. But anything I said would come out wrong. After everything that had happened, we were all on edge. If putting a little space between Roxy and me gave Bethany peace of mind, it was a small price to pay. A new perspective might even jar loose an answer I'd overlooked.

"Okay, how about I tag you or one of the guys next time I need a little cross-think?"

22. Breakthrough

T HE RING WAS indeed brimming with the Shadow Master's energy. We used it several times with the globe to good effect, and the magic drain from each use didn't register at all. The hunk of jewelry offered unlimited tracking.

One function we couldn't seem to get out of the tracker-globe combo was a decent view of the location to which we'd be traveling. The dean's holographic movies that spied on the other end would have been useful. We had to settle for brief flashes that barely registered before dissipating.

But we did know two things. Most importantly, the Shadow Master had gone to ground and not moved for several days. Of notably lesser value was the fact he seemed to be working in an office setting. An early morning stop at the dean's old office confirmed both facts still held true.

With Mr. Gonzales stationary and the total lack of progress in tracking down Dean Gladstone, it was beyond time to act. Lars's cage was ready to go, and I planned to send Amos in as an advanced scout. Ensuring the spider devices didn't send us off into oblivion was the big issue. I was about ready to just rip the damned spider device off the mirror portal whenever Bethany was ready. Her drawings were our best defense against the Shadow Master's minions. And it was obvious at this point that the dean's team wasn't coming back on its own.

"Bethany?" I knocked on the door to her artist retreat in hopes of catching her before first period. No answer, but I heard shuffling and a voice inside, so knocked again. "Open up, I need to talk to you."

I was about to knock a third time when the door opened just far enough for the person inside to peek out. But instead of Bethany, Owen scowled around the edge of the door. His hair was an absolute mess, and he seemed out of breath.

"Keep it down will you?" He frowned at the hand I'd raised to pound on the door. "She's not here."

"Yeah, sure." I smirked. "And you're just taking a nap in her private studio."

"Nothing like *that*!"

"Geez, I know." I pushed past him into the small room. "Bethany, we need to talk."

She was bent over a table that I'd never seen in there before, apparently wrestling unruly wires. Her tight leather pants and high-heeled boots caught me off-guard and made the view way too interesting. I coughed and forced my gaze away as she straightened, then did a double take.

"Mon?" That explained the clothes, but raised a bunch more questions that must have crossed my face when I turned back to Owen.

"And nothing like *that* either!" Owen's squawk of outrage sounded genuine

I sure hoped not. Mon and Bethany were together, weren't they?

"Instead of being a twelve-year-old, tell us what you think." Mon waved at the room.

The space had started as a small storage closet similar to my own workshop. The room had been gutted and rebuilt. The industrial metal shelves were gone. Bethany's drawings now hung by clips on braided steel wires that lined the walls in parallel rows. Low wooden shelves beneath held her sketchbooks and offered a slanted top with a lip so a few books could be left open for display.

Soft white light bathed the walls from LED strips along the ceiling. Mon had been bent over a stylish rolling art desk, complete with compartments for supplies and a work surface that could be slanted to the optimum working angle. A rolling chair fit snuggly under the desk, and Bethany's nest of pillows and blankets was neatly stacked next to a neon pink beanbag chair.

"You did all this?" I asked.

"It's a surprise birthday present." Mon nodded and bit her lip. "Do you think she'll like it?"

"Don't worry, she's going to love this!"

"Good, because there's no turning back now," she said. "And look at this."

Mon scooped a small white remote off the desk and pushed a button. The LED strips faded from white to purple and back again.

"Very cool. You're in on this?" I asked Owen.

"I'd never have gotten the shelves out or this desk in without him." Mon brought the lights back up to normal. "But let me guess, you want Bethany's help with whatever's in your pocket."

"Now who's being childish?" I'd never known Mon to kid around, especially when it came to Bethany.

"Don't be crude. There's something magic in your pocket." At my grin she held up a warning finger, and then lowered it to point at my left front pocket. "Not nice magic either. And it's trying to… I don't know…talk to something in your bag."

I dug in my pocket, pulled out the little cloth bag, and dumped Mr. Gonzales's ring out onto the table. Mon nodded as if expecting as much, but that she'd even been able to sense the ring inside its pouch came as a shock. Due to the dark nature of its magic, Ms. Eisner had insisted the ring be kept in the magic-resistant pouch when not being used to ferret out the Shadow Master.

"There's only one thing in my bag with any magic." I slid out the pair of spider devices and, sure enough, felt a faint stir within them. "Hang on."

I dove back into the bag and pulled out the leather case holding my spectrum goggles. I fit them over my head and studied the gadgets on the table under each of its lenses. Flipping down the standard yellow crystals on their wire arms revealed a dark aura pulsing around the ring, the kind of black energy I'd come to associate with demons and their workings. Similar energy radiated from the spider devices, but at a much reduced level. The red lenses showed a thread connecting the spiders. A whisper of power coursed between them.

"This has never happened before." I was certain I'd had these things in my workshop at the same time. "With the spiders awake, I might be able to get some answers."

I flipped down the final set of blue crystals, which did something wonky. I pulled off the goggles, cleaned the lenses with the tail of my shirt, and tried again. A wash of dark energy extended across the wood surface. Rather than the midnight black feel of the ring, this was shot with brighter flecks that turned it more charcoal-gray. The energy in the artifacts flared in response to the flecks. The gray shadow didn't extend all the way across the desk. It pooled in that one corner of the room, in roughly a sphere that extended from the floor and stopped just shy of the ceiling. Mon stood at the shadow's center.

"Can you step back?" I waved her away from the table. The shadow receded and the trace of energy in both spider devices winked out. "Now forward."

"What the hell—"

I cut Owen off with a chop of my hand and coaxed Mon back to the far side of the desk. Nothing happened when her charcoal-gray shadow—her magical aura, I supposed—touched the ring, but when it fell across the devices, all three artifacts flared to life.

Mon was good enough to humor me while I used her like a yoyo and flipped between crystals to verify the interaction I suspected. After a couple of minutes I was satisfied and pushed all three lenses up. I blinked, momentarily disoriented when the magical overlays I'd been studying vanished.

"I'm going to need you at my workshop after classes," I said, a glimmer of hope rising in me.

"Yeah, I would need to know why." Mon eyed me cautiously, as if worried about whatever I'd seen, but Owen just looked amused.

"The best I can tell, you're some kind of magical catalyst for these things." I scooped up the devices I'd taken off the portal. "Your aura makes these interact. The spiders don't fully power up, but it just might be enough to figure out how they work."

I resisted asking about her aura or even the talent we knew nothing about. Of course I wanted to know, but Mon had that deer-in-the-headlights look, and would probably bolt if I tried to make this personal. Time was too short, the stakes too high.

The personal energy surrounding people, even mages, was supposed to be bright and colorful. The shades of color said a lot about a person and entire disciplines outside Attwater were devoted to the study of such things. Dark auras would be cast by evil creatures, the blacker the nastier, but as far as I knew those didn't sparkle. Nor had I ever heard gray auras mentioned in class.

Mon took significant convincing, a fair bit of cajoling, and just a dash of pleading, but finally agreed to help. I think my growing excitement had something to do with her capitulation. Conquering the secret of how the portals were hijacked would let us secure Attwater from further attacks and lead us to the dean. My enthusiasm must have been enough to overpower Mon's misgivings.

I left them to finish remodeling Bethany's studio with a grin stretching from ear to ear. Mon promised to drop by my shop later in the day. Concentrating on classes was going to be impossible. I was positively giddy in anticipation of getting to work on those devices.

So, of course, Owen had to ruin it.

"By the way" — he hit me with a Cheshire Cat smile just before I shut the door— "what did *you* get Bethany for her birthday?"

Bastard.

23. Through the Looking Glass

I WOULD HAVE rather recovered the dean first. That would have given us maximum firepower for going after the Shadow Master and been the smarter move. But cracking the code on those spiders remained problematic. With Mon's help, tests on the pair from our classroom showed they acted much like Wi-Fi repeaters, but instead of receiving and passing along radio waves these worked with portal magic. By extending the signal, a linked pair of spiders effectively redirected the terminus of a portal.

Understanding the underlying principle should have made tracking them possible, but some kind of security lock had been activated on the pair of spiders linked to the silver mirror. No amount of physical or magical prodding had made a bit of difference to the device on our side. That was undoubtedly why the Dean and his people hadn't been able to return through the portal, but it didn't answer why they hadn't found an alternate way back—at least to get a message through. Maybe like so many of the older generation, they'd simply forgotten how to text.

The silver lining in our utter failure to trace the dean's whereabouts was that Ms. Murdock declared the office safe from outside invasion and cancelled the twenty-four hour security detail. After two weeks, they could no longer afford to keep their small staff on the job. I was equal parts pleased and guilt-ridden to not have security looking over our shoulders for what we were about to attempt.

"Video feed still good?" I asked Mon.

"Frozen on his last transmission, but crystal clear. Still a bit dark though." Mon leaned back after consulting the laptop that would keep us in touch with my robot.

Mon's small frame and black outfit melded into the big leather chair behind the dean's desk, making her nearly invisible. That she'd stepped up to help showed Bethany's good judgment in friends and had me reassessing my lingering misgivings about the girl being part of our inner circle. Quiet, surly, and darkly dressed didn't make someone a bad person—damned first impressions.

"What do you expect? You've got Amos hiding in a closet." Owen stood by the big mirror hefting a tire iron and clearly ready for action.

I shrugged his comment away. After confirming our target, Amos had taken refuge on the other side of the portal. The move was risky, but so was bringing my robot back through. Any use of magic increased the chance of discovery and of spooking the Shadow Master into running before we arrived. Once the gateway was open, Amos's live feed would resume, allowing Mon and Chad to monitor the operation. Bethany, Owen, and I were the ones crossing over.

Our target had gone to ground in a subway station of all places. It was a lesser-used stop on the yellow line outside Washington, D.C. He'd set himself up as king of the tiny admin suite just off the big tiled dome that was the underground station. Aside from a handful of sycophants coming and going over the past few hours, there only seemed to be two people working the office.

We'd shut down surveillance, sent Amos into hiding, and waited until after hours to give the human staff time to leave. Hitting the hideout when trains weren't running also kept innocents from getting caught in the crossfire.

Of course, there would be shadow demons—that was kind of the guy's thing. I turned to Bethany and had to smile because she was wrapped head to toe in one of Gina's black tactical outfits several shades darker than her skin, a sleek match to Mon's goth attire. Bethany caught me looking and patted the thick sketchbook clipped to her utility belt. The book held dozens of her more formidable drawings, ones that would make short work of the Shadow Master's minions.

The entire plan hinged on activating the portal so that it appeared just outside the office doors. A downside to the three of us taking point was that we'd be immediately recognized. But I hoped to use that to our advantage. The Shadow Master should go on the offensive and throw his shadow horde at us. Bethany's drawings would defeat his demons as we fell back, luring their master to follow. I felt reasonably confident he'd follow us through the portal and—if we timed it just right—straight into the leafy cage Chad would swing into place. Once trapped, his power would be nullified.

If a few shadows snuck through, Mortimer and Tina would be waiting for them along with a bevy of other animated drawings. A casual glance around the big office revealed splashes of color nestled among the dean's precious clocks. It was easy to miss the details: a transparent rodent here, a cartoon character there, and more.

Bethany's private army was ready for action. Harder to miss—if anyone was to look up—was the giant blue octopus wedged into the piping and vents. Tina was the ace in the hole of our operation, more than a match for any shadow demon ever born and, in a pinch, able to hold onto the master himself for a short time.

For my part, I went to battle in jeans and a Seether tee-shirt emblazoned with the band's logo and a reminder to "keep the faith." Not exactly a memorable outfit, except I also was styling with my new tinker's hat. The dust and grime had practically fallen off the sturdy leather, leading me to think the hat was enchanted. If so, the spell only kept it magically clean, and of course made the wearer dashing and debonair. After a brief wrestling match with my conscience, I'd decided the dead tinker would want to pass his headwear on to a worthy successor.

"You ready?" I asked the others, and ran a finger along the hat's brim in a kind of salute.

A round of thumbs up and grim smiles answered, and I reached for the globe. Before I could activate the portal, the office door crashed open.

"Wait!" Lars rushed into the room, panting and holding a leafy blanket.

"Okay, we really need to lock that." After pinpointing the obvious flaw in our preparations, I turned on the interloper. "Thanks for the cage, but the plan's all set. Unless you're spoiling to get in on the fight, I suggest you get out of here because it's go time."

I slid my index finger along the hat's brim for emphasis, finding the motion helped focus my resolve.

"Yeah, and we all know the plan is crap." Lars sighed and shrugged. "Well at least a little crappy. Chad's got to block the portal with my cage right after you three rush through, then hope shadow-dude comes next, but not too fast so he can secure the door. So I made you this!"

He held up the green blanket, pride lighting his pudgy face.

"A blanket?" I took the offered gift, unable to keep the skepticism at bay as I unfolded material made of fine shoots and budding leaves.

"It's a net with the same properties as the cage," Lars said. "I've been working on it day and night."

"Doesn't weigh much." I hefted the fragile looking thing, hoping it didn't fall apart in my hands.

"Keeping it light was the tricky part and why I couldn't be sure of getting it to work. Finally had to order spider silk cuttings. It's a super strong vine from the Congo region and took forever to get here. That's the secret to getting high tensile strength and durability. Use it like a normal net and it'll leaf out for that magic-blocking effect. The thorns will be much shorter of course, more like brambles, but four handles are woven in along the outside. Use those to keep from skewering yourself once it blooms."

"Lars, you're awesome. This is a game changer." I smiled, probably the first genuine smile I'd ever bestowed on my childhood nemesis.

We took a few precious minutes to ensure we knew how to throw a net over someone who didn't play nice and stand still to be captured. The fundamentals of the plan stayed the same, but Owen and I would use our new toy and then just drag our quarry's sorry ass back through the gate instead of trying to finesse him through. Chad and Mon would still stand ready with the cage in case things fell apart.

"We had better get to it." After the third run through, it felt like we were stalling. "Lars, thanks again. We'll let you know how it goes."

I waved him to the door, but he walked over to the cage instead. "If it's all the same to you, I'll stay in case you need an extra pair of hands."

Well, what do you know?

"Chad, lock the door." I gave my signature brim swipe. "To your places everyone."

We stepped through the portal right on the edge of the tiled subway tunnel platform, so close to the admin area that I almost smacked into the steel-framed door. As it was, I had to quickly step right to keep Bethany from plowing into me, and she had to do the same to make room for Owen.

Wire mesh embedded in the security glass of the upper door made it like looking through chicken wire. But at least we could see into the office area. An empty desk sat to either side of the outer bullpen. Two more desks would be out of sight at opposing ends of the long office running from right to left. The back side of a wooden door stood open on the left wall. That would be the storage room where Amos hid.

A glass partition straight ahead led into the manager's office, so that the entire area formed a tee-shaped layout beyond the short hall we'd have to enter through. A man sat in the far office with his back to us. If it hadn't been for Amos's surveillance, I wouldn't have recognized Mr. Gonzales. I couldn't see his face from this angle, but he'd let his neat buzz-cut grow out into an unruly mop, and the video footage had shown the bushy moustache he proudly wore now drooped low and thick.

I eased the door open and motioned the others forward. We crept a few steps closer to where the entry hall opened into the main room. My mental link with Amos sang. I felt the brave little robot as a warm presence in the back of my mind, the bond we shared snug beneath my breastbone. But something felt off. The invisible tether vibrated with anxiety.

I looked to the man at the desk, but he still hadn't budged. The room ahead was quiet, the desks in our line of sight neatly organized like window displays for the discerning administrator. A Xerox box sat at the foot of each desk and a column of the white boxes stacked four high stood to either side of the door to the inner office. Those hadn't been there a couple of hours ago, and I cringed at the thought of killing that many trees for such a small operation. What on Earth could they possibly be making copies of that called for that much paper? Even a demon-possessed manager ought to consider going paperless.

The quiet buzz of small motors drifted from the closet concealing Amos. The sound of his gyro-stabilizers was easy to recognize, as were the soft clunks of the actuators that moved his arms and legs. But when the noise didn't subside, I knew what was wrong.

"Amos is stuck," I whispered.

The Shadow Master was too far away to hear him struggle, but I sent a calming directive for Amos to keep still. We'd free him later from whatever obstacle had tripped him up. My designs were top-notch and hardly ever exploded nowadays, but there were still some situations that even the best of robots couldn't overcome.

I hefted the net, making certain its pleats were draped neatly so that it would open wide when I threw. With a nod, I crept forward, and the others followed. The bright office grew dark as the long fluorescent bulbs in the ceiling fixtures dimmed to the point they were difficult to make out.

As quickly as it had come, the darkness receded—no, it coalesced, gathering into irregular shapes overhead. Light showed between the shapes, most of which now sported arms and legs, teeth and claws. Before I could call out a warning, the shadow demons fell on us.

A sleek, dark cat the size of a puma hit the floor and sprang at me, leading the charge. Shadowy claws raked across my middle, slicing through shirt and skin. Fire seared across my stomach, and I hissed out a breath, hoping the wound was shallow. Shadows were too insubstantial to easily trap, but their magic certainly let them interact when it suited them.

I swung the net out of the way, brought up my free hand, and let loose a burst of mage light. The blue aura drove the thing back with an airy snarl, doing no real damage but buying time to put a few feet between us and our attackers.

"Time for phase one." I yielded the open bit of floor to Bethany.

This was what we'd prepared for. Bethany opened her sketchbook and swiped her hand up from the bottom of the first page. Crimson ink flew into the air before her. She flipped the page and repeated the motion in rapid succession across each of the facing pages. The three red clouds twisted, each expanding into a broad, three-dimensional rendering that dropped to the floor on four squat legs. A dimpled mound like a shell rose behind each beaked head, heads protected by horny plates. Wicked spikes ringed the edge of their bodies. The long prehensile tails each ended in a spiked ball.

The drawings resembled miniature ankylosaurs that stood knee-high, except the ancient herbivores hadn't used their tail like a scorpion to attack from overhead. And I supposed they hadn't developed a taste for shadow demon flesh either.

The trio charged, spiked balls smashing and beaks crunching. Conventional weapons and much of our magic couldn't touch the wispy substance of the shadows. That was why bottle traps and the newer battery traps had been developed. I patted the makeshift bandolier that held a half dozen of the latter against my chest.

Although Bethany's creations were definitely not demons—I'd had that argument often enough when she got depressed—their substance and magic was such that they could physically interact with the shadow spawn. As icing on the cake, her drawings drew sustenance from any shadows they consumed, growing bigger and stronger as they absorbed demon energy.

Despite being outnumbered, the dinos held their own until a massive canine shadow caught the base of a flailing tail in its jaws and tore it clean off. Without its main weapon, the poor thing went down under a pile of dark shapes. Bethany staggered and let out a sob as the shadows turned on the other two looking to capitalize on their advantage.

Owen and I both threw out mage light, giving our allies a short reprieve. Head down, Bethany tore through the pages of her book, firing out reinforcements and setting her personal army free. I'd seen the woman in action before, and the sight was awesome and terrifying in equal measure.

The bulk of her forces were reptiles or insects, modified with weapons well beyond what would be needed for survival in the wild. I cringed as a winged snake with two heads strafed the room, spewing inky acid that had the shadows howling. A deceptively useless looking toad worked its way through the melee, whipping out a spiky blue tongue and swallowing smaller demons whole. The toad swelled with each meal, growing larger as it went. A vaguely badger-shaped shadow attacked the toad from behind, landing on its back with raking claws, but the blue warts along the bumpy hide erupted in puffs of ink. The shadow badger staggered away as if drunk off its ass.

Amidst the carnage, one inky predator reigned supreme. If I didn't miss my guess, Bethany had drawn a dragon, complete with bat wings and vicious claws. But the monster was thick and had the distinctive head of a T. rex. Shadows fell before it and were finished off by the lesser drawings.

Even without blood, the battle was fearsome to watch. The stench of tar and burnt hair rose from the demons, charcoal and almonds from the drawings. My hand slipped away from the battery traps. We wouldn't need those. The intense fighting ended as suddenly as it had started.

The commotion died, leaving a small sea of swaying drawings awaiting their next task. Bethany walked among the survivors, patting heads and scratching behind ears. But I knew she was busy cataloging injuries to mend with her pencils, pastels, and pens once everyone was back on the page.

And still, the Shadow Master hadn't moved.

"I smell a rat." Owen had noticed the same thing.

We moved fully into the room. A gray-bearded man sat at the far right-hand desk that had been out of sight, and a young woman with mousey brown hair pulled back into a bun occupied the desk to our far left. Each wore dapper blue station uniforms and had a blocky company hat sitting in the middle of their desk.

"May we help you find your destination?" They asked in mega-creepy unison.

"Did you think I would not notice your childish attempts?" The Shadow Master stood at the door to his office, a self-satisfied smile stretching his lips. "I have been hunted for too many centuries to be taken unawares."

24. Out of Control

T HE MAN I'D known had always been lean, but under the Shadow Master's neglect, Mr. Gonzalez had grown thin and gaunt. It was as though the demon lord couldn't be bothered with the needs of his human host. The abuse made my face flush with anger.

"Yet here we are," I said, angling to wipe the stupid smile from his face. "Your shadows defeated. Three against one."

"Yes, your spy did so very well in keeping you informed." He threw his arm forward like a drama queen, or a gameshow host, and dark magic flared.

I ducked, but the spell slid past. A low squeak had me glancing over my shoulder to where the closet door slowly creaked open. Amos stood in the center of the small room, wrapped from foot to neck in silver duct tape. His camera had been left clear so that it still could transmit. The poor guy hadn't simply been stuck.

"That's going to take forever to get off him." Even if I used goo-away and a scrub brush, he'd end up scarred for life with sticky residue. "You couldn't have used rope?"

The drawings slid silently past, fanning out to cover most of the open floor space. Bethany was about to go for it. I took in the room as I turned back, trying to decide which side offered the best angle for netting our prey.

The two employees looked to the Shadow Master and pushed up from their desks. With her head turned, I caught sight of black markings at the base of the woman's neck, a sigil. The glint of red in her eyes and those of the old man confirmed it—they were both shadow possessed.

A high, thin squeal like air escaping from a balloon came from one of the original ankylosaurs as it fell sideways against a Xerox box and clawed the air. Across the room a similar seizure took hold of the blue toad, which flopped weakly, trying to push to its feet using a box of paper for support.

"What are you doing?" The question had barely left Bethany's lips when a third drawing went down.

A black claw raked at the substance of the squat red dinosaur, and a four-armed demon ripped its way out of the white cardboard box. These couldn't be shadow demons because the scaly black claws that tore away great clumps of ink extended from arms covered in brown fur. Matching apparitions grappled with the toad, and the second drawing to go down had been torn to shreds.

"Lurkers!" I pulled my hand from the trap I'd been fumbling for and called up fire.

The stacked boxes to either side of the main office exploded as four more lurkers spilled from hiding. From the shoulders up these new demons had pale, scaly skin. Pointed teeth lined their lipless mouths, and stubby tails jutted out behind each.

There was no way to throw fire without incinerating my friend's drawings, but I kept the spell ready. At the rate things progressed, there soon wouldn't be any drawings to worry about. The attackers were badly outnumbered, but Bethany's creations had no defense. Her drawing were uniquely suited for fighting shadows. Their clawing, biting, and thrashing only served to enrage the lurkers and leave colorful smears on their opponents' furry bodies.

"Pull back!" Retreating to the portal had been the original plan, and I couldn't think of anything better.

That the Shadow Master had aligned with lurkers shouldn't have come as a big surprise, but from all our reading I had the impression the demon lord worked alone. He specialized in controlling shades and shadows. What deal had he struck to gain the backing of lurkers? If anything commanded the ugly brutes it should have been a mimic—not that I wanted to deal with one of the high-ranking demons that we'd been told to never confront.

The answer to the riddle came clear when one of the lurkers slashed out at the nearest drawing. A pair of black interlocking diamonds within a circular border was burned into the scaly hide on the thing's neck. Shadow demons possessed the lurker demons. How far did the Shadow master's control stretch? How many could the man who'd once been my friend control? The ramifications were frightening. This had to stop.

Owen and I brought up the rear as we backed toward the door. Bethany called in her troops. Those that could disengage from the lurkers formed a defensive circle around us. Those that couldn't break free died. I snaked a bit of power into the storage room, snapped the tape around Amos's legs, and ordered him through the portal. There was nothing more he could do.

"Fire and fur?" Owen's teeth flashed behind his smirk. "I'll take the four on the right."

"Leaving four more for me," I agreed.

Having vertically challenged forces worked in our favor. Frosty crystals crept down the walls to either side as we gathered heat for our spells. We both let loose with fireballs that roared over the colorful ring surrounding the exit. The dino-dragon was the only one tall enough to be a problem, but we avoided burning him easily enough.

Fire splashed against hairy chests, adding the unique odor that was sure to be stuck in my nostrils for days. Owen was faster on the draw than I was, and had three lurkers engulfed in fire to my one by the time the Shadow Master threw out a spell to quench the flames that threatened the others. Still we backpedaled, drawing our quarry toward the trap.

"We can take them," Owen said.

I nodded. Even without Bethany's help, we could handle the few remaining lurkers. The Shadow Master himself was the wildcard. The net draped over my left arm remained our ace in the hole, but we'd certainly lost the element of surprise, not that we'd ever truly had it.

Just as I prepared another volley, the two station employees pushed between the demons and came for us, red eyes glowing. I grounded the spell, unwilling to fry someone just because they'd been possessed.

The pair stomped toward us, wading through the crowd of living illustrations. They snarled with hands raised, fingers curled into claws. I recoiled at the rage twisting these normal people into rabid animals, shuffled back faster, and stepped on Bethany's foot.

She reached up, grabbed me by the ear, and pulled my face down. Her nails dug in painfully, but I guess that was the point.

"You're running away from an old man and small woman." She grated out her words, tugging my lobe for emphasis. "They don't even have magic. Just wrap them in air and pitch them through the portal. Tina will pull out their shadow demons. We've got bigger fish to fry."

"Got it." I couldn't meet her gaze, but felt it boring into me as she huffed out a breath and released my tortured ear. Maybe the woman coming at us wasn't much of a threat, but I knew another tiny woman who scared the pants off me—for good reason.

Bethany was right, of course. Apparently the sight of demon possessed normal people freaked me out more than actual demons. Owen and I could probably have just grabbed the two by their shoulders and walked them off. But with four singed lurkers regrouping in front of their master, time was indeed of the essence. Feeling stupid, I screwed up my resolve and called on the elemental force of air.

Our spells pushed the man and woman through the gateway to Attwater as we backed out into the cavernous station. We must have injured the Shadow Master's pride because he didn't even hesitate to usher his paltry force through, following with murder in his dark eyes.

"We've got these clowns!" Owen's confidence was just what I needed.

Better yet, the comment drew the man's focus.

That's it, go for the smart ass. A few seconds of distraction would give me an opening. I fingered the net and kept hold of the air spell that would guide my throw.

The floor rumbled, and the Shadow Master smiled—not a pleasant expression. The man straightened and crossed his arms, waiting. In that instant, my opportunity to catch him off guard slipped away. The vibration rose to a roar, and wind rushed through the room. *What magic is this?*

I shot a glance over my shoulder to find...a subway train whooshing from its tunnel lair, brakes squealing as it slowed at the platform. Dozens of heads bobbed behind the windows as the passengers got ready to disembark. *Crap!* The last thing we needed was a carload of innocent bystanders.

"Bethany," I called over my shoulder. "Make sure those people don't wander over."

I kept my eye on the Shadow Master, ready to block any move to use the passengers against us. I didn't have a good sense of his power and wanted to avoid going toe-to-toe in a duel of magic. The three of us might be able to take him in an outright battle, but he'd pretty much vanished into thin air the last time the dean had confronted him.

"Jason, this isn't good," Bethany said as the train's doors hissed open.

"Just keep those people back." I crouched low to make myself a smaller target, eyes on our opponent. *Go ahead, make my day.*

"They aren't people." Her voice cracked and the heat from the fireball she launched warmed my back as it streaked off in the opposite direction.

"What the hell?" I spun around to see what had possessed her to attack.

Lurkers poured from the train cars, lots of them. Bethany's fireball splashed against the nearest ones, doing little damage. They lined up like troops, three and four rows deep, awaiting the Shadow Master's command. There had to be a super pissed off mimic out there wondering where the hell their minions had gone.

"Boss?" Owen's confidence was gone.

"That's" —I struggled for the perfect reply, for words of inspiration in our darkest hour— "a lot of demons."

I shot a furtive glance at the shimmering portal, wondering if we could escape without getting cut down from behind. Bad odds were one thing, but making a stand against the horde of lurkers would be suicide. And these weren't just the four-armed furries who guarded their smirking master. The heavy scales and stony bodies of these wouldn't burn. Two were as big as the monster that had impersonated that dumpster back on the day I'd met Roxy, and I wondered if they'd actually been inside the train or ridden on top.

The shapes and varieties were too much to take in. Worse than that, magic gathered in the hands of a phalanx in the back. Those demons were tall and gaunt with heads bowed beneath ragged hoods. We were in serious trouble.

For some reason, Amos hadn't gone back to Attwater yet. He just stood behind the portal, arms still taped to his sides, taking in the scene. No time to worry about robotic disobedience. My attention was already split between our quarry and the lurkers pressing forward.

"Looks like you guys could use a little help."

I turned at the familiar voice, wondering how Amos had managed to sound like Gina. The smoky haze of battle must have been playing tricks on me. A disembodied head poked through the shimmering oval that was our way home. The mass of dark, frizzy curls pivoted, and Gina smiled at me—a seriously ghoulish sight considering her neck was cut off by a glowing line at the portal's surface. Her gaze traveled to the train platform, and her eyes went round. "Or maybe you need a lot of help."

She gave an eerie nod and sunk out of sight. Moments later, Gina flew through the gate like a ninja, dressed in her midnight commando outfit.

Instead of being mad at Amos, I needed to give the stubborn robot a reward. Mon and Chad must have called for backup when they saw things going south on the video feed.

But as much as I appreciated Gina jumping into the fray, an extra body wouldn't improve our odds much.

"You're heading the wrong way!" I shook my head and waved the others toward our exit. Live to fight another day seemed like a wise move. "We're done here."

Instead of spinning on her heel and leaving, Gina put a balled fist on one hip, turned to the gateway, and let out a piercing whistle. Oh, she was one of those. The volume made me cringe. Dark shapes flowed from the gateway at a jog.

Five, ten, fifteen, twenty black clad people spilled out into the station, more than were left in the entire security branch. I recognized several faces, all set with firm resolve. Gina had mustered her student detail.

They hadn't come empty handed. The first row of students threw canisters into the ranks of lurkers. The flash-bang explosions sent a wave of magic through the demons that had them scattering. The robed figures closest to the train released a volley of their own. Yellow-red flares soared into the air and burst.

"Shields!" Gina yelled as sizzling yellow strands fell from above.

Four people across the back raised their hands and sent a sparkling blue barrier to meet the falling magic.

"My people will handle this lot." Gina sent her team forward with a series of curt hand gestures.

Under the protection of their shielding, the students surged forward and split off into a well-rehearsed maneuver. They worked with purpose, corralling the main body of lurkers and cutting out the lumbering giants to be dealt with separately.

More flash-bang devices echoed off the high tile ceiling, making a path for a squad led by a middle-aged man with slick black hair and a uniform that fit him like a wetsuit. The tactical unit attacked the tall magic-wielding demons at the back. Spells and sparks flew in a flurry of exchanges, but the Attwater crew clearly knew what they were doing.

"Close your mouth or you'll catch flies." Gina moved to my side, bumped her hip against mine, and then hauled back and slapped me on the butt. "Go get your boogeyman. Bike Boy and I will clear the way."

I gaped as she winked and waved Owen forward to attack the tangle of furry demons. *She slapped my butt.* It hadn't hurt, but who did that? I shook off the distracting train of thought before it could gain momentum. We weren't out of the woods yet. Fireballs fizzled out on contact with the spell protecting the Shadow Master's guards. My friends shifted to air and earth magic, sweeping the now-howling lurkers off to the side.

The Shadow Master had had enough. I saw it in his angry glare, smoldering eyes promising future pain. He backed through the doorway, and smoke rose around him as he prepared to flee. I threw the net aside and used a whisper of air magic. The material unfurled out of his line of sight and scooted up the wall to dangle above the doorway.

"This isn't over." His low growl was muffled behind the shroud of magic that enveloped him.

"Big words for a body snatcher and coward." I lunged forward, desperate to keep him talking. Any second now the man would wink out of sight, and we'd be back to square one. "Do the mimics know you steal from them too?"

I wasn't sure if the insult or accusation caught his attention, but one of them certainly struck a nerve. The shimmering dark smoke that would transport him to safety receded until it roiled around his knees like angry fog.

"Do you know what it's like to have power over others, Jason?" He stalked forward, teetering on the threshold, his face twisted with scorn as he spat out the question. "To hold the soul of another in your hands? These so-called mimics with their grand plans are nothing more than puppets. Not of my making, but puppets nonetheless. They dance at the whims of others as they plot and scheme, thinking themselves clever."

"Cleverer than you." I stepped back, hoping to draw him out of the doorway. "You've been discovered twice now. How's *that* feel?"

The fight raged on. I tried to ignore the screams and stench of magic rising behind me. Likewise, I blocked out the thrash of bodies as Owen waded in to grapple with the demons, tire iron alight with magic.

"They waste time paving the way for others." His demon eyes shone with fanatical intensity. "I seize the moment, do what is needed to solidify my hold, and am castigated— shunned by those who would hand the treasures of your world over to others."

"And you're sooo much better." I heaped sarcasm into the words.

"Here, I am a god!" Spittle flew as he screamed his insanity and took a step. "I will—"

My air currents flung the net down over his head. The lightweight material billowed out and quickly settled over the man's shoulders and torso. His hands tore at the flimsy weave, but Lars knew his plants. The net stretched and creaked, holding fast.

Vines along the bottom contracted, cinching the net tight around his feet. The gaunt features stretched, his face elongating into a fierce caricature as the Shadow Master howled. Black nails sprouted from each fingertip.

He raked at the net, magic sparking against the green stems. The vines thickened as needle-sharp thorns sprouted along their lengths. Leaves and a blush of delicate pink flowers burst forth, forming a fuzzy pink cocoon. The Shadow Master's power flared and…winked out.

As he raged within his prison, the net drew tighter to restrict the Shadow Master's movements until he finally grew still. An eerie wail rose from all around, and the rhythmic sounds of battle faltered. Half the lurkers were already down. Those still standing stumbled about as if dazzled. A dark thick snake rose from each as the shadow demons controlling the lurkers separated from their hosts.

Bethany's creatures seized the opportunity and surged forth to deal with the shadows even as Gina's people waded back in to dispatch the dazed lurkers. It was more of a slaughter than a battle and over quickly.

To be honest, we didn't really know what happened to dead demons. Our demonology class maintained that their essence was simply banished from our world and returned to the chaotic void from which they'd escaped. Even so, clean-up was going to be a bitch. The hungry drawings took care of the shadows, but we'd have a long night ahead mopping up lurker guts if we didn't want the local authorities freaking out.

"Nicely done." Gina staggered over, looking like a car windshield coming out of bug-infested swamplands.

"Thanks. Um, you've got a little something there." I pointed at her big grin, not wanting to know where the fuzzy brown bit stuck in her front teeth came from. "Let's get this asshat home. I want Mr. Gonzalez back."

25. Light Waves

T RUSSED UP AS he was in the neutralizing net, the Shadow Master could do little more than rage during his transfer through the portal. We all breathed a sigh of relief when he was finally secured inside the cage back at the dean's office. Although it was surely uncomfortable, I left the netting in place as an added layer of security while we pulled together the needed equipment.

Thankfully, the administration wing outside the office was empty for the night, so the blistering curses and promises of painful retribution didn't draw unwanted attention. If we were still at it come morning, I'd have a lot of explaining to do to Ms. Eisner. The acting dean had been grateful for our help in searching for Mr. Gonzales, but hadn't gone so far as to sanction a rescue. With the primary security forces tied up on other matters, I'd made the command decision to go after him, figuring it was easier to ask for forgiveness than permission.

During the twenty minutes it took to assemble the equipment we'd staged, our prisoner fell silent, no doubt biding his time and waiting for us to make a mistake.

"That's about got it," Owen said after he and I strong-armed a cylinder the size of a small barrel onto the top of the cage. "Let's get it all plugged in and hope we don't blow a fuse."

Electrical wire trailed from the cylinder and three tall panels spaced around the cage. We'd rolled the entire contraption into the corner of the room for easy access to the power strips along the back of the dean's workbench.

Owen and I plugged everything in and made certain the switch for the unit on top was within easy reach. I got the feeling we'd only have one shot at this and looked to Bethany. We were betting an awful lot on what she'd managed to glean from old texts, but this was the best any of us could come up with to simulate how the monks had dealt with this particular demon lord. You could cut the tension with a knife, but after circling the equipment one last time Bethany finally gave her nod of approval.

"Lars, release the net," I said.

Mon and Bethany stood ready with magic in case something went wrong. Owen and I teamed up to run the gear. Lars reached a hand through the leaves of the outer cage. At his touch the pink blossoms withdrew into the vines and the weave unraveled. The net slithered off our prisoner. Lars jumped back, clutching the wispy vines, just in time to keep his hand from being lopped off by the black nails slicing down at his wrist.

Chad stood by the door like the proverbial Black Knight, his body language saying clearer than words that "none shall pass." Aside from myself, Chad had the biggest grudge against the Shadow Master. In his bid to take over Attwater, the demon master had damaged the very heart of the school, an unforgivable offense in the eyes of our friend.

"Here goes nothing." Owen flipped on the main switch and purple light flooded from the three upright panels.

"Oh, please." The Shadow Master's voice dripped with scorn. "I expected more from you, Jason. Didn't your precious Mr. Gonzales teach you anything?"

His glib attitude almost had me fooled, but a trickle of sweat ran down his temple. And we'd only just gotten started.

"Leaves." I waved Lars forward again.

Luckily he didn't have to reach past the cage walls this time. With a light touch on one of the carry handles, the greenery withdrew into their vines like startled coral. With the shade withdrawn light bathed the man. He hissed and raked a clawed hand across the vines. Sparks of magic rose and several woody stems parted.

Without leaves, the magic dampening properties of the cage were greatly reduced. This was the riskiest point in the plan. I cranked up the ultraviolet lights to full intensity, driving him back from the cage walls.

"It's working," Bethany said. "The monks chained the host out in the desert sun, sometimes for several days. This should drive the demon out quicker."

Lars had come to the rescue again in constructing our demon lord banishment contraption. The botanical department called in a favor or two to get the industrial grow lights from a commercial greenhouse they staffed.

"Why's he smoking?" I asked.

"It's the demon's substance trying to shield itself," Bethany said. "Look, the UV burns it away."

Black wisps rose off his skin to shroud him in smoke. For a moment his entire body was obscured, and I worried he'd teleport out of the trap. But Bethany was right. The light thinned the smoke like sun burning off morning fog. A snarl of rage tore from the man's throat as his neck stretched and his face sharpened into that of a feral predator. He howled, claws raking the air as if he meant to drive back the light.

And still the smoke rose off his body. A new fear gripped me, worry that the intense light would blind or even kill the man we were here to rescue. The monks had been brutal in their pursuit of demon cleansing. Of the few times they'd documented driving the Shadow Master away, they'd only succeeded in saving the host once. More often than not, the person died of exposure. We didn't expect to be at this long enough for exposure to be a problem, but hadn't counted on the physical reaction ultraviolet light would have with Mr. Gonzales's demon-imbued flesh. His crisp uniform scorched where the smoke rose.

"Tina, be ready!" Bethany called toward the ceiling.

Blue tentacles tightened around the pipes overhead in anticipation. Tina was our last line of defense if the Shadow Master broke free. She was clearly more than ready for a rematch.

The smoke gathered thick around the man's head, but then pulled upward as if caught in a draft, exposing Mr. G's twisted features. The elongated bones of his face stretched even further as the smoke condensed into a solid looking mass trying to lift him off his feet. Two slits opened in the dark mass, angry yellow eyes. The mad gleam left Mr. Gonzales's eyes and his features sagged back into the normal proportions of a haggard man.

"He's leaving." Bethany waved Lars and me in for the final stage. "Get ready!"

A two foot column of darkness rose from the back of the man's head, stretching longer and thicker by the second. But unlike his shadow snake slaves, the Shadow Master rose from his host like a dark scarecrow, mouth gaping in a silent roar and eyes blazing hatred. The thing lunged at me with shadow claws, pulled back at a flash of power from the leafy cage, then tried for Lars. And still it rose. The lower half of the demon's body slid from the back of its human host, and Mr. Gonzales crumpled to the cage floor.

"Now!" I yanked open the access panel under the cylinder perched atop the cage.

Lars reached out with his talent, and an opening formed in the woven ceiling of the cage. Nothing stood between the Shadow Master and the dark interior of the cylinder. The shadowy figure sped upward to escape the intense light. On its way past, an arm shot out through the gap in the magical wards, black nails raking the air inches from my face.

As soon as the creature disappeared inside, I rammed the panel closed, trapping the thing that was truly the Shadow Master in the cylinder. Owen turned on the juice.

The cylinder's control unit thrummed with power, feeding electricity to a final array of ultraviolet lights inside the mirror-lined chamber. The room dimmed from the power drain, but the overhead lights quickly stabilized. Instead of simple grow bulbs, this last part featured high voltage sanitation lights, a kind of ultraviolet doomsday weapon for large scale germicide in hospitals and water treatment plants.

A piercing, hollow shriek no human throat could form tore from the cylinder. I'd welded the walls myself from heat-curved sheet metal. The sides vibrated so hard that I worried the seams would burst. But my work held, the inhuman noise faded to a thin keening, and the cylinder went still.

We stood tense, gathered around the cage and straining to hear movement over the hum of the lights. I caught myself holding my breath and released the air from aching lungs as quietly as I could.

"How long do we wait?" Mon whispered into the silence.

Bethany shrugged. "Another five?"

Nervous nods accompanied the whoosh of others releasing their breath. Five minutes turned into ten. *Go team procrastinate.*

"Feels like we're just stalling now." I shot a questioning look to the group and wrapped my hand around the handle that would slide back the bottom of the cylinder.

When no one argued, I slid the panel open and jumped back. Mage light flared to my fingers as something dark drifted from the light chamber. But it was just ash and powdery soot. The Shadow Master was no more.

I sheepishly snuffed out my light, but hadn't been the only one to call up magic.

"Is he gone?" Chad asked from his station by the door.

I looked to Bethany, the closest we had to an expert.

"I think so." She nodded. "The ash is a good sign. He didn't just teleport out."

Unfortunately the ash fell right onto Mr. Gonzales, who was still crumpled into a ball at the bottom of the cage. The residue dusted him with black flecks. I breathed a sigh of relief when the Shadow Master's remains didn't magically reconstitute and possess the man.

"What's going on?" Mr. Gonzales sounded hoarse and exhausted, but pulled himself up to a sitting position and blinked at me. "Jason?"

He tugged on the wooden bars of his prison, but talons didn't spring from his fingers.

"Don't worry. We'll get you out of there in a jiffy and explain everything." I knelt and grinned as he took in his surroundings, eyes going wide at spotting the octopus slithering its way across the ceiling.

Then he did something good, something very good. He stuck a hand through the bars and grabbed my shoulder. The Shadow Master wouldn't have been able to simply reach past those vines. Mr. G. was finally home.

26. Memories

"I T STILL FEELS like a dream," Mr. Gonzalez said as he picked up the other end of the workbench. "I get flashes of memories, but they feel like they belong to someone else."

We were busy rearranging his shop, undoing changes he'd made while under the Shadow Master's influence. The six-foot-long table went into the center of the room so that shelves of materials sat behind it and Mr. G. could keep an eye on the door while he worked.

"That's got to be weird." I squared my end up using the grout line in the tile floor. "I'd be having nightmares for a year."

After spending a week at home, Mr. Gonzales insisted on coming back to work. As a bachelor living alone, I think he felt more connected at the school. We'd all certainly missed him, but the acting dean didn't want him working full time without assistance so had kept the current maintenance staff working, with Mike Gonzales consulting.

The arrangement gave security time to interview our recently returned staff member. He had a standing appointment for an hour a day, something I didn't envy. But I understood the need. Ms. Eisner had to be absolutely certain

Mr. Gonzales was no longer under demon influence, and until she was, he wouldn't be left unsupervised.

You'd think that focus would have spared yours truly from getting royally reamed out for going in to rescue the man—but you'd be wrong. Mary Eisner was none too happy with any of us for going behind her back on our little subway raid. The only thing saving us from losing our Attwater scholarships was the fact that Ms. Murdock from security had been so closely involved during our vigil waiting for the dean to return on his own.

Plus, Gina and her team were basically picking up the slack for the missing security forces. She'd become a de facto second in command, so having her along to pull our bacon out of the fire lent something close to legitimacy to our rescue mission.

I think what really concerned Ms. Eisner the most was that we'd brought the Shadow Master back inside Attwater when she'd been doing her best to lock down the school. I'd been pegged as the ringleader, but would have argued the rescue had been a group effort.

We all took our community service punishments in stride and promised never to do something like that again without her approval. She was holding us to that promise by declaring the mirror portal off limits for chasing after the dean—at least until we had solid information on where he and the others were sent.

"I can handle the dreams," Mr. G. said, and it was good to see some of the sparkle back in his eyes. "It's the voices that worry me."

"The what?" My own voice squeaked high.

"The incessant voices, Jason." He walked like a zombie with arms out in front of him to my bag by the door and started to rummage through it. "The ones that tell me you have a candy bar." His words rose in pitch and power. "A choc-o-late confection. That I must...devour!"

He brandished my afternoon snack, held it to his nose, and inhaled deeply before bursting into laughter—short and forced, but laughter nonetheless. I shook my head and heaved out a sigh.

"*That* was not nice." I waved him off when he moved to put the candy back. "Keep it. You've earned it."

"If you insist." He started to close my bag, but reached back in and pulled out one of the spider repeaters. "Now this looks awfully familiar."

"From one of your memories?"

It had to be. The spiders hadn't shown up until after Mr. Gonzales went missing. Which also meant we'd driven the Shadow Master out of Attwater well before portals started getting hijacked. Given the timing, I'd assumed he hadn't had anything to do with the dean's disappearance.

"Yes, this has a certain feel to it."

I pulled out the other half of the pair, and we sat them on the work bench. Whatever glimmer of insight he had faded, so I recapped the small amount I'd been able to discover with Mon's help.

"But I have no idea how to track where the ones on the mirror portal may have sent the dean," I concluded. "That's the real problem. It doesn't help that I can't even poke around without Mon being present."

"These require a magic key." Mr. G. turned over the spider I'd pried open and peered inside. "Your friend must have a unique magic talent."

"She doesn't do it on purpose," I said. "Something about her aura acts like a catalyst. This pair basically powers up to standby when she's close. But I need them fully operational. Who would have those keys?"

"I'm not talking about a physical key." He waved the notion aside and tapped his temple. "We need a spell crafted with elemental forces in just the right proportions. Think of it as a cryptographic key like the kind that secures your email. Talking helps me remember bit and pieces."

"Do you recall how the Shadow Master snuck back in with these?" I hated the thought that he'd had access to Attwater after we sent him packing.

"He didn't." Mr. G. closed his eyes and spoke slowly, chasing his thoughts. "I'm pretty sure he never came back here. But he was…familiar with these devices. I feel like he might have used them against the other demons at some point. There wasn't much love lost there."

"You said something similar—or at least the Shadow Master did—back at the train station. He'd been possessing lurkers and made it sound like he was at war with some high-level demons."

"That sounds about right." He shook his head, a rueful gesture. "Teamwork wasn't in his makeup. Now, let me think about this. The spirit element probably formed the basis of the key since setting these up took a force of will. And I seem to recall fire forging the spell together."

He spent the better part of the lunch hour fiddling around with the spiders and grasping at fleeting insights for the proper key. I left him to it and went to class, not willing to fall even farther behind.

I returned to find Mr. Gonzales slumped over the table fast asleep. It was a miracle that he hadn't fallen out of his chair. Fully recovering from his ordeal was going to take time. I took the opportunity to look through his collection of tools, always interested in seeing what other people favored.

"Jason?" He stirred and rubbed his face. "What time is it?"

"Three-thirty. My last class let out early for a change so I figured I'd see how things were going. Maybe you should go home and rest."

"Cat naps do wonders." He shrugged off my suggestion and slid the two spiders into the center of his worktable. "I took a break after finishing."

"You got them to work?"

"Almost," he said. "Come see for yourself."

With a wave of his hand a complex knot of intermixed magic flared and sank into the closest device. I didn't quite catch all the connections, even after scrambling to slip my goggles on. Hints of earth and air were mixed in with the spirit and fire elements. A dark shroud resembling the aura Mon exuded pressed the components together into a knife edge that Mr. G. touched to the body of one spider. A golden thread of power sprang up between the two spiders.

"Take this to see the details." Mr. G. passed over the open end of a linking spell.

Teachers often used the simple spirit spell in tutoring sessions. Linking into the magic an instructor cast helped students see the composition of the spell and get a clearer idea of how to cast it themselves. I tied off the loose end to my own spell and waited for the surge of energies to settle out, indicating we had a stable connection.

He picked up the other device and moved it to the far end of the tabletop. The line of power connecting the two fanned open to cover the surface with a regular grid of energy floating just above the wood.

"It's a map!" At least, I thought it was.

"You're right." Mr. G. nodded and rotated the view. "And it can be set to relative or absolute depending on how the portal trap is to be programmed. This view is relative and shows the offset to be applied to travel. I can't share the scale and some of the other controls, but that bright spot is where the portal will exit as compared to the expected location."

He pointed to a red dot like a laser pointer makes. The spot burned brightly on a distant gridline well away from both spiders.

"Seems like doing that would probably just kill anybody using the portal," I said. "Unless you had a really accurate way to measure out how far to shift the exit so it didn't land in a tree or something."

"Not as difficult as you might think. Portal magic has improved over the years to include built-in safety measures. You'd need stronger magic than these devices to force a portal into solid matter or to open at a deadly altitude. In those instances, the terminus would simply appear at the closest safe location. Now I'll shift to absolute coordinates. Tell me if anything looks familiar."

The magic subtly shifted and the grid reconfigured into irregular outlines recognizable as a map. A wide column off to my right ended in a familiar pointed toe with opposing heel, resembling a boot. A bright red target lit the front of the ankle area.

"We *were* in Italy!"

"Right around Pompeii," he agreed.

"So we could find the ruins again?" I grinned at his nod. This was the breakthrough we needed. "Will the same key work for the spider on the mirror portal?"

"Without the device from the far end, I won't be able to activate relative mode, but an absolute map should let us see where it leads. Once reactivated, that is where travelers will go."

"We need to talk to Ms. Eisner."

27. Retrieval

T HERE WAS NO covert operation involved with going after Dean Gladstone. This time we launched a fully sanctioned assault with Ms. Eisner's blessing. Considering she'd pulled every last security person in and even borrowed a few from our sister schools, I felt privileged that my friends and I were included in the operation. Since Mr. G. and I had figured out how to safely work the portal, I got to be nominally in charge of planning—as long as I worked with the team assigned by the acting dean.

As usual, my leadership role was loosely shared with Bethany and Owen. With no shadow lord to deal with, Lars had begged off of the weekend raid. And although Mon shared a teary goodbye hug and extracted Bethany's soulful promise to be extra careful, the goth girl did not accompany us. Her omission was largely a matter of not wanting her strange aura to interfere with the reactivated spider devices. For his part, Mr. Gonzales would keep watch in the dean's office to ensure the link between the spiders remained stable and allowed us all to return.

Gina and Melissa Murdock would lead their respective teams through, and heaven help the demon that tried to stand in their way.

"I believe all is ready," Acting Dean Eisner said from the big leather chair, looking very much in control even if her feet didn't quite reach the floor.

Owen had worried the unassuming woman with the ready smile wasn't dean material, but our teacher had risen to the challenge. Mary Eisner's short black hair bobbed, and determination glinted in her dark eyes as she nodded for us to proceed.

For the duration of the rescue mission, she planned to camp out in the main office, which was fully stocked with carafes of strong coffee and meals from the kitchen. A small first aid station had even been erected by the fireplace and was staffed by two volunteers.

My friends and I stood by the mirror gate with Mr. Gonzales, but the contingent of several dozen security personnel stretched out into the hall. Mr. G. keyed the spider device set in the mirror's frame, bringing it to life. He left the portal itself inactive while examining the coordinates programmed into the device.

"Very odd." A frown creased his forehead, but he hurried to explain. "Not a problem, just strange. The portal has been redirected to take travelers deep underground near Kīlauea."

"The volcano in Hawaii?" I asked.

"That explains why they haven't been able to return." Ms. Eisner nodded as if a great piece of the puzzle had just been revealed.

"I thought portals had safeties so people didn't end up landing in things like molten lava." My heartbeat thundered. We were too late—and had been from the start.

"They do. Not to worry." Ms. Eisner made a note in the journal she'd been using for the mission. "Volcanic rock is resistant to magic so would block their return once the portal closed and the spider device in the cave went inactive. Mr. Gonzales, let's bring our people home, shall we?"

Gina and the other team lead called back along the line for their people to stand ready. Because the spiders had been programmed with absolute coordinates, once activated they redirected the portal. If a relative offset had been used, we would have needed to know exactly where the globe had tried to send them the first time around.

Magic flowed and the mirrored surface shimmered as it shifted into the familiar swirling energy that marked a portal gate. Mr. G. double checked his readings with a nod and we moved out.

Gina, Ms. Murdock, and two of their guards stepped through first with weapons drawn and magic shields at the ready. I went through next, followed by Owen and Bethany.

Dank air and darkness met me as my feet crunched on what sounded like shards of broken pottery. Soft yellow mage light illuminated the black walls of a huge tunnel. The damp air carried a strange scent like a match had been struck, but there was no smell of smoke.

The three of us stuck to the plan and moved off to the side to let the trained forces file through and regroup. Bethany and I threw out our own lights, blue-white balls that drifted up to the ceiling to join the others.

The cavern was maybe twenty yards across, and deserted as far as we could tell. Of course it stretched on into darkness beyond the lights ahead and behind the portal.

"They've definitely been here," Gina said, joining us after it became clear there was no immediate threat. "Even before our people came through, there were plenty of footprints in the sand. They cleared a path through the shattered bits that look to have fallen from the ceiling."

"But where are they now?" Bethany asked.

"We'll have to fan out and see where the tracks lead," Gina said. "Looks like an extensive cave system. This could take a while."

Tracks headed off in all directions as if the dean's group had also been searching for an exit. It only took twenty minutes to figure out they'd settled on forging ahead in the direction that the portal pointed, which also happened to be uphill.

"Do either of you know anything about caves under a volcano?" I asked as we hiked along behind Gina. "It doesn't feel hot in here, so I'm guessing we don't need to worry about lava."

"I've read a little," Bethany admitted, which earned an of-course-you-have eye roll from Owen. "We're probably in a tube that carried lava hundreds of years ago. These ridges in the walls are from backed up molten stone that would have drained out to leave the cave system. This could go for miles."

"Wonderful. We're in the volcano's plumbing," Owen said.

"Deep in it according to Mr. Gonzales." I ran a hand over the dark stone, which appeared smooth but felt rough. "If volcanic rock is resistant to magic and there's a mountain of it above us, no wonder the dean got stuck. They're probably still wandering around looking for an exit."

"I doubt they came prepared for something like this." Owen scowled and spat. "Maybe there's water down here, but there sure isn't any food. You don't just keep walking without both, not for weeks on end."

He was right. After two hours, the tunnel leveled off and widened into a kind of hub. Short passages shot off in several directions. None went far before dead ending. The main tunnel we'd been following continued up a much steeper slope, but the tracks in that section went in both directions.

The hub level was crisscrossed with tracks, and a long-cold fire pit in the center contained only ash, which had us wondering what they could have used for fuel. We fanned out looking for clues.

"They stayed here for a while," I called back over my shoulder after peeking my head into a low-ceilinged chamber with a sandy floor that had been cleared of debris.

Owen and Bethany joined me. There'd been a lot of activity in this room. Depressions around the base of the wall looked suspiciously like sleeping spots. An odd scrap of paper here and bit of fuzz there were pretty good clues that our people had hunkered down here, but the marks carved into one wall were the dead giveaway.

"Sixteen days. Has to be." Bethany ran her fingers over the scratches.

Groups of four vertical lines with a fifth slashed diagonally were followed by a lone vertical mark that would have been the start of a fourth group. More searching uncovered a handful of spilled coins and a key fob with the Attwater logo. The tip of the sole metal key on the attached ring had been ground down flat so was likely what they'd used to mark off days.

"Crap!" Owen backed out fast from the side passage farthest from the sleeping area. "I found the latrine."

"I've sent runners on ahead to see how far the tracks go," Melissa Murdock said as everyone regrouped around the fire pit. "But it seems obvious to me that they backtracked to this spot to await rescue. There's a refuse pile down that right-hand spur that tells us they had some edibles along, even a couple of canteens. But I'm guessing they were in a bad way for water before long."

"If they hit a dead end farther on or just decided to wait because the caverns seemed endless, then where did they go?" I couldn't help asking the obvious; it was kind of my thing.

No one had a ready answer.

We waited a solid three hours while runners continued on and others went back to check the less obvious trail that headed downslope from the portal. The latter patrol came back first, saying the entire tunnel had collapsed ages ago and was totally blocked.

The last scouts reported back that the trail we'd been following went cold a few miles ahead. The tunnel split off in two directions that inexplicably looped back on themselves, another dead end.

With little more to do, the security people filtered back down to the portal. Ms. Murdock promised to call in forensics experts to help ferret out what had happened. With her student security cadre on their way back to the school, Gina joined Bethany, Owen, and me by the fire ring. Sitting in the sand with heads hung low, no one had much to say.

"We were so close." I wanted to roll back the clock and get a do-over. "I shouldn't have dragged my feet on going after the Shadow Master."

"None of that now." Gina slid her hand into mine and bumped shoulders. "You can't blame yourself. Taking on that beast any sooner could have been a disaster."

"I'm not giving up." Bethany shook her head, braids flapping. "Dean Gladstone will show up. Mark my words. The man's a legend. Isn't that right, Gina?"

Gina wasn't listening. She poked through the ashes with her free hand, rubbing them between thumb and fingers, totally absorbed.

"Um… Gina?" I squeezed the hand I still gripped to get her attention.

"Huh?" She looked up wearing a quizzical expression. "Sorry, it's just…" Her attention drifted back to her sooty fingers. The ghostly outline of a little lizard crawled from her palm to stomp around in the swirling ash. "There are traces of magic here, more than just what they used for warmth. I think this is where they tried to break out of this place."

The translucent lizard—if it wasn't my imagination—crawled back under her hand and disappeared. If it was one of Gina's salamanders, it didn't have any flames or embers to give it substance.

"I sure as hell would have been trying every spell I know." Owen put the boast into action by raising his right hand and launching fire at the ceiling.

The spell left his hand as a lance instead of the ball we'd all been taught, and envy rose at seeing his level of control. But as impressive as the blast was, it simply winked out as the energy came into contact with the lumpy black stone overhead.

"Magic resistant rock. Remember?" Bethany shook her head with a sigh. "But I think Gina's point is that residue of whatever they tried can be found in the fire ring and maybe even the sandy floor."

"We'll have to hope those experts piece together what happened." Hope—I found it a difficult sentiment to conjure at the moment.

28. Bittersweet

T HE DAYS GREW longer as the semester rushed to a close. Additional information wasn't forthcoming from the investigators, and the acting dean had sealed the mirror portal just in case the demons could access the devices they'd planted.

I supposed that it was just as well. With no demon plots to distract me, schoolwork and building up my welding skills again took center stage. Gina even broke away from her graduation prep to give the occasional one-on-one tutor session. The woman was a master with all manner of welding gear, and I picked her brain to tease out as many tricks of the trade as possible.

The dean's absence weighed heavily on staff and students. Between additional protocols and physical checks, getting through our classroom portals took so long that hardly any time was left to deal with Mr. Manning's demon du jour. By the end of the semester, we'd worked our way up to low-level lurkers, fluffy legless blobs reminding me of tribbles from *Star Trek*. I got that he didn't want to freak anyone out, but dealing with the innocuous critters was laughable given what my friends and I had been through.

Ms. Eisner continued pro forma updates about the hijacked portal situation at the start of each student assembly, but provided little in the way of actual information. All we really knew was that the dean and his security detail were still missing, and that the administration remained optimistic they'd find a quick resolution.

On the global-fight-against-the-darkness front, something in the world had shifted. As the days warmed, assaults on industrial facilities dropped off. The prevailing opinion called this a temporary reprieve at best. But at least reduced problems in the field gave everyone time to breathe.

Of course, some people couldn't help but look a gift horse in the mouth. Rumblings of demonkind's nefarious new plans sent an ugly undertone through the school's preparations to send a new class of certified technicians out into the world.

Regrettably, Mon was among those who foresaw dire times ahead, and she pulled Bethany into her deep-state theories. Roxy provided a bright counter-opinion to the drama and had backed down the conspiracy mongers on more than one occasion. She simply asked them to prove their claims that the mimics were coming for Attwater, a polite tactic that never failed to derail naysayers. It was even more entertaining to watch her debunk the growing story that the dean had been devoured by the dark and would return as a powerful, undead lich. I understood being on edge, but, honestly, the school was turning into a gossip mill, which served only to fuel fear and distrust.

"You'll do fine," Gina assured me at the end of our latest tutoring session. "Mr. Martin isn't the kind to ding a few wavy welds, and everything you produce passes quality checks."

"Hope so." I shoved the inert gas tank we'd been using into its spot in the shop's rack of canisters. "Now I just need to fall asleep before two in the morning."

"More bad dreams?" She asked.

I'd had some doozies since rescuing Mr. Gonzales and losing Dean Gladstone. The standard nightmare usually involved my elemental spells having no effect and me being unable to figure out how to use my tinker skills to save my friends. Which wasn't far from the truth of things. My skill in repairing items grew exponentially, but you couldn't exactly fix your way out of being possessed by a shadow or torn apart by lurkers. Dealing with the elusive mimics didn't even bear thinking about. Bethany—and on one occasion Chad—proved to have talents most suited to confronting the enemies that threatened. For all his cool exterior, even Owen's mechanical abilities just didn't come into play in a fight.

My ears burned hot under Gina's gaze as she waited for an answer. Bad as they were, those nightmares weren't what currently kept sleep at bay. My main problem was coping with the end of the semester and the fact that a certain woman I really liked would soon be moving on with her life.

Gina had yet to share where she'd be landing jobwise. Last I knew, her offers included a research facility on the gulf coast and a shipyard in San Diego. Both offered excellent opportunities for her to pursue the underwater certification she coveted. Both were ridiculously far away.

"Come on, out with it." Her dimples grew irresistible as she tried to needle an answer out of me—literally, with index fingers poking all over in an attempt to lighten my mood. "Why suddenly so grim?"

How did you tell someone that you wanted more time with them? I opened my mouth before having any real idea of what to say, and was saved by a stringent ringing from behind her.

"Hold that thought." Gina held up a finger, dug into her back pocket, and pulled out her phone. "I have to take this."

"How can you get calls inside?" I think my mouth was hanging open.

"A perk of working with security." She covered the mic with two fingers. "And before you ask, no, you can't get the access code. Only rising stars are allowed to override the cell-dampening magic. Now, shush for a minute."

Funny, I hadn't been the one talking.

The one-sided conversation only took a minute, during which Gina gave one-syllable responses and nodded a lot—for all the good that did. She hung up looking excited, but I couldn't tell if it was over good or bad news.

"Murdock's calling in all the security leads for a meeting, so gotta run. You okay cleaning up the rest of this?" She swept an arm toward our visors, gloves, and a few other items.

"Sure," I said with little enthusiasm.

"Don't sweat your tests. Get some rest, and you'll do great." She gathered up her bag and turned to leave.

"See you later?"

And the academy award for most eloquent, love-struck leading man goes to Jason Walker—not!

"How about this—" She turned back, but dropped her eyes to watch my feet. "You go ace your exams tomorrow, and to celebrate, you can take me to dinner. Your treat."

For being backward and upside down, her offer yanked me out of the doldrums fast enough to make my head spin.

"Uh, sure thing. It's a deal." I tried for calm and collected, forcing myself to not grin like an idiot, then noticed her frowning. "I'd really like that."

"Nice save, Romeo." Gina pinched my cheek a little too hard, then patted it gently, her warm fingers lingering deliciously before sliding away.

I watched her saunter off, slower and…swishier than expected given the apparent urgency of the phone call. Not that I minded, not one bit. Especially given *she'd* just asked *me* out. Hadn't she? And right before graduation. What did that mean?

Yeah, I didn't imagine much sleep was in the cards.

* * *

I caught up with the rest of the crew in the commons before heading home for the night. Bethany and Mon sat across from Owen, and Chad had his back against his favorite stone column.

"I agree, something is definitely off," Chad was saying to the others.

"Not you too." I slid in at the end of the guys' side of the bench and pointed an accusing finger at Mon. "Don't take advantage of the poor, confused cowboy. He's fragile."

"Yeah, right!" Mon slapped my hand away and almost smiled. "I didn't say a word."

"I bet." Given all her help, I'd been making an effort to include Mon more, but the conspiracy theory thing was really starting to get under my skin.

"She didn't—much." Chad added the qualifier after a moment's hesitation, and then patted the stonework by his head. "But Attwater feels it too. She's been healing steadily from her ordeal, but there's this vibe, like something's lurking in the halls that shouldn't be here."

"What about those redirection gadgets planted on the portals?" Bethany piled on. "That alone gives us enough to worry about."

"But wasn't that the Shadow Master?" Owen's position in the natural order of our group was scribed in indelible ink as devil's advocate, so it was strange to see him play peacekeeper.

"As much as I hate to disagree, no." I grimaced at my own words. "Mr. G. swears the Shadow Master didn't plant the spider devices. Unfortunately, I believe him."

"Vindication!" Mon crowed, and Bethany nodded.

Owen had maneuvered me right into their clutches. Maybe he *was* still poking the hornet's nest, and I just hadn't noticed. His grin as I worked through that thought had me shaking my head. I'd definitely been played.

"Listen, the demons are always going to be a threat. That's why we're here training." My outlook had brightened considerably since talking to Gina. I tried to share the newfound optimism because my friends seemed to be spiraling. "It sucks that the dean's missing, but the semester has been a win. The school's quelled tons of demon uprisings, Bethany figured out how to fight an ancient super-demon, and we saved Mr. Gonzales from a fate worse than death. We're getting stronger all the time. So we keep our eyes open, do what needs doing, and stay one step ahead. QED."

I took their non-committal shrugs as agreement, and the tide of conversation shifted to focus more on recapping our adventures than worrying about the future. As the tension unknotted, Chad leaned back into his resting-cowboy pose with hat pulled low, and a smooth sigh of air escaped the ventilation above. Even our semi-sentient school was happy to put off worrying for a while.

"So on a brighter note." Owen's open smile should have been warning enough. "Is everyone ready for finals?"

The deluge of half-eaten food that pelted Owen was a good sign. We hadn't completely lost our collective sense of humor.

Epilogue

G INA MET ME in the commons after finals, dressed to the nines in the sparkly green top she occasionally rocked. I was sitting with Lars, of all people, trying to figure out how the guy could be so helpful one day and back to his snide insults the next.

"Lookin' good." Lars added an inappropriate whistle as Gina came over.

"Yeah, you do look nice." I rushed to get my own compliment in without it being an awkward imitation. *Thanks, Lars.*

"Gentlemen." Gina nodded and took a seat next to Lars. "How are evaluations going?"

"Slammin' 'em back hard," Lars said before I could jump in. "Botanical identification and growth will be tomorrow, but I'm not worried."

The way Lars fell into his alter ego was really kind of mesmerizing. I sat there dumbfounded as he preened and crowed about how he was acing everything from advanced common core to his talent training. If you flipped open a dictionary to poser, there'd probably be a picture of Lars leaning in way too close trying to impress Gina while fondling his gold chains.

For her part, Gina did a lot of nodding and um-humming, unable to stop the landslide of unwanted information Lars chose to share. Her eyes sparkled with barely contained amusement, and she did an extraordinary job of keeping a straight face when he started in on how he'd been helping Ms. Schlaza perfect a new spell using earth magic.

"Fascinating," I interjected when Lars paused to breathe. At his glare, I smoothed away the sarcasm. "No, really. It doesn't feel like we've even scratched the surface of how some of the elements could be used."

"Well, yeah…we could do more…" He trailed off.

"We've got to run now." I struck while he puzzled over my agreement and pushed to my feet. "Welding trade manual stuff. You understand. Hey, good luck with tomorrow's exam. We'll catch you later."

Sharp as always, Gina follow suit and edged her way toward the exit. Before he could come up with a reason to stop us, I hurried Gina out into the hallway.

"Okay, thanks. Uh…later," Lars called.

"Oh, you're bad." Gina giggled as we ran for the student exits.

"Sorry." I stopped and made as if to head back. "Did you *want* to hear more?"

A look of horror stretched Gina's mouth into an oval under wide eyes. She spun me around by the elbow and pushed me onward. We used the old Beer Barn exit to my neck of the woods. Along with her superpower of now having cellular service on campus, her security connections allowed Gina to use any of the student portals. If I'd tried to use a different portal without getting permission first, it wouldn't work or would just send me back home.

We stepped out onto the cracked asphalt of the quiet little parking lot. Dusk was well on its way, and the dingy yellow streetlamp clicked on just as we headed for my car.

"What do you feel like eating?" I asked.

"I'm hungry, not picky."

"There's a decent tavern in town with good food." I belatedly scurried around the car to get the door for her.

The mid-week crowd downtown was light, and we got a nice corner booth. Between the dim lighting and little oil lamp on our table, reading the menu proved challenging. I picked out the specialty burger, and Gina ordered a personal pizza with the works. Since Lars had monopolized our earlier discussion, Gina took the opportunity to grill me about my exams while we waited for our orders.

I should have reveled in the fact we were finally on our first date, but talk of school made me somber. And when Gina compared her own first year results in Mr. Martin's class to mine and went on to talk about how important arc welding, cutting, and brazing skills would be for our careers—well, all I could think of was the fact she'd be leaving for her own job in just a few days. First date or not, odds were we wouldn't ever get a shot at a second.

"What's eating you now?" Gina asked when I fell silent and poked at my newly arrived burger.

"Nothing," I lied, trying to think of a new topic. Only one thing came to mind, so I screwed up my courage. "Guess I should ask, which job did you accept?"

"I was wondering when you'd turn the tables on me." The gleam in her eye told me her new position was something special.

"You took the gulf coast one, didn't you? I figured you'd go for the job near scuba diving."

"No, not Florida." She held up a finger to forestall my next guess. "And not California either."

"Where, then?" I hadn't heard about her other offers, but it stood to reason she had more to choose from.

"You're being such a sourpuss that I'm not sure I should tell you." Gina crossed her arms, pouted, and arched an eyebrow to see if I was biting, but I wasn't in the bantering mood. "I think you'll like it." She sung the words tauntingly.

"I think I won't." I meant to singsong my response, but it came out as more of a growl.

Her lower lip stuck out further. The twinkle in her eye said she suppressed a smile. My mood darkened. Teasing me with the information that would crush our chances to get to know each other was...cruel. Gina wasn't a cruel person, which meant she'd never really seen a future for us. She didn't think of me romantically.

"Attwater," she said.

I waited for her to continue, to say how the school had prepared her for whatever great opportunity awaited. But the seconds stretched.

"Attwater...and?" I suddenly felt tired and just wanted the night to be over.

"There's no and, just Attwater." Gina smiled, dimples deeper than I'd ever seen, eyes alight. She shook her head, hair whipping into a curly mess that framed her round face. "I've taken a job with the school. Isn't that great?"

"But why?" I wasn't sure I understood. "I mean, how? Mr. Martin is the welding instructor. He's on my schedule next semester."

"I'm going to work in security." She beamed at me, and her infectious smile burned through my sour mood. "Ms. Murdock was so impressed with our train station raid that she wants me to stay as her deputy. The department is stretched too thin because of the missing personnel. Five other grads are staying to help beef up the ranks."

"That's awesome!" I couldn't wipe the stupid grin off my face, despite embarrassment about the childish funk I'd been in all evening burning my ears.

"It's a full time position with excellent pay. Even if we brought the dean and others back next week, the job's guaranteed at least through next semester." Gina reached across the table to squeeze my hand.

Those words sobered me. But the grin stayed, and there was no way in hell I was letting go of her warm fingers. "I think you're safe from that happening."

I went back to poking at my sandwich, taking mental inventory of the layers and trying not to dwell on our lost people. My emotional rollercoaster had peaked with the news that Gina was staying. I refused to let it plunge over something we couldn't control.

"I wouldn't be so sure," she whispered and leaned in close. "It hasn't been announced yet, but the analysis of the spells used in the lava caves yielded an interesting conclusion."

"Do the investigators know where they went?"

Gina nodded slowly and replied with one word. "Back."

"I don't get it. Back where?"

"It sounds weird saying it out loud. But I told you about the dean's special talent, the one that goes beyond just *repairing* clocks?" She made little counter-clockwise circles with the index finger of her free hand.

"Sure, and I've been trying to find out more about those monks with the hourglass tokens like his." I'd come to suspect that Dean Gladstone was a Chrono-monk—at least an honorary one. "Are you saying he jumped back in time?"

"That's what the residual magic suggests." She nodded.

Sweat was building up between our hands. I reluctantly let go as I tried to imagine our trim, dapper administrator ferrying his security team into the past.

"But why?"

"They were trapped in magic resistant rock. We figure the Dean hopped backward looking for a time before the tunnel collapsed. Or maybe he was trying to go all the way back to before it existed."

"That would be tricky," I said. "The tunnel would have been full of molten lava when it formed."

"Good point. No one knows much about the Dean's talent. Maybe he has some sort of safety mechanism like the portals."

"So what's our next step?" Time traveling wasn't a common skill.

"That's the question of the day." She took a bite of pizza and considered. "A few higher-ups are scouring records at all three schools, looking for anyone else with time-distorting talent. A Chrono-monk would be our best option. They could trace where the dean landed along the timeline. But every last monk basically vanished a decade back. Their defenses at the edge of the world still keep most of the bad things out, but I don't know if the order maintains its magic from hiding or if the spells were just designed to not need much maintenance."

"You'd think they'd get a message back to the school." Even in science fiction, time travel made my head hurt. "Being in the past would give them all the time in the world to mail a letter or send a package." I felt the beginnings of a headache.

"But if the dean did manage to send word, it should have shown up the moment the group went missing."

"Unless they've gone so far back that mail doesn't exist," Gina said. "But the search is also on for any unopened postage."

"Between this news and the lava rock, it's no wonder the dean's globe couldn't locate him." I'd been afraid it was because they were all dead, but wasn't certain this was much better. "So what do we do now?"

"*We* let the experts do their thing." Her emphasis on the pronoun sure made it sound like she was just talking about me. Gina would probably be on the case as part of her new job. "You focus on getting through your last semester. You'll be going out on more training missions and need to complete your formal certifications." She held up the one slice of pizza she'd managed a bite of. "And this food isn't going to enjoy itself."

"But—"

"Let's not borrow trouble." She held up a finger to silence further argument. "But I do need you to answer one very important question." She continued at my nod. "Who in their right mind puts ham and cheese on a hamburger?"

"Asks the woman with dead fish on her pizza." I shook my head at her feigned shock, and proceeded to describe the delights of Cuban-inspired burgers.

Gina's smile brightened the dim room. Sure, we still had problems at Attwater. Hell, the world had problems, and that wasn't going to change anytime soon. Worrying about those facts wouldn't do anything except ruin our first date—something I wasn't willing to risk now that there might be a chance for a second.

~

Loved it, hated it, somewhere in between?

Let people know!

I'd be eternally grateful if you'd share your opinion of *The Silver Portal* or any other books on my Amazon author page.

https://amazon.com/author/steinjim

Your review need not be long, only takes a minute, and is super helpful to new authors. — Jim

Excerpt from *The Forgotten Isle*

"I HEARD THE raid didn't go so well," Bethany said as I joined her and her girlfriend Mon at our usual table in the commons. "Don't worry, you'll get them next time."

Bethany seemed even more upbeat than usual, with hazel-brown eyes shining above a brilliant smile. The youngest of our Attwater group, I tended to think of her as baby-faced, but something was different. Her rich cocoa skin might have a bit more glow, or maybe she wore makeup to make her high cheeks rounder? It was difficult to tell with those thick black braids hanging down.

"Hey, your hair's longer!" I put my finger on the difference almost immediately and wondered if Mon's magic somehow made hair grow fast. We didn't know the Asian girl's exact talent, but she'd be graduating in cosmetology. "Like, since yesterday."

"Looks good right?" Bethany swung her head and the braids slapped her shoulders. "Don't sprain your brain, Sherlock, they're called extensions."

Ah, so no magic involved. That made sense. Mon compressed her lips as if trying hard not to comment and settled for shaking her head. Her own hair was a glistening raven-black match to Bethany's, but fell straight to her shoulders. Mon had a year on Bethany's nineteen and about an inch on her five-foot-four frame, though the latter was hard to judge without an algebraic equation to account for heel height on any given day.

The two had grown close over the past year, Bethany's bright bubbly personality complementing Mon's quiet introspection. I'd upgraded that last from sullen brooding as we all got to know each other, but at times Mon could still be off-putting. Her black lipstick, eyeliner, slacks and halter didn't help. If anything the contrast between Goth outfit and pale skin tended to amplify moods like her current disgust at my apparent ignorance of advanced hair styles.

"Yep, hair's awesome," I said carefully before deciding to focus on the botched demon raid. "Security isn't going to be checking out any more leads from Mr. Gonzales for a while."

"Can't blame them, if the Shadow Master left bum info in his wake." Chad's voice boomed from behind as the big cowboy strode over to the table and squeezed himself onto the bench alongside Mon so that he could lean against the stone column.

"Geez, keep it down." I scanned the room and pumped my hands palm down like the gesture would lower the volume on his Midwestern draw.

Thirty or so students sat scattered around the big room, and a few more loaded up lunch plates in the kitchen area along the back wall. No one seemed to notice or care that Chad was talking about a sensitive topic. Hopefully his words had been lost in the general hubbub and excited discussion of classes or lost into the pipes and ventilation high overhead.

Mon actually smiled, just a tick up of her dark lip liner, and squirmed closer to Bethany so the big galoot could settle his butt down. Chad Stillman ported in from a barn in Montana each day, so much cooler than the old beer barn that was my local Attwater branch-slash-portal. At six-two our cowboy was big as life with an annoyingly square jaw and perpetual tan. He also happened to be a marshmallow who'd formed a special bond with the school building—a fact that was painfully clear by the way one hand caressed the stonework at his back. Attwater responded with a gusty sigh from the vents above. He even pulled off the cowboy hat with disturbing ease. Today's was dark brown to match his plaid shirt and boots. I could pull off a hat too, but refused to don my new headwear inside.

"Sorry," Chad said with an easy smile. "I forget that not everyone's read in on last semester's events."

"But you're right and apparently everyone knows about yesterday's mission," I admitted. "Three nests in a row have been deserted. Each was definitely a demon stronghold, so Mr. G's info is right. It's like they knew we were coming."

Order your copy of *The Forgotten Isle* on Amazon today!
https://www.amazon.com/dp/B08RVLZ478

About the author

Jim Stein hungers for stories that transport readers to extraordinary realms. Despite sailing five of the seven seas and visiting abroad, he's fundamentally a geeky homebody who enjoys reading, nature, and rescuing old pinball machines. Jim grew up on a steady diet of science fiction and fantasy plucked from bookstore and library shelves. After writing short stories in school, two degrees in computer science, and three decades in the Navy, Jim has returned to his first passion. His speculative fiction often pits protagonists with strong moral fiber against supernatural elements or quirky aliens. Jim lives in northwestern Pennsylvania with his wife Claudia, a grandcat with a perpetually runny nose, and the memory of Marley the Greatest of Danes.

Visit https://JimSteinBooks.com/subscribe to get a free ebook, join my reader community, and sign up for my infrequent newsletter.

Made in the USA
Middletown, DE
08 November 2023